PLAGUES AND PAPYRUS

- EGYPTIANS -

LIGHT OF NATIONS
BOOK TWO

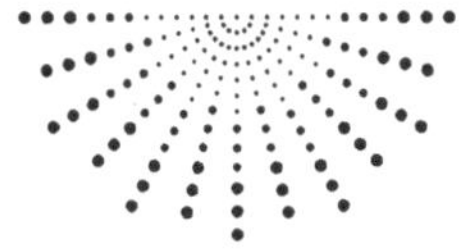

CHRISTINE DILLON

LINKS IN THE CHAIN PRESS

With grateful thanks for those who commit themselves to the often unseen ministry of prayer. As a child of missionaries and then as a missionary myself, I have had more people praying for me than most people ever do. I feel the encouragement of that privilege every day.

Thank you not only to those who pray for me, but for those who pray for my writing. So much of what has been achieved is because of those prayers. Pray on!

I will make you as a light for the nations,
that my salvation may reach to the ends of the earth.

Isaiah 49:6b (ESV)

But I have raised you (Pharaoh) up for this very purpose, that
I might show you my power and that my name might be
proclaimed in all the earth.

Exodus 9:16 (NIV)

LIST OF CHARACTER AND PLACE NAMES

Fictional Characters

Kheti - an Egyptian living in the Nile delta region. Second son of a farmer, **Hepu** (senior), who farms papyrus and crops.

Pentu - Kheti's older brother. Married to **Iset** and father of young **Hepu** (an infant son). He concentrates on the crop side of the family business.

Avraham - a Hebrew slave. Husband to **Sara**, and father of **Yosef**, **Havvah**, and **Noach**.

Tia - younger sister of Kheti.

Nanny - an old woman who helped raise Mosheh and Pharaoh.

Nophret - a neighbor. **Intef** is her younger brother.

Biblical Characters

I have chosen to use more Hebraic-anglicised versions of the familiar names. This helps us approach the story with different eyes and hopefully makes the biblical parts, feel less familiar.

Mosheh - (more familiar in English as Moses). Raised in Pharaoh's palace for forty years and then fled to the wilderness for forty years. Married to **Zipporah**.

Pharaoh - the king of Egypt. It is unknown precisely which Pharaoh he was. Three possibilities are:

a) Thutmose II (c. 1493-1479 B.C.E.), a pharaoh with a brief reign and no legitimate son to succeed him. In addition, his mummy showed evidence of scars and cysts from possible disease.

b) Rameses II is a more popular candidate (reigned c. 1279-1213 B.C.E.).

c) Merneptah, the pharaoh who succeeded Rameses (reigned c. 1213-1203 B.C.E.).

Aharon - Mosheh's older brother.

Miryam - Mosheh's older sister.

PROLOGUE

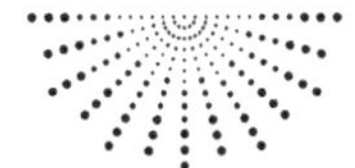

Goshen, Nile Delta, Ancient Egypt

"Grab it!" Kheti squeaked in excitement, ankle deep in the squishy mud on the edge of the Nile River.

Just as he was about to capture it, the frog gave a mighty leap out of his encircling hands.

Kheti stood up and swung his head around. His older brother, Pentu, was nowhere to be seen. As usual.

Kheti scanned the riverbank. There was his slippery target, trying to hide behind a clump of papyrus. Kheti splashed through the refreshing water.

"I'll help," said a nearby voice.

Kheti turned as another little boy came running over.

Kheti focused back on the frog and crept forward. Mud squished through his toes. He beckoned to the other boy to approach the grass clump from the other side.

"Slowly," he commanded in a whisper. Together they should be able to trap the frog.

The wet frog was motionless, gleaming like a dark green jewel.

Kheti squatted and the other boy copied him, moving cautiously at half speed. Kheti grinned. It was good to have a friend. Pentu said he didn't have time to play with Kheti.

Slowly, slowly they both reached toward the frog.

"Come away from there," a sharp voice said. "Mother wouldn't want you playing with a slave."

The frog gave a mighty leap and disappeared under the water with a splash.

Slave? Kheti looked over at the boy. The boy plunged his hands into the river, not seeming to notice Pentu. With a shout of glee, he raised hands cupped around what must have been the frog they had pursued.

As if sensing Kheti's desire to continue his game, Pentu grabbed him by the shoulder, fingers digging in.

"If you ever come near my brother again," he snarled at the boy, "I'll get my father to have you and your father whipped."

Kheti had never seen his Papa whip anyone, boy or beast.

The delight that had recently been on the boy's face was replaced by fear. Trembling, the boy bent and released the frog from the cage of his hands. It used its powerful legs to escape into the reeds.

A woman scurried down the slope toward them. "I need your help, Yosef," she said, voice thin and not looking at Pentu. She gently tugged the boy's arm.

Kheti watched sorrowfully as Yosef was led away, his heart pounding as if Pentu had threatened him too. Pentu gave him a sharp prod to direct him toward the house, forcing him to turn his back on Yosef, who walked hand in hand with his mother up over the rise of the riverbank. Why shouldn't they play together? It wasn't as if Yosef was dirty or diseased. Kheti's mother never let him talk with the Hebrew slaves, but Yosef had seemed like an ordinary boy before Pentu said he was a slave. Well, Mother and Pentu must know best. Kheti turned his eyes to the river, blinking at the brightness of the reflections off the water.

"The river is life, Kheti," Papa had often told him as he dug two hands into the soft wet earth and offered Kheti the rich black soil to consider. "See the river's gift. See how our great gods make us rich." Kheti saw mud, not riches, but there was much he did not know about the world, so much he had yet to learn about the river, its frogs and gods, and why some boys were slaves and others were not.

* * *

Several days later
Near Kheti's home

*K*heti had been left to play on his own because Pentu was off helping their father. Kheti sighed as he thought of the boy he'd played with down at the river. If only Yosef had been allowed to stay. There was no one else of similar age around. He leaned against a stone wall, his mother and grandmother with their backs towards him, were seated on the wall above his head and hadn't noticed him.

"They breed like sandflies," his mother said.

Who did? Kheti slid down the wall. He risked a stinging pinch to the ear if his mother caught him eavesdropping, but Papa always said he needed to pay attention to learn about the world.

"Pharaoh had the right idea—kill the lot of them," his grandmother said.

Kheti blinked at the spite in her voice. He'd gladly see annoying sandflies exterminated, but he didn't think his mother and grandmother were talking about sandflies.

"Didn't work," his mother said, matching his grandmother's

tone. "Those Hebrews are a plague in our lands, even after Pharaoh commanded that all boys be killed at birth."

Kheti's heart pounded so loudly in his own ears that he was afraid they could hear it too. Kill the boys? He was a boy. He sucked in a mouthful of hot air.

"The midwives were ordered to kill all the boys. Any babies found hidden, the soldiers threw in the river," added his grandmother with an air of satisfaction. "But they're like those wretched flies. There's always more."

Vomit rose in Kheti's throat. His mother had always warned him not to swim in the river because it was full of crocodiles as big as horses that loved to feast on the unwary. There were angry hippos too, although they were easier to see and avoid. He trembled.

Why did his mother and grandmother and Pharaoh hate the Hebrews? There didn't seem to be anything particularly nasty about them. There was a family of them living over the river. Kheti had never been allowed near their hut, but he'd seen the children playing together at a distance, heard their laughter, and wished Pentu would play and laugh with him.

"And to think it was one of our own pharaohs who invited them here. Let them settle on our land. Let them farm our delta. The best land in Egypt!" Grandmother slapped her leg. "Our land. Our water. Our crops. Our fruit."

"Why didn't they put them out in the desert?"

"That would have kept their numbers down." His grandmother cracked her knuckles. "Only the sandflies can breed out there."

In stories, the desert was described as an empty expanse that couldn't have been more different from the lush green of the delta, planted with wheat and barley, beans and peas, spices, and watermelons. Kheti's mouth watered at the thought of sinking his teeth into a slice of sweet, juicy melon.

"They don't belong here anyway," Grandmother continued.

"They should have gone back to Canaan after the famine, not stayed here and stolen the best of our lands. Fat and happy, taking what was ours for generation after generation."

Silence fell between the two women. Kheti held his breath so they wouldn't notice his presence.

His mother spoke again. "How long have they been a curse on our lands?"

"For a long, long time. They were around even when my grandmother was a child."

Kheti tried to imagine how long ago his grandmother's grandmother had lived and gave up. His grandmother was one of the oldest people he knew. Old and wrinkled and with a tongue that cut like a knife.

"Well, why haven't they gone back?" his mother asked.

"They're wanderers. I'm not sure they even have their own land."

"Well, this is not their land, and their welcome expired long ago," his mother said in a tone that brooked no argument.

"Once guests, now pests," his grandmother added in a singsong voice.

His mother chuckled. "Yes. And what a mistake it was to treat them well when they are vermin."

"Mmm," his grandmother said. "But still we must feed them."

"Just enough to keep them fit for work." His mother sniggered.

"But not enough for them to have energy to plot mischief."

It made Kheti sad to see how little food their house slaves were given. He'd been sneaking extra to them since he'd first been unable to resist their hungry eyes as they watched him eat. He'd seen Papa do the same when his mother wasn't looking.

His grandmother shifted her seat. "We'd be fools to feed them too much. That would risk their raising an army to overrun us."

Kheti widened his eyes.

"I doubt they have the wit to work together," his mother said.

There was a pause, and Kheti held his breath again.

"They breed like flies, but they work like ants," his grandmother muttered. "That's why Pharaoh made them slaves in the first place. Didn't want them supporting our enemies to get rid of us."

His mother gave a little whimper. "Don't scare me."

"Don't you worry, honey. We have the wit and the whip. They have empty heads and empty bellies. Like ants, they can't stop working, or they won't get fed."

Kheti shivered. The slaves might be ants, but he'd seen ants lift a dead beetle many times their weight.

"Although there might be trouble if that fellow Mosheh comes back," his grandmother said.

Mosheh? Kheti pricked up his ears. A name he didn't know.

"Raised in the palace. Given airs unfitting for a slave. The previous Pharaoh was a fool to let his daughter keep a Hebrew child, and a greater fool to let Mosheh escape."

"But they tried to find him, didn't they?" his mother said, her voice tight. "Surely he died somewhere out in the desert."

"They didn't look hard enough, I say. You don't risk leaving a fellow like that alive. Not if you know what's good for you."

What had the man done, and why did Grandmother's voice shake?

"But nothing has been heard of him during my lifetime."

"Maybe not, but as I said to your aunt when he fled, 'That one will cause trouble, you'll see.'" Grandmother would be wagging her finger.

"Come on," Kheti's mother said, her knees creaking as they always did when she stood. "That's enough of a rest for now. Can you make it home?"

Kheti made himself as small and silent as a mouse hiding from a falcon hoping they wouldn't glance over to his side of the wall.

The shuffle of their footsteps and the murmur of their voices faded. He waited to make sure they were well away before scuttling off on the shortcut home. Who was Mosheh? How could he find out more about the man? Even his name sounded mysterious, but a Hebrew raised in the palace sounded even more intriguing. Why had Pharaoh's daughter kept him if everyone hated the Hebrews so much? Why had Mosheh fled? Was he still alive? And if he was alive, where was he now? Would Yosef and his family know? Thinking of Yosef's smile when he'd caught their frog, Kheti was hit with a sudden flood of sadness. It was no use thinking about Yosef. He'd never be allowed to talk to him again.

CHAPTER ONE

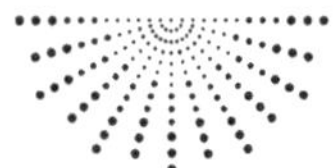

10 years later
Goshen, Egypt

Kheti pushed the papyrus boat out into the flooded River Nile. All along the edges of the river, the water eddied in languorous currents. The river would recede after the next moon, leaving behind the silt that made the delta so fertile. Kheti almost licked his lips thinking of all the fruit and vegetables to come. Before the planting, he and his father and brother would make another offering to Hapi, the river god, to thank him for the fertility the inundation brought and to plead that the river would stay within its boundaries until after the harvest. Most years, the gods answered their prayers.

The prow of his boat nudged its way between the purple flowering water lilies and toward the next clump of papyrus. Papyrus was the source of their family's wealth. They made paper or boats with the best of it and wove sandals and baskets with the offcuts.

Reaching a clump that grew well above his head, Kheti pulled the first stalk up by its roots. With a swift cut of his knife, he severed the root clump and let it drop back into the river. After laying the main part of the reed at an angle across his papyrus-reed boat, he reached for the next stalk.

A pair of otters frolicked in the water ahead. The white of their throats caught the sun as their lithe bodies twisted and glided through the water.

Kheti's mother thought this job was beneath him. She told him to send the Hebrew slaves to do the harvesting, but he loved to come and soak in the serenity. Overhead, the sky was awash with streaks of orange and palest pink. The intoxicating smell of the sacred blue water lilies, a symbol of the sun god, Ra, and a sign of rebirth, filled his nostrils. He sniffed and scared a frog off the papyrus. It plopped into the water and swam away with vigorous kicks of its back legs. On mornings like this, Kheti could imagine the world was perfect.

Out here he could escape his mother's endless nagging. His workday was never finished in her eyes, and she had a new refrain. "Pentu was married at your age, Kheti. Will I die before I see your sons?" Out here he could forget the extra busyness of harvest season. His workers had been sick yesterday, and they hadn't managed to get more papyrus ready for soaking. They'd have to catch up this afternoon.

Kheti cut the final stalk in the first clump of papyrus and paddled the boat toward the next. Each stalk came up with a squelch and a few air bubbles. He kept up the rhythm. Pull, slice, place. Pull, slice, place.

At each clump of papyrus, he only harvested the larger stalks, leaving the smaller to continue to grow. Ra, praise him, had once again conquered Apep, the serpent of darkness, and now sailed his boat across the sky, warming Kheti's back. He'd fill up the boat and head back to the soaking vats. Behind him, he could hear the calls of the other gatherers. They tended to keep together. Unlike his mother, he permitted the slaves to talk as long as it didn't impede their efficiency. Not that his mother actually got her hands dirty with any part of the process. She loved being able to live as a woman of leisure. Kheti's father preferred to supervise the making of papyrus reed boats, a task performed later in the year after the reeds had fully dried.

Kheti continued to move from clump to clump until his boat was full. He dug his paddle into the water and used the water flow to swing the boat around, ready to return home.

Midway through the turn, he heard a scream, then another. A crocodile? He completed his turn and froze, fear prickling his skin. What in the name of Ra was wrong with the water? The river between him and the other boats glowed red. He glanced at the sky. No, it wasn't a reflection from the sun, for the sunrise was long gone. He looked back at the water, recoiling to see the redness spreading toward his boat. A vague salty-sweet smell filled his nose. He'd never seen anything like this. What was this phenomenon? The slaves were paddling for shore, shouting to each other in their barbarous language, not caring that some of the harvested stalks were falling back into the water.

Kheti clicked his tongue in annoyance and yelled after them, but they took no notice. Red now crept around the edge of his paddle. Reaching forward, he lifted some of the dripping stalks abandoned by the slaves onto his boat. The stained water was warm and unnaturally viscous. He sniffed at it cautiously. Where had he smelled that smell before?

On the riverbank, the men had pulled the boats out of the water, dragging them from the front rather than walking into the shallows and carefully beaching them. He yelled again, telling them not to damage the underside of the boats, but they ignored him and then gathered in a nervous huddle well away from the water. Maybe his mother was right. Maybe Kheti had been too soft with them.

Kheti kept paddling, picking up each one of the abandoned stalks. The smell had increased, and now his stomach threatened to disgorge his breakfast. He recalled the first time he'd been to a temple and seen the animals slaughtered for sacrifice. Blood? He bent to examine the river more closely, and stretched out his hand to place one finger in the red water. It felt warm. He brought his finger close to his nose and sniffed. He stuck out his tongue and touched it to his finger. Ugh. He spat into the river and then spat again.

Blood. How could the water be blood? Even as he looked, the surface of the river seemed to boil as fish floated to the surface, lying belly-up, mouths gasping in the air.

Dread struck Kheti's belly. Plunging his paddle into the river, he bolted for the riverbank. What devilish trick was this? What had Egypt done to come under Hapi's curse?

As he approached the riverbank, he again caught sight of the slaves huddled in fear. He swallowed, took a deep breath, slowed his paddling, and sat more erect. He must not let the slaves see the panic dancing through his limbs. A master must always be in control of himself.

The prow of the boat crunched against the bank. "Come! Help!" he called.

No one jumped at his command. Finally, after a whispered consultation, two men approached, assisting him to drag the papyrus off the boat but not putting their feet anywhere near the water.

Once the boat was emptied, Kheti schooled his face to calm and then stepped into the water. It swirled warm around his calves. He wanted to dash, screaming, out of its sticky embrace, but for the sake of his pride, he held his head high and strode toward the shore. He gestured to two of the men, who half-dragged and half-carried the boat to a safer spot on the riverbank. Blood clung to the boat in a sticky tideline.

He clamped down his terror and pointed at the slaves. "Come! Carry the papyrus back to the soaking vats."

They muttered amongst themselves but after a brief delay, hoisted the reeds onto their shoulders, ready for the short walk home. Kheti looked back at the river. As far as he could see, the river was red and the stench was heavy in the air. He turned to follow the others. Away from the dying fish. Away from the horror. Away from the river of life that had turned to death.

The men whispered among themselves in their own tongue as if the river had turned into a monster they now feared to awaken.

Kheti took surreptitious deep breaths. The air was full of the smell of metal. Looking down at his feet, he shuddered. The blood had dried, and his feet were sticky. Little tufts of dried grass and sand now rubbed at his soles.

He stopped and waved his arm. "We'll go via the lake so we can wash."

The slaves looked up and nodded, gratefulness evident in their haunted eyes. It wasn't far out of their way. Kheti often used the lake for quiet swims after a long day in the papyrus sheds. The lake was filled by a spring and free of any dangerous creatures.

They marched in silence. As they approached the lake, birds flew over in a huge flock, the air full of the beating of their wings. Not their familiar graceful flight, but frantic flapping, as if they were panicked. Kheti squinted as he watched.

Kheti's throat tightened. Not waiting for the slaves, he rushed to the top of the small hill ahead, heart pounding, and looked down at the lake. From shore to shore, the waters were red like the Nile, and the air pungent with the smell of death.

Hapi, why are you angry? The only answer was the beat of the birds' wings as they fled.

The river and the lake. How far had this curse spread? The men lined up on either side of Kheti, silent and still, then each spun around to head back to the farm.

Kheti reached down to brush the sticky sand and grass strands off his feet. There was plenty of water at home, and he'd make sure they could all wash. But he wished he could have washed before his mother saw him covered in blood.

The papyrus sheds were still some distance away when a shout went up.

"He's back." His father and brother came striding toward him. "What's going on?"

"What do you mean?"

"All the vats are full of blood," Pentu said. "What's happening?"

The slaves wailed.

"Shut up," Kheti yelled, failing to keep his voice measured. They looked startled. He seldom yelled at them.

"Go over there." He pointed. "Put the papyrus on the ground, and don't go near the vats."

He turned to his father and brother. "The river and the lake are the same. Everything has turned to blood." Seeing their faces awash in disbelief and incomprehension, Kheti indicated the drying blood painting his legs.

"Everything? What about the water jars at the house?" his brother asked.

"You'd better go and check," Papa said, voice shaking.

Pentu set off at a run, while Kheti turned to his father. "Can you show me the vats?"

Papa motioned for the slaves to sit, then he and Kheti went toward the sheds where they soaked the papyrus. A hole in the roof above the main shed let light into the cool darkness. The smell of blood was overwhelming. Kheti leaned over the edge of one vat, and the light bounced off the red surface of the water.

"Praise the gods, the workers were unable to prepare most of the papyrus yesterday. We should only lose one vatful," Papa said.

One vat was loss enough, given each vat was the size of four oxen. "What do you think we should do?"

Papa stood rigid, still staring into the blood-filled vat. "I don't know. No one has ever heard of this kind of curse."

Pounding steps came from outside the shed, and Pentu burst back in. He rushed over to them, panting. "Every water jar and every pot is full of blood. Mama is screaming and accusing the house slaves of some sort of sorcery."

Maybe she had a point. If this wasn't a curse sent by the gods, sorcery was another possible explanation. But who had the kind of power to turn all water to blood? He'd heard that Pharaoh's magicians were powerful, but why would they want to harm Egypt? Without water, everyone would suffer, even sorcerers.

"Father, should we drain the vats?" Kheti asked.

"If we don't, we might never be able to clean them."

"But if we drain them, the blood will dry and pollute the mud," Pentu said.

"Son, I don't know what to do. I'm more worried that the blood will set. Blood thickens and coagulates." Papa walked over to a storage area and took out a heavy hammer. "Pentu, knock the stoppers back into the vats and let the liquid out. I must go and see if we can save the papyrus."

Kheti shook his head. He doubted papyrus soaked in blood could ever be useful.

Pentu took the huge hammer from Papa and found the plug of the first vat. He swung the hammer, and it thudded against the wooden plug. It took five hits before the plug released the liquid to gush into the channels dug in the earthen floor. Leaving the first vat, he moved to the second, empty of papyrus but still full of blood.

"Kheti, come with me to check the papyrus," Papa said.

They went over to the furthest vat. Papa took the long pole leaning against the wall and plunged it into the crimson waters. With a grunt, he lifted the pole and held it steady, allowing the excess liquid to stream off the strands of papyrus.

"They're definitely pink," Kheti said. "If we had clean water to wash them off, we might save them."

"But if we just dump them, there is no possibility of using them. We must try."

"I'll call the workers." Kheti went outside and beckoned the foreman of the group. "We are going to prepare the papyrus as usual."

The foreman turned and spoke to those behind him in his own language. There was much shaking of heads and muttering.

"What are they saying?" Kheti asked.

"They don't want to touch the papyrus." The slaves must be petrified of blood to risk disobeying.

"Beat the lot of them," Pentu said before Kheti could open his mouth.

"Now, now." Papa hurried toward the group. "Beating won't help the situation. Let's think of a compromise."

Papa always compromised if possible. Maybe it was the secret of his success. He certainly had a lot less trouble with his workers than any of the other slave masters in the area.

"Avraham, if we got the papyrus out of the vats, would your men be willing to lay them out on the racks?"

Avraham consulted with the others. With much nodding, they agreed.

"Kheti, could you please go and ask your younger sister to join us? The four of us will have to lay out the papyrus."

Kheti nodded and set off to summon Tia.

CHAPTER TWO

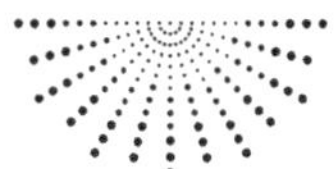

Kheti licked his dry lips. With no water to drink they'd been taking sips of beer, and Papa had passed around goat milk at midday. How long would there be no water? No water for drinking, no water for washing, no water for the papyrus. If this continued, the livestock would die like the fish had, along with all the papyrus in the river. Kheti's mother had been making offerings all day, but they still didn't know whether a god was responsible for the catastrophe, or something else.

"Master, come and look," Avraham said to Kheti's father.

Kheti looked up from where he was weaving the strips of papyrus to form the outline of paper. Half the strips were horizontal and half vertical.

"What is it, Avraham?" Papa said. "We have no time to waste if this is to be done by nightfall."

"There seems to be some clearer water in one of the channels."

"What do you mean?" Kheti asked, seizing the chance to stretch his back.

"There was a blockage in that channel." Avraham pointed

towards the shed. "And where the liquid filtered through the earth, it's much clearer."

"Show us," Papa said, putting down the sodden strip of papyrus that his not-so-nimble fingers had been trying to weave into a sheet of paper.

They went into the shed. Sure enough, the water below the blockage was running much clearer. Papa stood for a long moment, rubbing his ear. "Avraham, can you think of a way we could filter the water through sand and earth to get cleaner water?"

Avraham looked around him.

"Abba." Avraham's son tugged his arm. "What about if we dig holes near the river and carry the water back?"

Avraham slapped him on the back. "Clever boy." He looked at Kheti's father. "Can we go and try?"

"Yes, and I'll come with you. If we could rinse the papyrus, its value won't be lost." He looked across at Kheti and Tia. "Could you finish weaving a few more sheets of the stained papyrus? I want to see what happens when it dries."

Kheti nodded. One of the reasons Papa's business kept growing was that he was always learning. Kheti had noticed the speculative gleam in his eye when Avraham's son had come up with the idea. If one idea had come out of that young boy's head, there might be more ideas. Profitable ideas.

* * *

"Where's your father?" Kheti's mother asked, coming around the corner of the shed. The contents of the vats still gushed out of the shed, spreading out in bloody pools. Mama held her nose and stepped cautiously over towards Kheti.

"There's no water in the house, and I'm thirsty."

Mother was thirsty? What about everyone else? She'd probably been sitting with a slave fanning her while the rest of the family labored. The sun was now high in the sky.

"Father's working on it," Kheti said.

"Where is he?"

"Down there." Tia pointed to the riverbank.

"What's he doing down there? We need him here."

Kheti took a breath. His mother wore him out with her constant demands.

"I'm certainly not going down there in all that muck. Priests' daughters must remain clean."

Priest's daughter indeed. There hadn't been a priest in the family for generations, and Mother refused to talk about whatever had happened to break the priestly line. Yet she kept claiming a priestly birthright as a convenient excuse to keep her from doing anything she didn't want to do.

"I'll go, Mama," Tia said, tucking the edges in to complete her sheet of paper. She rubbed her hands on a cloth and set off down the hill toward where Avraham and the men were digging their series of holes.

Water must already be seeping into the holes. Hopefully cleaner water, because otherwise Papa would have to bury the whole vat of papyrus.

"Mama, I doubt the water is going to be drinkable, but there's plenty of wine," Kheti said. "I'll get some beer for the workers."

"That's our beer," she snapped.

"We have to give them something, or they won't be able to keep working." That was an argument she should accept.

"Humph. You'd better water it down. We don't want them drunk."

Kheti laughed. If they had water, they wouldn't need beer. "We'll have to wait and see whether the water they find is drinkable. There's no point making anyone sick."

"I can't stand around here all day," Mama said, turning away. "I've got things to do back at the house."

The stench was definitely worse now that the full force of the sun was blazing down. The wind blew toward Kheti, thick with the smell of dead fish. Could blood ever become water again? A few more days of this, and the stench would be unbearable. And livestock would start dying. Then his mother would have something to complain about.

Tia crested the hill, her forehead glistening with sweat. "They've got cleaner water, and they'll start bringing it up to put in the smaller vat so you can rinse the papyrus."

He blew out a gusty breath. Praise the gods. They were saved. He put the plug in the vat, then went to find his brother to yoke up a pair of oxen.

* * *

"*Much* better." Kheti's father withdrew the first of the rinsed papyrus. "It will still be pale pink, but hopefully the color will fade as it dries." He looked outside for Avraham and called him over. "Would you take two men with you to bring the water? And have the others prepare the paper with us?"

Avraham was back almost immediately. "My son and the others will make the paper."

"Good," Papa said. "Kheti, please keep an eye on things. I'm going back to the house for a while."

Kheti nodded and assigned two of the workers to get the papyrus out of the vat. They draped each piece over long poles next to the weavers. He and Tia and some of the more nimble-fingered, worked to lay the paper out on sheets of felt.

He completed weaving the piece of papyrus and put another layer of felt on top. They built a stack, alternating papyrus and felt.

Each stack would dry for seven days before a final drying in the sun.

* * *

At the first sound of birdsong in the morning, Kheti turned over and stretched. He took a deep breath out of habit, and gagged. The blood. The stench was far worse this morning, and it brought back the calamity that was yesterday. The disgust, the fear, their powerlessness to do anything about the blood, and the looming threat of financial ruin.

He stumbled out of bed and went to find Papa, who was already outside peering toward the river. Kheti hawked and spat into the bushes.

"Papa, what are we going to do?"

Papa turned toward him with a grim smile.

"I talked to some of the neighbors last night. Everyone is going to work together to gather the rotting fish and dig them into the soil." Rotting fish would enrich the soil.

"And?" Kheti was certain Papa had more than one plan.

"And we will go to the capital as usual and deliver paper."

"I doubt the priests will accept pink papyrus."

"Remember, I always keep some back from each batch."

Kheti did remember. He'd protested when Papa had made them store it.

"I'll have to admit, I was wrong about that."

Papa chuckled. "A real man is always willing to admit his mistakes. Remember the story I used to tell you about the hippo?"

It was Kheti's turn to chuckle. When he'd first started trailing along after Papa as a young child, his father had taken the time to teach him skills and tell him the ancient stories. Kheti had lapped up the wisdom, but then there'd been a long stretch of time when he'd copied Pentu's contempt of what he called "superstitious myths."

Kheti had seen the hurt in Papa's eyes, but at that stage Kheti had wanted Pentu's admiration more than Papa's. He'd been a fool. It had taken a few years before he worked out that Pentu was only interested in one person—himself.

"Let's check how much papyrus we still have." Papa led the way.

The storehouse was well away from the vats and any source of moisture. Unlocking the door, they went into the cool, dry, darkness inside. The papyrus was laid on racks so that air could circulate underneath.

"Yes, there's more than enough," Papa said.

Kheti laid a hand on Papa's shoulder. "How did you know we'd need this one day?"

"I didn't, son, but a wise man never presumes that the gods will always smile with favor. We live in a land of floods and hail and locusts. Something can always go wrong."

CHAPTER THREE

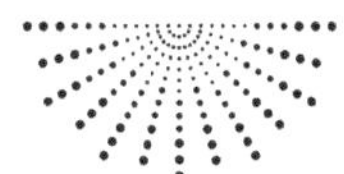

Kheti and Papa left for the capital before dawn to deliver the papyrus.

"Look, Father." Kheti pointed toward the river. All along its banks were long shapes.

Papa shaded his eyes. "I had no idea there were so many crocodiles in the river, but they can't survive there at the moment."

"And they'll eat all the fish that Pentu wanted to improve the soil."

Papa chuckled. "I'm sure your brother will work out a way to frighten them off and get his share. Although, it might be harder to shift those." Further along the bank, a group of hippos greeted the sun with huge yawns.

Kheti had wondered if the blood was a local problem, but every pond and water storage area along the way to the capital was red and reeking.

Two roads met ahead of them, and there were crowds of people sitting motionless. As Kheti and Papa passed, most sat listlessly. One or two of the more energetic ones held out their hands and called, "Water, for pity's sake, water."

Papa didn't stop until he was well past them. "Go back and give a single scoop of beer to those most in need. Then run back here before they mob you. Do you understand?"

Kheti shuddered. *May the gods see our good deeds and protect us.*

He offered the first scoop of beer to a woman clutching a nursing child. She only slurped a few mouthfuls before a man grabbed the scoop and spilled precious liquid on the ground.

"Look what you've done," a woman screamed.

In the end, Kheti was only able to give three or four people a drink before he had to run to avoid being mobbed.

When would this curse end? If it was not soon, some of those people would be dead by the time Ra next rose in the sky.

As they got closer to the capital, the river was lined with crowds of people digging, digging, digging, trying to filter any water they could. The rest of the roads were quiet, as people tried to conserve what energy they had.

As usual, Kheti and Papa visited a temple outside the city before heading for the palace stables. The chanting of the priests and the smell of incense always made Kheti shiver with awe. Father liked to pray for the success of their journey in a bigger temple. Presumably prayers offered in temples nearer to Pharaoh himself were more effective.

At the stables, Papa unhitched the oxen and gave them to the slaves. Within minutes, a group of slaves arrived to take the papyrus to the magicians' and priests' storage area.

"Stay here, Son. I'll go and get the payment and try to find out what I can."

Papa had all sorts of contacts among the priests and magicians. If they weren't the source of the problem, they'd be working on a solution.

"I'll talk to the stable hands and then sit over there." Kheti indicated a small courtyard nearby.

The stable hands only confirmed what Kheti already knew.

They too had had to dig down beside the Nile for fresh water, and they were worried about the animals in their care.

Kheti took a handful of dried raisins and figs over to the courtyard. It was deserted except for a wizened old woman sitting in the shade of a doorway. Even on tiptoe, she'd only reach his chest, but by the look of the hump on her back, straightening would be impossible.

"What are you looking at, boy?" the old woman said.

He drew himself up tall. "I'm no boy. I've lived through seventeen inundations and been considered a man for some time now."

"Time will tell. Time will tell." She cackled. "There's some boys that become men, but many boys never grow up."

She obviously didn't have a high opinion of men. This lady might look ancient, but her tongue hadn't slowed down like the rest of her.

"Times are going to get interesting. Take Pharaoh." She gestured back toward the entrance. "I have my doubts that he'll prove to be a man."

"Shh," Kheti whispered, finger on his lips. "You'll get us killed."

"They won't kill me. Looked after him as a baby, I did, and let me tell you there was nothing godlike about him. Pooed and screamed like any other child."

Who was this? She couldn't possibly be Pharaoh's mother, not wearing a simple linen dress and sitting out here on her own.

"In fact, royal children are harder to look after than the non-royals. They're told from babyhood that they're something special." She rocked back in laughter. "Bet I'm the only one alive to have ever spanked a pharaoh."

"You didn't!" His voice rose.

She giggled. "I did. He'd slapped Mosheh and called him a stinking slave."

Mosheh? The name sounded familiar. Kheti turned to go. There didn't seem much point in wasting time with a woman who told such tall tales.

He walked across the courtyard. Wait a moment. Mosheh? Wasn't that the man he'd overheard his mother and grandmother—may the gods carry her soul to peace—talking about long ago? What was it they'd said about him? Something about him being raised in the palace and running away.

Kheti turned and walked back to the woman.

She was still mumbling to herself as though he hadn't left. "Now Mosheh, he's someone to be watched. He might prove to be a man. A leader worth following."

He squatted down near her. "Were you Mosheh's nanny as well?"

"Of course." She nodded emphatically. "Running through the palace corridors after him and those other young monsters from sunup to sundown."

Papa hadn't yet returned. He must still be in the depths of the palace, getting the best price for the last of their best quality papyrus.

The woman's birdlike eyes darted here and there, and she probably had nothing better to do than listen to the gossip. She might know a lot more than the stable hands.

"Do you know why the water's turned to blood?" Kheti asked.

"Know?" She looked at him scornfully. "Of course I know. It was Mosheh."

Mosheh? Was he some sort of magician then?

"He met Pharaoh on the bank of the Nile as he went down for his morning bathe. And bold as you please, he said, 'The Lord, the God of the Hebrews, has sent me to say to you: "Let my people go, so that they may worship me in the wilderness. But until now you have not listened."' Of course Pharaoh hadn't listened. Never listened as a boy. Stubborn as a hippopotamus." She sniggered to herself. "So what does Mosheh tell him next? 'This is what the Lord says: "By this you will know that I am the Lord: With the staff that is in my hand, I will strike the water of the Nile, and it will be changed into blood. The fish in the Nile will die, and the river will stink; the Egyptians will not be able to drink its water."' I'm not familiar with his god, but sure enough the river has turned to blood."

It was as though a cold wind blew through the courtyard. Who was this Mosheh and who was this god of the Hebrews? Kheti shook his head. No, the woman was just telling tall tales of spanking Pharaoh. But maybe she did know something, for the way she spoke the words of Mosheh's so-called god sounded like the truth. And the river had turned to blood, and the fish had died. Even now, the fish were lying along both sides of the river.

Kheti turned to look at the woman. "But it wasn't just the river."

"No. They didn't just strike the water of the river. Apparently Mosheh's god told him, 'Take your staff and stretch out your arm over the waters of Egypt—over the streams and canals, over the ponds and all the reservoirs—and they will all turn to blood.'"

And so even Kheti's bathing lake had been polluted.

"He said the blood would be everywhere in Egypt, even in vessels of wood and stone," the old woman continued.

And the blood was everywhere, just as Mosheh had said.

"And what about Pharaoh's magicians?" Kheti asked. "What did they do?"

The woman snorted. "The magicians? Useless bunch of boys that they are, they managed to produce blood as well. Blood, blood, and more blood."

"Doesn't that show that they're as powerful as Mosheh?"

She turned to Kheti, and tapped him on his head. "Hello, anyone home?"

Anger coursed through him. How dare she? He wasn't going to stay and be insulted. He stood to move away from her.

"Not so fast, boy," she said. "What use was it for the magicians to produce more blood? It's water that we need, not more blood."

She was right, though Kheti hated to admit it. "And couldn't the magicians get rid of the blood?"

"Nope." She rubbed her snowy white eyebrows. "They tried, of course, but when they failed, they went back into their quarters, and Pharaoh followed their lead. I haven't seen him since."

There was still no sign of Papa. Perhaps he'd talked to the palace diviners and determined the real source of the blood, rather than listen to some old woman's ramblings. But was there some truth in her tales? Or were her tales merely the mumblings of a failing mind? In her old age, Kheti's grandmother had muddled up her past and present but remembered the stories of her youth as though they'd happened yesterday. "Where did this Mosheh come from?"

The woman raised an eyebrow. "It's a long story, laddie. Have you got enough time to hear it?"

He sat down again. "I'll be here until my father returns." And that could be a long time.

She wriggled on her seat. "I do like the company."

He shifted his position. "Mosheh?"

"It's a story of terrible times. Pharaoh's father was scared of the Hebrews multiplying too fast, so he decided to deal with the situation."

The conversation that Kheti had eavesdropped on so long ago was coming back to him. "Didn't he try to kill all the boys?"

She fixed him with her gaze. "You going to let me tell the story?"

"Please go on," he muttered.

"Killing the baby boys was one of his sillier ideas. First, he instructed the Hebrew midwives to kill any boy at birth, but they wouldn't kill their own. If Pharaoh had wanted the job done, he should have sent soldiers."

The old woman had a point.

"So the midwives came up with the excuse that Hebrew women were so quick in birthing that the babies were born well before they arrived." She chuckled. "Trust women to outsmart mere men. Then Pharaoh sent soldiers to toss all the boys into the river, but that didn't always work either because the parents hid their children."

"And Mosheh was one of the hidden ones?"

"Mosheh's parents—" She wrinkled her brow. "I hate forgetting names, but foreign names are so hard to remember. Amram, that's right. Amram and Jochebed. They hid Mosheh for a while, but when he was three moons old, he couldn't be hidden any longer. They wove a papyrus basket and covered it with pitch and hid it among the reeds on the edge of the river."

"Sounds like quite a risk," Kheti said, thinking of all the crocodiles he'd seen on the river's edge that morning.

"Yes and no. They had Mosheh's sister watch the baby."

Mosheh had obviously survived.

"Pharaoh's daughter went down to bathe at the river and saw the basket hidden among the reeds. When they opened it, there was Mosheh, crying like his heart would break."

"And what did Pharaoh's daughter do?" Kheti asked.

"She couldn't resist such a handsome, healthy child with cute dimples. Mosheh's sister came and asked if Pharaoh's daughter would like her to find a wet-nurse, and she brought Mosheh's own mother."

Kheti whistled. "Brilliant."

"A woman after my own heart. Not only did Pharaoh's daughter let Jochebed nurse the baby, she paid her to do it. When Mosheh was weaned, he came to live in the palace, and I looked after him in the royal nursery. Pharaoh's daughter never had any other children, so Mosheh got the best. Training in reading, writing, and the arts of war."

Could this old woman have truly been a palace nurse? But what of her story of Mosheh and his god, the river and the curse? Kheti glanced toward the palace, willing his father to return with more news to clarify her tale, but also wanting him delayed so he could find out more.

"But Mosheh has been away somewhere, hasn't he? Do you know where he's been?"

She snorted. "Of course. I was there. Mosheh's mother weaned him late. He heard her sing the stories and songs of his people." She shook her head. "We always thought of Mosheh as Egyptian. He spoke our language, ate our food, and wore our clothes, but he wasn't blind. He saw the sufferings of his people, and he knew he was one of them. One day, Mosheh saw an Egyptian beating a Hebrew, so he killed the Egyptian and buried him in the sand."

Kheti leaned forward. "And someone saw?"

"Someone saw. The next day, Mosheh intervened as two Hebrews quarreled, and one of the men demanded, 'Who made you ruler and judge over us? Are you thinking of killing me as you killed the Egyptian?' When Pharaoh heard about the Egyptian's death, he wanted Mosheh dead, so Mosheh fled into the desert."

Footsteps emanated from the doorway beside him, and Papa appeared, squinting in the blaze of light. Kheti stood. "Sorry, I must go. Thank you for speaking to me."

"Come again anytime," the woman said.

She sounded lonely, but it was unlikely they'd meet again, so Kheti wasn't making any promises.

CHAPTER FOUR

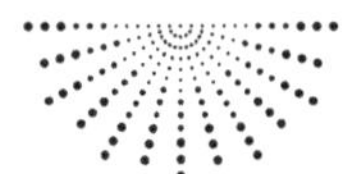

The necks of the oxen strained with effort on the return trip. Kheti's father had a principle about never wasting a journey with an empty load, and he'd bought goods to sell: jars of olive oil, beer, and bags of grain.

Before they'd left the capital, they'd found another cart traveling further south to send some goods to Mama's sister. Kheti never saw his aunt because she'd looked down on them ever since she'd married a wealthy man, but his mother was constantly trying to get back in her favor.

Kheti walked alongside the oxen, encouraging them occasionally with a long switch. He'd excitedly told Papa everything he'd heard from Pharaoh's nanny, and Papa had confirmed the stories she'd told.

"She looked after many royal children, but now she's largely forgotten. Cultivating her friendship may be worthwhile, because I don't think we've heard the last of Mosheh."

They were coming to a larger town. "Let's drop in on the marketplace. See if we can lighten our load by selling some of the produce," Papa suggested.

Kheti took the nearest ox's head to turn it, and they plodded forward. Traveling with oxen was slow, but they were better than donkeys for heavier loads.

The market was still bustling. Drawing up under a tree, Kheti and Papa stood up on their cart. "Olive oil," Kheti called. "Barley."

"Have you got anything to drink?" a man called. "We're parched, and our supplies are running low."

"Beer," Papa said, "And wine."

The price of beer in the capital had risen, but they'd still make a profit.

"I'll take beer," the man called, hastening forward.

"And me," said a second and a third.

Soon they had a line. Within a short time, they had sold everything they had.

"Maybe we should go back to the city," Papa said. "Make a few trips before anyone else thinks to do the same."

"What about Mother?" Kheti asked.

"She won't worry until tomorrow or the next day. If she complains, a gift of linen and honey should sweeten things."

* * *

*K*heti and Papa made two more trips with most of the loads being drinkable. The prices continued to rise each trip, but his father still made a small profit each time.

"Why didn't you charge more?" Kheti asked as they headed for home.

"People remember if they've been overcharged. I would have made more money this time, but they wouldn't buy from me again in the future. Son, always think of the long-term."

Kheti nodded. Another piece of wisdom to note.

Now that most of the load was sold, they were riding in the cart.

"Did you find out anything from the magicians when you delivered the papyrus?" Kheti asked.

"Yes and no. They didn't say much, but it's obvious there was a story there. I suspect they came off the worst in whatever encounters they had with Mosheh."

"I thought there was only one encounter."

"That was the impression they wanted to give, but I went and asked around, which is why I took such a long time getting back to you."

"And?"

"And the turning of the water to blood wasn't the first encounter between Mosheh and Pharaoh. He apparently reappeared in Egypt more than a moon ago."

Kheti turned to him. "That long?"

Papa nodded. "I pieced together a rough account from various people."

Again he went quiet. Papa wasn't much of a talker and tended to thoroughly think through things before he spoke. There was no point in getting impatient.

"Mosheh and his older brother, Aharon, approached Pharaoh soon after Mosheh returned to Egypt. They told Pharaoh their god's message: 'Let my people go, so that they may hold a festival to me in the wilderness.'"

Give the slaves a day off? They'd have more luck asking for all Pharaoh's gold.

Kheti flicked one of the oxen to keep it in step with the other. "I can't imagine Pharaoh was too impressed."

"Indeed. He basically said, 'Who is your god that I should obey him? I don't know him, and I won't let you go.'"

"Sounds too polite," Kheti said with a grim laugh. "He probably told them he was the son of the great Ra and follower of Hapi, and Sehkmet, Anubis, and Osiris."

Kheti had only seen Pharaoh once in his life, but Pharaoh had stood on the raised platform, skin oiled and gleaming with gold, like he owned the world, and other Egyptians were ants beneath his feet.

"He told Mosheh and Aharon to stop distracting his slaves with festivals and get back to work," Papa said. "And Pharaoh issued an order to all the overseers that the Hebrews were no longer to be given straw to make bricks but must gather their own and still produce the same number of bricks."

Kheti gasped. "That's impossible."

"It is, but Pharaoh believed that if the Hebrews were worked to the bone, they'd have no time to think about going out into the desert to offer sacrifices to their god. Pharaoh has always feared a Hebrew uprising." Papa frowned. "Feared them uniting under one leader."

Fear clutched Kheti's throat. "Mother and Tia—you don't think they're in danger from our slaves, do you?"

Papa shook his head. "Not yet. According to those I asked, the Hebrews are angry at Mosheh for increasing their pain. If he hadn't spoken to Pharaoh, then they wouldn't have an even greater work-load now. Pharaoh must have thought he'd effectively silenced Mosheh, but now Mosheh has cursed the Nile."

Cursed with blood that threatened to bring chaos and death if the situation wasn't soon reversed.

"But surely Pharaoh's attitude has changed since Mosheh's power has been demonstrated in so dramatic a way?"

Papa shrugged. "Mosheh has caused the blood, but the question is whether he has the power to heal our land. The magicians don't, and I suspect that was why they wouldn't talk to me. They've been humiliated."

And now everyone, including Kheti, was wondering what had gone wrong. What power did Mosheh have that the magicians didn't?

"Did you hear anything else?"

"Only one more thing," Papa said. "Before the Nile was cursed, Mosheh and Aharon went back to Pharaoh and repeated their demands, and Pharaoh asked them to prove themselves with a miracle."

Kheti turned toward his father. "And did they do one?"

"They did indeed. Aharon threw his staff on the floor, and it turned into a snake."

Kheti whistled through his teeth.

"Our Pharaoh didn't lose his head for a minute. He called the magicians in. They threw down their staffs, and they also became snakes."

Awe filled him. Magicians had always made Kheti's skin crawl, but they were the mediators between men and the gods. He'd heard they had many miraculous powers. "But if Pharaoh's magicians could create snakes, why won't they talk about it?"

Papa frowned. "I had to ask that question three times before anyone would answer me."

"And?" Kheti raised an eyebrow.

"And Aharon's snake swallowed the magicians' snakes."

Kheti gulped. That was not a good sign. It suggested that Aharon, a slave, was somehow superior to the palace's best. Kheti squared his shoulders. There was no reason to give up yet. Mosheh and Aharon hadn't proven that they could solve the blood problem. Tonight, Kheti would pray to Hapi, god of the inundation, and Sehkmet, goddess of blood. Together they controlled the level of the inundation and ensured the fertility of their land. Together they should be more powerful than one elderly man and his brother, and a god with so little power that his people had fled famine into slavery.

But if Hapi and Sehkmet had ensured the bountiful harvests and the greatness of the Egyptian nation, why hadn't they sorted out the situation and restored all things to their order? If all the fish were already dead, then all the creatures who relied on the fish would be next. Soon the plants of the river would also die, and the plants of the river were Kheti's family's livelihood.

CHAPTER FIVE

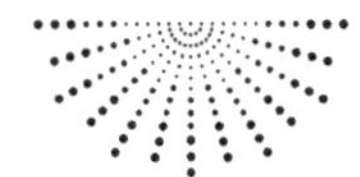

Kheti and his father were nearly home when the wheel of their cart broke. It took a long time to repair, and they'd had to spend the night huddled in their cart to protect its contents. In such troubled times, robbers had multiplied and become bolder.

In the morning, the oxen grumbled about being hitched back into their yoke, and a cantankerous ox kicked Kheti.

Yet again, it was too much beer and too much bread for breakfast. Without the bread, the excess beer would be making his head spin. Kheti longed for water, but there was still no good water to be found.

"Ready, son?" Papa held his switch ready to touch the lead oxen's rump.

"More than ready," Kheti muttered, swinging up onto the cart.

They moved forward, climbing the last slight rise. At the top of the incline, the whole Nile delta spread before them, a profusion of channels, newly turned black earth, and lush grass. The water sparkled in the sun.

Wait.

Sparkled?

"Papa, the river is water again!" Kheti called, excitement coursing through him. "The blood's gone."

Papa swiveled his head to look at all the water in sight. He leaned against the cart and let out a long breath. "Just in time to save our stock."

"You said the magicians were confident they could heal the land. They must have changed the blood into water."

"I hope so," Papa said. "I hope so."

Why was there such hesitancy in Papa's voice? Didn't he believe their gods had made Egypt mighty? Mightier than the kingdoms before them. The Hebrews might have their own gods, but of what use was a god whose people were slaves?

As their cart approached the farm, Tia dashed out. "Water! We have water."

Avraham came and unhitched the oxen. "They'll need a good rest," Papa said. "They've been back and forward a few times to the city."

"Do you think the river's safe now?" Avraham asked.

Papa rubbed his chin. "I think we should take some extra precautions in case of crocodiles."

"They've eaten a lot of rotting fish," Avraham said "The young master didn't get as many as he wanted for the fields."

Which meant Pentu was likely in a bad temper. Not that bad moods were too unusual, if his new wife's expressions could be trusted. Did Kheti's brother take out his moods on her? They'd been married the papyrus season before last, and she'd brought great joy to their family with the birth of her first child, a son. Little Hepu had been named after his grandfather, and Kheti and Tia visited as often as possible. Kheti could have wasted hours holding Hepu, staring at his perfectly formed fingers and toes.

His parents' marriage wasn't one that Kheti wanted, but he'd never seen Papa take out his frustrations on Mama, although at times Papa must want to roll his eyes at her behavior. He'd once told Kheti to look at the heart when he chose a wife, not the outside. As most of Papa's wisdom came from daily life, Kheti assumed this was a lesson learned the hard way. His mother was beautiful, but she behaved like a pharaoh. Kheti needed to make sure Tia got out more, so that she wouldn't become like their mother.

* * *

"*P*entu and Tia," Kheti said, later that afternoon. "I'm going to the lake to bathe. Do you want to come?"

"Mama, can I go?" Tia asked, bouncing up from where she was seated.

His mother fixed her gaze on Kheti. "She can go, if you keep a strict watch over her."

Tia squealed and hurried to get ready. Pentu scowled. "I don't want to go if she is going to make that kind of racket."

"You were young once," Kheti said.

"Not that young," Pentu said.

Would Pharaoh's nanny label Pentu *man* or *boy*? Now that Pentu was married, he claimed to be a man, but Pharoah's nanny would probably still say, "Time will tell, time will tell."

Tia returned, having covered her head and arms. Their mother insisted that she not let her skin darken like some farm slave. According to Kheti's mother, the paler a girl's skin, the higher her chances of marriage. Marriage seemed to be all his mother cared about.

Usually Kheti was the only one at the lake, but today there were several people at the far end. Pentu rushed straight in. Kheti would have done the same if he had been alone, but he'd promised to look after Tia. She'd never been given the opportunity to learn to swim. In fact, he'd been surprised his mother had agreed to her coming at all. Maybe being around someone with so much energy tired Mama out more than she liked to admit.

"Come on, Tia. Leave your veil on the beach and come in. There's no need to be afraid. It's shallow until further out."

"Ooh," Tia said as she placed her foot in its papyrus sandal into the water.

"You'll get used to the cold," he said. "Come in deeper. It's only up to your waist here."

She waded in with further *oohs* and *aahs* as the cold water rose higher. Kheti tried not to feel envious of Pentu as he swam to and fro in the deeper water. Today was about giving Tia a good time. She had none of the freedoms he and Pentu had.

The water was now up to Tia's chest, and she giggled as she pushed down her billowing clothes.

"Now duck down like this." Kheti demonstrated. The cool, clean water closed over his head and the fear and uncertainty of the last few days washed off him.

He popped out of the water, and Tia laughed. "Your hair is all plastered down like black fur."

He grinned. "It feels great. Now I am going to rub all the dust and grime out of it like this." He dipped his head under the water and scrubbed his scalp. His hair and skin always felt better after swimming.

"Mama will get cross if my hair is wet."

"She won't know," he said. "It will be dry before we reach home."

Tia looked around as though fearing their mother had somehow followed them, then pulled out the leather tie and unraveled her braid. Ducking under the water, she followed his example before standing up and spluttering. "You're right. It does feel good."

Kheti showed her how to rub her feet with the fine sand, and she ducked under the water a few more times.

"Show me how to swim," she said.

Kheti swam up and down a few times, reveling in the silky coolness of the water on his skin. He'd learned to swim by watching frogs. The strokes looked odd, but they worked.

"Can I come swimming with you again?" Tia asked.

Selfishly, Kheti wanted to say no, to say this was his special place. But it wasn't her fault that she was a girl. Pentu certainly wouldn't bother to take her.

"Next time, I'll give you another swimming lesson."

Tia flashed him a smile that warmed his heart. He hadn't thought she was lonely, but maybe she was. Their mother had never allowed her to play with the neighbors because of all that, "We're descendants of priests" nonsense. Avraham had a daughter Tia's age, but slaves were definitely off the possible playmates list. Poor Tia.

Something tickled Kheti's feet and he lashed out. What was that? He put his head under the water and peered through the blurriness. There was a flash of silver, and another and another. Fish? How could there be fish? Hadn't all the fish died?

"Tia, come and look. There's fish."

"But they all died." She waded toward him.

"That's what I thought," Kheti said. "But here are fish and there's no trace of the blood at all. It's like it never happened. When I went to scrub the bottom of the boat, the red waterline had disappeared. I thought maybe Pentu had washed it."

She snorted. "Did you really think Pentu would have done your work for you?"

It had surprised him, but Kheti hadn't had any other explanation. He scanned the shore of the lake. Nothing. He'd have expected there would still be a red line and dead fish, but it looked like someone had come and scrubbed the whole area clean. He shivered as though a cool breeze had blown across his wet skin. Did Mosheh have this sort of power?

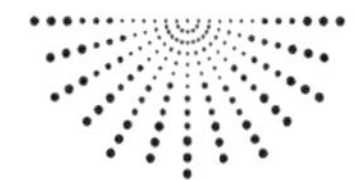

CHAPTER SIX

"Kheti, come!" Papa called a few mornings later.

Kheti groaned. Papa got up even earlier than Kheti did.

"Hurry. Come and look."

Kheti got to his feet and, still rubbing his eyes, went outside. Papa pointed at the river. Oh no. Once again, the river's surface was dark. Surely the blood wasn't back.

Kheti rubbed his eyes again. No, this wasn't blood. The surface of the water was churning, and a writhing, pulsating tide of blackness was leaving the river.

"What is it?" he asked.

"I don't know, but we'd better go and see."

Heart pounding, the two of them hurried toward the water. Whatever it was, the dark mass was coming toward them, widening and spreading across the ground.

"It's hopping," Papa said. "Could it be frogs?"

They were frogs. Frogs Kheti had assumed were dead. Could they, like the fish in the lake, have been miraculously replenished? His skin prickled. He'd been right to fear the magicians.

Their power was much greater than he'd imagined. Much greater. Or was this plague also the work of Mosheh and his god?

"Could the frog spawn have survived the blood?" Papa asked.

"But it's only been seven nights since the river first turned to blood, and a few since the blood disappeared. That's not enough time for the eggs to hatch and the tadpoles to grow legs. It's like what happened at the lake."

Papa turned to him with his eyebrow raised, and Kheti told him what he and Tia had observed.

Croak, croak, croak. The swarming frogs were drawing close. The throbbing chorus grew louder until Kheti covered his ears with his hands.

Kheti stood frozen beside Papa. Had he truly woken up, or was this a nightmare?

But as the first frogs reached them, Papa grabbed his arm too tightly for a dream and pulled him toward the house at a run. "We've got to close the doors and cover the papyrus vats," he panted as they ran.

"Do you think they'll come that far?" Kheti asked.

Papa gestured over his shoulder. "Look back and tell me if they're stopping."

Kheti turned. The ground behind him was completely black, and still the tide of frogs came up out of the river. He would never have believed the Nile contained so many frogs, but the croaking, hopping proof was right behind them.

They reached the house.

"Tell Tia and your mother," Papa said. "Then come to the sheds as soon as you can."

The lids to the vats were heavy to maneuver. Papa would need all the slaves to help.

"Mother. Tia," Kheti shouted as he ran into the house. "Hurry! Close all the doors!"

His mother stumbled out of her room, her hair in disarray around her shoulders. "What's the emergency?"

Kheti pointed out the window, and her eyes widened and face paled. "What is it?"

"Frogs, more frogs than you've ever seen. Coming this way."

"Why?" she wailed. "Who is out to destroy us?"

Kheti didn't have time for her questions. He rushed to the front door and locked it. Tia came into the front room, looked out the window, and ran toward the back door.

Kheti and Tia rushed from door to door, window to window, their actions accompanied by their mother's wails.

Holding the last heavy wooden shutter, Kheti dared to take the time to look out. The writhing glistening mass of frogs were mounting the front gate.

"I must help Father. Don't leave the house," he yelled over the roar of croaking.

"Go out this window," Tia said. "I'll fasten it behind you."

"I'll knock if we need to come back in." Although he doubted anyone would hear any knocks over the croak-croak-croak of the seething mass of frogs.

Kheti ran around the backs of the buildings, where the ground was still clear, and used another window to climb into the shed. Inside Papa was directing the slaves, who were making a horrible grief-stricken moaning as they covered the last vat.

"The house is closed up, Papa," Kheti said, panting.

"Master," Avraham said. "All is done. May we go?"

Papa looked at the fearful men dripping with sweat in front of him. "Yes, yes. Go home. Secure your own dwellings."

The slaves clambered out a window and took off at a run.

Papa turned to him. "The job isn't done. There are holes everywhere. Block them with anything you can find."

Kheti and his father worked steadily, stooping to fill the holes with cloth and stones. The draining of the vats the previous week had created new runnels and entryways through the walls.

Kheti finished three sides of the shed and stood to see how Papa was managing. Papa was mopping his brow with his arm and leaning against the earthen wall of the vat.

Already Kheti could see the frogs leaping outside the final unsealed window. It was time to shut himself and Papa into the darkness. First, Kheti lit a small clay lamp. Outside the window, the ground was covered in a pulsating carpet of frogs. They'd looked black when they'd come out of the water, but now he could see individual frogs. Some were dark green with a stripe of paler green and others were gray with red blotches. He'd have thought them pretty if he'd seen an individual frog, but in these numbers? They were terrifying.

Kheti pushed the shutter closed, closing out the daylight but not the noise. Now the small clay lamp was their only source of light. Kheti went over to the drinking bucket and carried a scoop of water to his father. Papa was breathing hard, and he splashed his head and neck before drinking.

"Now we wait," he mouthed at Kheti. The croaking made talking impossible. They sat and waited, listening to the throbbing sounds from outside. Should Kheti be here or with Tia and his mother? His mother would be of no help to Tia at all.

Beneath Kheti's feet, a louder croak rang out. Looking down, he saw that the sheer volume of frogs outside had pushed the cloths up a drain, and a few frogs had found their way into the shed. He tamped in the cloth more securely in the drain then pursued the frogs, gathering them in his hands. Then he tentatively opened the window shutter. Finding it still clear, he flung the frogs out.

In the distance, he could see Avraham heading toward them. He carried a broom and swept a way clear for his feet. Kheti watched him until he reached the window and then hauled him in. Avraham gestured to them that he'd stay, so Papa pointed for Kheti to head for the house. Avraham handed him the broom and lowered him quickly out the window, but not quickly enough. Some extra high jumpers made it in through the open window before Avraham could close it.

Outside, the frogs were over knee-deep in places, and the broom was useless. Kheti gave up, and keeping his eyes away from the frogs, strode forward, trying to ignore the squelching as he crushed frogs underfoot. His sandaled feet slipped, but he made it to the window of the house, managed to attract attention, and clambered inside. Tia greeted him with a pale, teary face and a clinging hug.

They spent the rest of the day repelling determined invaders and blocking up each hole again and again until Papa returned, and then they all collapsed onto their sleeping mats.

Some time later, a scream rang through the house, and Kheti woke, heart pounding in the dark. He stumbled out of bed and there was a slippery squelch underfoot. The frogs had found another way into the house.

There was another scream. "Get it out! Get it out!"

Kheti navigated safely out of his room.

"I can't see any more," Papa said.

"I can't see them, but I can feel them," Mama shrieked. "Do something. I refuse to have frogs in my bed!"

Papa came out of the bedroom as Tia arrived from another. "Kheti and Tia, we'll have to search for where they got in."

They lit some oil lamps and set off to search, holding the lamps in the palms of their hands. Wherever the first frog had gotten in, plenty had followed. There were frogs in the kitchen pans, frogs in the drinking water jars, and frog eyes shining at them from every corner. Outside, the whole chorus of them seemed to be laughing.

Tia waved Kheti and her father over and pointed to a new hole behind a stool.

A few more frogs hopped in before they found more cloth to

block the hole. Then they picked up as many frogs as they could and placed them in a bag.

"Drop the bag out the window," Papa shouted. "We'll deal with them in the morning."

Lying on his mat, Kheti couldn't get back to sleep. Their family, and all of Egypt, relied on the Nile and had believed Hapi and the other gods controlled its rhythms, but now the river was rebelling. First the blood, and now the spewing out of all its frogs. Where would this end?

The next day was spent fighting to keep the frogs out of the house and shed, but it was a losing battle. At nightfall, Papa returned to the main house and Kheti's mother insisted they make a sacrifice to Heqet. "After all, it's her responsibility to get rid of this plague."

His mother prepared an elaborate food sacrifice and burned incense in a censer. In her prayer, she apologized to Heqet for not being able to get to the local shrine to pay the priest to make the offerings on the riverbank. Kheti thought the gods would understand.

During the second night, his mother's screams woke them so many times that Kheti gave up on sleep and simply guarded the door of his parent's room, dropping any frogs he caught into a large pottery jar where their cries reverberated like a musical instrument.

The following day was a repeat with new screams from the kitchen as his mother discovered more frogs among the foodstuffs and cooking pans. Kheti would have found the whole debacle funny if it wasn't for his pounding headache and lack of sleep.

On the third night, he prayed to any god he could think of to get rid of the frogs so they could sleep. It must have worked, because he did manage to fall asleep while leaning against the wall outside his parents' room.

When he woke in the morning, something was different.

Outside the house he heard a screech of birds, and then more screeches as they squabbled.

The frogs.

Kheti jumped to his feet. There was no more croaking of frogs.

He went to the nearest window and pushed open the shutter. No, the frogs hadn't disappeared, but they were silent and still, their skins dull in the rays of the sun. He climbed out the window. The frogs lay in piles against the walls of the house, stiff legs stretched out. He reached down and prodded one with his finger. It was quite, quite dead. Pentu was going to have all the rotting things he needed to plow into his fields after all, and they'd better get to it quickly before the sun rose and brought back the stench of the week before.

Kheti rubbed his face, weary to the bone. What would come next? Did this plague have anything to do with Mosheh or was it just a coincidence?

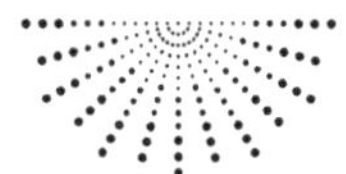

CHAPTER SEVEN

"Kheti." Papa sounded as exhausted as Kheti felt. "I need you to return to the capital and find out what's going on."

It had taken three days to clear up the frogs and bury them. Three days of heat and muck and a stench that seared their noses. Three days of back-breaking work, shoveling the frogs into piles and loading them in the cart to take to the fields.

The season of Akhet was nearly finished, and they were already behind on plowing to get ready for the season of Peretor.

"I do not want you to go alone," Papa said. "I cannot spare Avraham, but would you be willing to take his son with you?"

"I will, Father." Avraham's son, Yosef, had grown up thin and scrawny and quiet, far different from the little boy who'd briefly played in the mud with Kheti that one time. Yosef didn't look like he'd be much use if they encountered any bandits along the way.

"We need the oxen for plowing, but I'll send you with donkeys." Papa scratched his chin and thought for a long moment. "You can sell some of the rope we have stored and buy olive oil." He gave a weak attempt at a smile. "Then, if we're hit with a plague of mice—

gods forbid—we'll at least have exchanged the rope for something non-perishable."

* * *

*K*heti and Yosef were sent off with heads full of instructions and more gifts to send to Kheti's aunt. Papa had also given Kheti the name of the rope buyer and told him to bring back jars of olive oil as something less susceptible to loss.

Yosef was shy but willing and eager to be helpful. They both spent most of the trip with one hand holding their noses to block the reek of rotting frogs, and the other waving to keep the accompanying flies away from their faces.

When Yosef saw the capital, he was silent for a long while before firmly gripping the donkeys' halters. Apparently, he'd never been to the capital before. Yosef waited outside the temple while Kheti made the usual offerings, then followed behind him as Kheti led the way through a gate and into the noisy streets beyond.

Due to his father's references and contacts, the business was quickly concluded. Kheti left Yosef at the palace stable with the donkeys while he looked for the old woman. She was exactly where he'd seen her last time, as though she had grown into the seat.

"Hello, boy. Back again for some palace gossip?" she said with a cheeky grin.

Kheti nodded. He'd been worried he wouldn't find her again or that she wouldn't talk.

He squatted beside her and drew a small pot of honey out of the pouch around his waist.

Her eyes gleamed. "How did you know I like honey? Trying to buy my favor, are you?"

He smiled. He'd given her honey because she didn't have many teeth left.

"Did the frogs come here?" he asked.

She nodded. "Hopping into every house and every bed."

So they'd been cleaned up quickly. "Even the palace?"

Her eyes twinkled. "Even the palace. Pharaoh managed to avoid being too inconvenienced by the blood because he had vast stocks of wine, and he was always happy to avoid bathing, even as a little boy." She wagged a finger. "But the frogs were harder to ignore. Hopped right into the palace. They didn't know they were invading his sacred space." She thrust her face uncomfortably close to Kheti's, so he could see her few remaining teeth. "When he woke in the morning there were two sitting looking at him." She giggled. "I named them Mosheh and Aharon because they've been as pesky as frogs."

Kheti chuckled. "Was this Mosheh's doing?"

She stared at him. "It's them who brought the frogs."

Kheti had hoped that the two plagues hadn't been linked. That perhaps this had nothing to do with Mosheh and Aharon. That perhaps they'd given up after the plague of blood. Obviously not.

"Seven nights after the Nile turned to blood, Mosheh and Aharon came in to see Pharaoh and repeated their demand, 'This is what the Lord says: "Let my people go, so that they may worship me."' Their god also said, 'If you refuse to let them go, I will send a plague of frogs on your whole country. The Nile will teem with frogs. They will come up into your palace and your bedroom and onto your bed, into the houses of your officials and on your people, and into your ovens and kneading troughs. The frogs will come up on you and your people and all your officials.'"

It was like a drum beating out the same rhythm. Request. Refusal. Punishment. Request. Refusal. Punishment.

Punishment for everyone. Days of frogs invading every place they could access. It was good to know that even Pharaoh and his officials hadn't been exempt. During past floods, droughts, and storms, the people in Kheti's area had complained bitterly that

Pharaoh was protected from the hardships of ordinary people. At least this time it was not true.

"And again Aharon stretched out his staff over the streams and canals and ponds, and the frogs came out of the water at their command."

"And Pharaoh's magicians? What did they do?"

She sighed. "Oh, they somehow made more frogs come out of the water, but they couldn't do a thing about stopping the frogs."

Kheti frowned. "But the plague did stop."

"Yes, but that had nothing to do with the magicians. It didn't take Pharaoh long to have had enough of the frogs." She grimaced. "He soon summoned Mosheh and Aharon and begged them to pray to their god to take the frogs away. Pharaoh promised them he'd let them go and make their sacrifices."

Kheti's shoulders relaxed. Things would be fine now. Now Pharaoh had given in to their god's demands, their country could return to normal.

"And?"

"And Mosheh said, 'Pharaoh, I leave to you the honor of setting the time for me to pray for you and your officials and your people. I will pray your houses will be free of frogs and the only frogs left will be the ones that ought to be in the Nile."

Kheti leaned forward. "And what time did he set?"

"The very next morning."

Goosebumps rose on Kheti's arms. By his calculations, the frogs had indeed been dead at the time that Pharaoh had set.

"And what a reek that caused. Pharaoh should have asked their god to have them cleared away as well because he wasn't happy to have the palace full of dead frogs."

No one on the farm had been happy about the dead frogs either. They'd all been angry at the extra work, and Kheti was worried about the strain he'd seen on his father's face at the end of each long day.

"And what time did Pharaoh set for the slaves to have their festival?"

She shook her head. "He's not keeping his word at all."

A dread settled in Kheti's stomach. What if Pharaoh kept refusing? Would Mosheh's god send more plagues? How long would they last, and how severe would they be?

"And our magicians? What have they been doing?" Kheti asked, his voice tinged with desperation.

She snorted. "Precious little. I don't know whether they really have been producing blood and frogs. The red in the water could have been a trick. The magicians didn't let us get close enough to smell or taste their magic, and the frogs were already coming up in a continuous stream. How could we tell if they actually caused more to leap out of the water?"

"But the snakes," Kheti said. "They did turn their staffs into snakes."

She nodded. "Yes, they did. They have some power, but how much remains to be seen. They certainly haven't been able to solve any of the problems despite slaughtering a huge number of animals and praying constantly." She indicated the entrance beside her. "That drone you can hear? That's the magicians at their prayers. They're worried about what Mosheh might do next."

Kheti swallowed. "What do you think will be next?"

"I don't know, but I fear it." She shook her head. "I fear it. Mosheh's god's power has proved to be like a butcher with a very sharp knife. Where he says he cuts, he cuts. No hesitation. No misses. And Pharaoh has always been stubborn. He will not yield." Her voice dropped to a whisper. "I fear he might have met his match."

Kheti hoped not. All his life, he'd been told that Pharaoh was the incarnation of the gods. He didn't really know what that meant, but at the very least he expected Pharaoh would ensure order and wealth for their nation. If that order was lost, what would it mean for every one of Egypt's people? For Kheti's family?

"Thanks for the honey, sonny," she said.

When Kheti had seen how bedraggled and thin she looked, he'd wished he'd brought more than honey. He'd have to see what his father could spare next time.

"Can I come again?" Kheti asked.

"Anytime." She clutched the container of honey.

He stood to go but then turned back. "What am I to call you?"

She gave a toothless grin. "Nanny will do. That's what I'm used to, and not many people bother with me anymore." Her voice was sad.

CHAPTER EIGHT

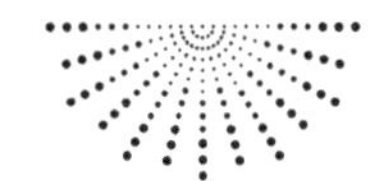

The donkeys plodded along with the precious jars of oil strapped on each side of their bodies. Kheti and Yosef walked alongside them under a cloudless sky as they headed towards home. Yosef wasn't much of a conversationalist, but the trip would feel even longer if they didn't talk about something.

"Do you remember trying to help me catch a frog?" Kheti asked.

Yosef raised his head. "I wondered if you remembered that day."

Kheti mainly remembered it because of how sternly he'd been rebuked for daring to play with a slave. "Your name was easy to remember; it's not common among my people."

Yosef looked across at him. "It is a common name among the Hebrews. Have you not been told of our Yosef?" He flushed, looking down at his feet as if fearful he'd done something that wasn't permitted.

"No," Kheti replied, curious why Yosef assumed him familiar with Hebrew history.

Yosef remained silent, scratching the closest donkey on the rump.

If there were more plagues to come, Mosheh's name would surely be remembered. But who was Yosef?

It didn't look as though Kheti would find out if Yosef continued to keep such a tight rein on his tongue. There was no one else around to see them talking, so why didn't Yosef relax?

The silence stretched on. Maybe Kheti would have to speak to tempt Yosef to say more.

"My parents named me after two famous Egyptians. A treasurer under Mentuhotep II and a famous scribe. They hoped I'd bring honor to the family."

"Yosef was also very well known and held in high honor."

Kheti walked on. If this man was so famous, why had he not heard of him? But then perhaps he had been a person who lived far away and in a different time who mattered only to the slaves. "I have not heard of your Yosef," Kheti said.

"He was once famous in Egypt." Yosef's abrupt tone suggested he was aggrieved that Kheti did not know this. Then Yosef clamped his mouth shut and looked at the ground in front of his feet. He had good reason—slaves who spoke to Pentu in such a tone could expect a beating.

Kheti's mother hadn't looked happy when his father had sent Yosef with him on this trip. What was she afraid of? A friendship between Yosef and himself seemed unlikely. Not with the ways they'd been raised, and not with society's views on what was proper curbing any natural conversation.

But there was no one here. No one to frown or criticize. Today was an opportunity to talk to someone whose language and customs were so different from Kheti's own.

"I have always wished we could have continued playing with the frog," Kheti said. "I was sorry about what happened."

"It was always going to end that way." Yosef glanced around as though to see if anyone was near. "Your kind don't often talk to my kind. Your brother has never even bothered to learn my name."

"I'm not my brother," Kheti said. "I want to talk to you, and the first thing I want to know is who was this Yosef you are named after?"

Yosef took a deep breath. "It's not a short tale."

Kheti laughed. "It's not a short walk home."

For the first time, Yosef raised his head and smiled. It was a shy smile, a smile that looked as though it hadn't been used often. Maybe it had never been directed toward anyone outside his own family.

"Many, many years ago there was a man named Avraham."

"Like your father," Kheti said.

Yosef nodded. "The first Avraham was the ancestor of all the Hebrews. He lived far away, in Ur near the Tigris and Euphrates rivers, and our God called Avraham to leave and follow him to the land that he would give him—"

Kheti had always believed that Ra was the creator of all, but Yosef definitely wasn't referring to Ra. Yosef talked about their god as if he could be known. As if he could be trusted. The Egyptian gods were unknowable, far removed from the affairs of men, and the tales about them were often fantastical and cruel tales of murder and violence and ugliness.

"—the Promised Land, the land of Canaan." Yosef pointed in the direction of the Red Sea.

Kheti had heard of it. It hadn't sounded like a place he'd want to visit, with lots of tribes warring against each other. Nothing like Egypt with its grand temples, palaces, and canals. Egypt was the envy of the whole world.

"Avraham's God promised that he would bless him and make him a blessing to the whole world," Yosef continued.

So Avraham's god hadn't kept his word. No one could call a bunch of slaves a blessing to the whole world. However, since Yosef had finally dared to talk to him, Kheti wasn't going to point this out.

"Avraham and his wife couldn't have children for many years, but they finally had a son when Avraham was one hundred and his wife ninety."

Kheti cocked an eyebrow. "That sounds like a legend."

"It was a miracle from Elohim, and it was the first of many—"

"Is that what you call your god?" Kheti asked.

"He has many names," Yosef said. "You'll have to ask Abba if you want to know the rest of the story. He's the one named after Avraham."

This was beginning to get interesting. "Go on."

Yosef held up his index finger. "Avraham had Yitzchaq, Yitzchaq had Yaakov, and Yaakov had twelve sons, one of whom was Yosef."

Now they were getting to the real story.

"But Yosef's brothers were jealous of him, and one day they sold him to some slave traders who took him to Egypt."

"And that's how you came to be here? You're all descendants of this Yosef?" Kheti asked.

"Not exactly," Yosef said.

One of the donkeys stopped walking. He did that sometimes: just stopped when he was thirsty. Kheti looked around and saw a pool and a little shrine nearby. "Let's give the donkeys a break."

The donkeys had a long drink, and so did Kheti and Yosef. Then they set off again.

"What happened to Yosef in Egypt?" Kheti asked.

"At first, he did really well. He was sold to Potiphar and quickly rose into a high position within the household. But Potiphar's wife accused Yosef of something, and he was thrown into prison."

Kheti looked at Yosef. "What was he accused of?"

Yosef flushed. "Rape, because he refused to sleep with her."

"And his master didn't believe him?"

Yosef rubbed his eyebrow. "You're joking, right?"

Kheti frowned. "What do you mean?"

"What master is going to believe a slave over his own wife?"

Now it was Kheti's turn to flush. He never thought about what it was like to be a slave. To be disbelieved simply because he had no status.

"So Yosef went to jail?" Kheti said quickly to cover his embarrassment.

Yosef nodded. "Even in jail he was soon put in charge."

This Yosef sounded like a man of integrity. A man like Papa.

"While he was in the prison, two of Pharaoh's servants had dreams. Yosef was given the power to interpret them."

Kheti stared at Yosef. "What do you mean, given the power?"

"Elohim gave him the power."

So Yosef was like the magicians? They interpreted dreams.

"And did Yosef's interpretations come to pass?" Kheti asked.

Yosef nodded. "Yosef had asked one of the men to intervene on his behalf when he once again became Pharaoh's wine taster, but the man forgot all about Yosef."

"That must have made Yosef angry," Kheti said.

The donkey swished its tail to get rid of a cluster of flies.

"Maybe," Yosef said. "But one night Pharaoh himself had a terrible dream that he mentioned to his wine taster. The wine taster remembered Yosef and told Pharaoh about him."

"I bet Pharaoh got him out of the prison super fast."

Yosef nodded. "Pharaoh had two different dreams, but their meaning was the same. One was about grain—seven skinny ears of grain swallowed seven fat ears. Pharaoh also dreamed of seven sleek, fat cows. Then he saw seven starving cows, which ate the seven fat cows, but afterwards they were still as skinny as ever."

Kheti could understand why the dreams disturbed Pharaoh. "Well, was Yosef able to interpret them?"

"Yosef said to Pharaoh, 'I cannot interpret your dreams, but my God will give Pharaoh the answer he desires.'"

This Yosef was not like Egypt's magicians. They would have claimed the power was their own. "And?"

"And the seven fat cows were seven years of plenty that would be followed by seven years of famine," Yosef said. "The famine would be so severe that the years of plenty would be forgotten."

Somewhere, sometime, Kheti had heard of such a famine. Had it been another of the things he had overheard his mother and grandmother talking about when he was a child?

"Yosef suggested to Pharaoh that he appoint someone to collect one-fifth of all the coming harvests to be stored away to prepare for the famine."

"He sounds like a wise man," Kheti said. "Your parents chose a good name for you, a name to live up to."

Yosef beamed. "Pharaoh too thought Yosef was wise, and so Yosef was appointed second-in-command for the whole of Egypt. Because of his preparations, Egypt was saved."

So this was why Yosef assumed Kheti would know of his namesake, but Kheti had never heard of this man. Was Yosef's saving Egypt merely wishful thinking concocted by the Hebrews, or was it a truth Kheti's countrymen had found convenient to bury?

Kheti frowned. "But you said you're not all descended from Yosef."

"No. The famine was severe enough that it affected the surrounding countries, and Yosef's brothers came to Egypt to buy food—" Yosef's jaw tightened and his face drained of color. His gaze darted from side to side. "We might be in trouble. Don't look too quickly, but there are men hiding behind that collection of rocks to the east."

Kheti swallowed. Papa had warned them to look out for thieves. He carefully turned his head and glimpsed movement among the rocks and shadows. There were at least three of them, and Kheti guessed there'd be more. These kinds of cowards didn't show themselves unless they were confident of success.

He turned toward Yosef and muttered, "Any ideas?"

"I'm praying," Yosef said, face pale.

"I was hoping you were doing more than praying."

"Abba always says pray first." Yosef's eyes widened. "Here they come, and there are six, seven, no, eight of them."

There was nowhere to run, nowhere to hide, and no one else in sight.

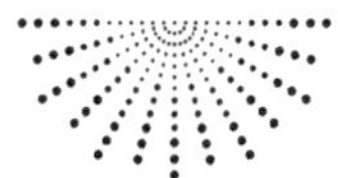

CHAPTER NINE

"Hold tightly onto your switch," Kheti said to Yosef, as he clutched his own. "We might need them."

The men approaching were only half-clothed, and their skin gleamed with oil, accentuating the bulk of their muscles. They swaggered forward, teeth gleaming in unpleasant grins like a bird of prey eyeing off a rabbit.

"What do we have here, men?" the leader said, his voice a low growl. "Two timid mice with their daddy's purchases."

Kheti drew himself up as tall as he could. Papa would not blame him if the goods were stolen, but robbers seldom only took the goods. His heart pounded in his chest. "It's only some olive oil." And the bandits looked like they had access to enough of that already.

"'Only olive oil,' the taller mouse says. Oil is easy to sell, and we'll be very happy to sell it for you."

Kheti's mind had been whirring since they'd first seen the men, but he'd come up blank. Maybe it would be best to just give them the oil. What a day for this to happen, when his only companion was Yosef. Not that Kheti was scary-looking himself.

"Feel free to take the oil," Kheti said, a wobble in his voice.

"Oh, we won't just take the oil, will we men?" The men around him nodded their heads without saying a word. "We'll take the donkeys too."

Kheti didn't see that they could do anything but hand over the halters. If the gods smiled on him and Yosef, they might get away without a serious beating. It all depended on the leader, because the others didn't seem to be anything but followers in his thrall. Kheti flicked his gaze toward Yosef in case he had come up with a plan. Yosef wasn't even paying attention. He was looking in the sky behind the group. *Great.* This wasn't a time to daydream.

Kheti stepped back, touching Yosef's arm as he did so. If he could flick the bad-tempered donkey on the rump hard enough, the ensuing chaos might give them enough time to get away, even if they had to leave the donkeys behind. It was a small chance, but the only chance Kheti could see. The robbers had chosen their ground well. He tensed his arm, ready to hit the donkey.

"Watch out behind you!" Yosef yelled, his voice cracking.

The thieves wouldn't have been human if they hadn't looked. Behind them, a vast billowing cloud of black fury descended, biting and buzzing.

The robbers screamed and slapped at their exposed skin, howling as the black insects, whatever they were, attacked their faces and their eyes.

Yosef grabbed Kheti's arm and pulled him toward the nearest donkey. Kheti grabbed the halter, narrowed his eyes to mere slits, and followed Yosef, who was leading the other donkey. The insects bit him around his ears and neck, leaving a trail of fire behind them. It took all his self-control not to join the bandits in jumping around and screaming.

"Keep walking," Yosef mumbled, keeping his mouth shut.

The donkeys shook their heads and half-bucked, trying to shake off the insects. Kheti concentrated on walking forward. Home was not far. All they had to do was to keep moving as quickly as possible and pray the robbers wouldn't pursue them.

The robbers' shouts were fading behind them, and ahead lay a patch where the infestation seemed less serious. Kheti and Yosef hurried forward, swinging their free arms as they went, to keep the gnats—for that was what they seemed to be—away from their heads.

Nanny had thought there'd be more plagues. Was this the next? The last two had been uncomfortable, but this one was painful. How many plagues would there be before Mosheh's god was satisfied?

A strong breeze blew into their faces, and Kheti opened his eyes as best he could. Yosef's face was covered in pink spots where the gnats had bitten him, and one of his eyes was almost swollen shut.

"Have we got any water?" Yosef asked.

Kheti uncorked the water bag, and they both splashed water on their burning skin. The breeze blew cool on them and brought a tiny bit of relief. When Kheti got home, he was going to submerge himself in the nearest deep water.

"The gnats must be fewer here because of the wind," Yosef said. "Let's hope there are some windy days coming or it's going to be miserable."

"Do you think this is another plague?" Kheti asked.

Yosef tilted his head to one side. "Yes, I do. I mean, I prayed for God's deliverance, but I don't think the miracle was produced for us."

"Why not?"

Yosef wrinkled his brow. "It seems a strange way to rescue us when God could simply have sent a caravan of merchants toward us."

"Come on," Kheti said, tugging his donkey's halter. "If it is another plague, then we'll be needed at home."

Yosef gave a snort of laughter.

"What are you laughing at?" Kheti asked.

"Those men kept insulting our size, but in the end, they were defeated by something far smaller."

Laughter bubbled out of Kheti's throat. "Revenge of the midges."

The donkeys brayed, and Yosef clutched his sides. "See, they agree."

* * *

Once they reached home, Kheti left Yosef holding the donkeys. He went to the house, but it was silent and deserted. Where had the family gone?

As he turned back toward Yosef, the skittish donkey bucked and let out an ear-splitting hee-haw. As if in answer, he heard Papa's holler. Where was he?

Yosef pointed toward the sheds. Once Kheti's eyes adjusted to the dimness, he bit back an exclamation. His whole family was submerged in one of the papyrus vats, with wet cloths draped over their heads.

"Don't laugh, son," Papa said. "It works."

"I'll unload the oil and feed and water the donkeys before I come and tell you how we went," Kheti said.

The gnats ensured he didn't take his time. Shortly afterwards, Kheti lowered himself into the vat with his family. "How long have you been here?"

"Ever since the gnats started biting," Papa said. "Tia's idea."

Tia grinned at him from beneath her unconventional head covering.

Kheti lowered himself into the water, feeling the slime of the papyrus on his feet. "Where's Pentu?"

"He took the oxen and some of the other animals down to the

lake." Papa waited until Kheti settled and then asked, "What's the news from the city?"

Kheti told them what he'd heard, and about the ruffians.

"You mustn't go by yourself again," his mother said.

"We might not have any more problems with them. The timing of the gnats' arrival was so perfect that they probably think we conjured them up." Kheti grinned at the memory of the robbers' howls. If the men had worn less oil and more clothes, the gnats wouldn't have had such an all-over effect. "Yosef was a good choice to send with me. He did well under pressure."

"I could see you were disappointed in his size when you first saw him," Papa said. "But sometimes heart is more important than brawn."

"Where is Yosef now?" Tia asked.

"I sent him home," Kheti said.

"I sent Avraham home too, but they should be here," Papa said. "There are plenty of vats."

"No." Mother slapped the surface of the water. "It wouldn't be right for the slaves to be here with us."

"If these plagues continue, dear," Papa said, "we're going to have to learn to work together."

"Not today," she said with a whine in her voice. "They have their place, and we have ours."

Kheti took a deep breath. It didn't matter why his mother was so against the Hebrew slaves. He intended to make up his own mind. Her attitude had prevented him from developing friendships with the only people nearby who were his age. He and Yosef had gotten along well once Yosef had realized Kheti meant him no harm.

"Father, I'll go and suggest they go down to the lake." Kheti stood.

"Can I come?" Tia asked.

"Tia, I'll need your help to think about what we'll do tonight," their mother said. "We can't sit in the water all night, and we don't know how long this will last."

So far, each plague had lasted a few days. If there hadn't been a few days between each, Kheti and his family would all be seriously struggling with lack of sleep.

Kheti got out of the water and the first of the gnats circled his head. "I'll take the donkeys to the lake as well."

* * *

*A*vraham and his family were not at home. Kheti dragged the reluctant donkeys behind him to the lake. "Come on. You'll appreciate the water once you're there."

Yosef waved to Kheti as he and the donkeys reached the water. The donkeys took off, showering him with sand as they dashed into the shallows, wading out until they were almost submerged. Kheti swam behind them, following their example of plunging his head below the surface for a few moments of cool forgetfulness from the stinging, buzzing haze around him.

Seeing the donkeys had no intention of leaving the water, Kheti swam toward Yosef and his family.

"Yosef has been telling us of your adventures," Avraham said.

Kheti grinned. "They might have ended badly except for his quick thinking."

"That's not what Yosef told us. He said he prayed, and Elohim sent the gnats."

"The timing certainly was perfect," Kheti said with a grin.

"Don't tease the young master," Yosef's mother, Sara, said. "Tell him what you've heard."

"My name is Kheti," he said, now uncomfortable with being called by a title.

"Thank you, Kheti," Avraham said. "A messenger arrived with news from the capital a short while before we came down to the lake."

The messenger must have traveled fast. Presumably he'd gone on to pass the same message to others.

Avraham looked across at Kheti. "Yosef tells me you have been enquiring about Mosheh?"

Kheti nodded. "I was told he sent the blood and the frogs. Are the gnats also his doing?"

"The messenger said that once again Mosheh and Aharon went to Pharaoh, and once again Pharaoh refused to listen," Avraham said. "So God told Aharon to strike the dust of the ground and all Egypt's dust would become gnats."

"There is a lot of dust in Egypt!" Kheti said.

They laughed politely at his joke, but Noach remained quiet, eyes wide.

"He doesn't know you," Yosef's younger sister, Havvah, said. She was about the same age as Tia. A serious girl with wide brown eyes.

"Abba, tell him what is different about this sign," Yosef said.

"Sign?" Kheti said. "We call them plagues."

"Yes, signs of Elohim's wondrous power," Avraham said, as if there was no difference between the words. "With all the previous miracles, the magicians were able to do something with their powers."

"Except rid the land of the blood or frogs," Kheti said.

"This time, they could not match God's power at all. The magicians came to Pharaoh and confessed, 'This is the finger of God.'"

The finger of god. A shiver rippled through Kheti. Nanny had scoffed at the magicians. She called them "boys puffed up with pride." What did it take for the magicians to admit that they could do nothing? To recognize that these wonders were beyond their powers?

Kheti had always assumed the gods were in control, and the

magicians were the mediators from the gods. Now it seemed things were not as simple as he'd believed. If even the magicians were acknowledging the plagues were the finger of god, what did this mean for Kheti's family? And for Egypt? Would the plagues get worse? More inconvenient? More painful?

CHAPTER TEN

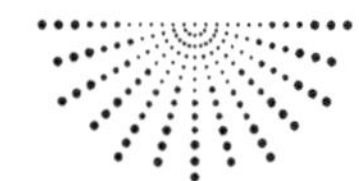

Kheti's mother lay back and fanned herself while Tia applied lotion to her mother's face and neck. Blotchy red bites still lingered, although the gnats had disappeared as abruptly as they'd arrived.

Kheti had spent the last few days rescuing the papyrus from the vats and drying as many pages as possible. The papyrus-making season was almost done, and Kheti and his father would soon make their final papyrus delivery trip to the city. Next they'd plant the crops, then move on to making boats with the reeds that had been drying for that purpose.

Every day when he woke, Kheti would peer anxiously at the sky and the river to check that no other disaster had descended on them overnight. Each day proved hot, dry, and normal, so he would breathe a sigh of relief.

"Tia, are you nearly finished?" Kheti asked. "Avraham's daughter has come to learn how to do the papyrus weaving."

The seasonal slaves had returned to their original master and now they only had Avraham and his family.

"Mama, can I go?" Tia asked.

Her mother waved her away. "Do what you like. Nobody listens to me."

Kheti stifled a smile. Not true. Both her family and slaves jumped at her commands.

Tia accompanied him to the work area, and he introduced her to young Havvah. Tia took some of the drip-free strips from the many hanging over the poles and deftly showed Havvah how to weave the papyrus over and under and how to tuck in the ends. The natural glue within the papyrus helped the ends adhere to themselves. The weavers worked in pairs so they could help each other lift the piles of felt drying pads.

Kheti had paired himself with Avraham so he could ask some of the questions that had been burning in his mind. Yosef had claimed his father was the best storyteller, and stories were just what Kheti wanted. "Yosef said you were named after an ancestor of your people."

"That's true," Avraham said. "And Sara is named after the wife of the same ancestor." He finished weaving the sheet of paper and added the top piece of felt. "Her name was the reason I initially noticed Sara. And once we decided we wanted to marry, your father was willing to give us permission."

"I am sorry you had to ask permission," Kheti said. "It doesn't seem right."

"It is what it is." Avraham's fingers laid out the vertical strips of another papyrus sheet. "I am grateful your father is our master. Life would be much harsher in the brick pits or working in the storage cities."

"Yosef said that Avraham and Sara didn't have any children until they were old. Were they truly so old?"

Avraham smiled gently at him. "Yes. Generation after generation was birthed from this first miracle, and the descendants passed on the history."

"But don't the myths change with time? They do in Egypt."

Avraham was silent for a long moment as though working out what to say. "My father made me repeat the stories over and over until I got them perfect. You have papyrus and stone to record your customs and traditions. We have only our memories and our songs."

Sometimes when the slaves were working in the fields or harvesting papyrus, Kheti had heard their songs. Mournful or joyful, they'd sung them with gusto.

"Avraham didn't die until he was one-hundred and seventy-five," Avraham said.

Kheti whistled, not sure that he believed any man could live to such a great age.

"At seventy-five, when God spoke to him, it started him on a journey south. He even made it to Egypt during a famine."

"Tell me more," Kheti said.

"It would be better to start at the beginning," Avraham said.

He and Kheti transferred their stack of felt to the bigger pile and placed some rocks on top.

"In the beginning," Avraham said, his fingers busy weaving the papyrus, "The heavens were formless and empty, and darkness was over the surface of the deep, and the spirit of Elohim hovered over the waters."

A tingle ran down Kheti's back. Avraham spoke as if he meant every word.

"And Elohim said, 'Let there be light,' and there was light. He separated the light from the darkness, and he called the light 'day' and the dark 'night.' And he saw that it was good, and there was evening and there was morning, the first day."

Egyptians respected gods who brought order, and here was order in Elohim's every word and action.

"Then Elohim said, 'Let the waters above be separated from the waters below.' The waters above he called 'sky' and the waters below he called 'sea.' And he saw that it was good, and there was evening and there was morning on the second day."

Kheti's fingers kept weaving, but his mind was full of pictures of this god bringing order out of chaos, one step at a time. He saw the dry land separated from the waters, as Avraham was describing it, and the creation of all the trees and plants, and fish and birds. Hundreds and thousands of plants and creatures, each unique, and each simply spoken into being by their master, followed by the recurring rhythm of the chorus, "And Elohim saw that it was good, and there was evening and there was morning, that day."

Kheti was reflecting on all the animals in the delta area when Avraham said, "And Elohim said, 'Let us make people in our image, in our likeness, so that they may rule over the fish in the sea and the birds in the sky, over the livestock and all the wild animals, and over all the creatures that move along the ground.' So Elohim created mankind in his own image, in the image of God he created them, male and female he created them."

The words were mesmerizing. Kheti's hands slowed, and he listened as Avraham said, "God blessed them and said, 'Be fruitful and multiply. Fill the earth and subdue it. Rule over the fish in the sea and the birds in the sky and over every living creature that moves on the ground.'"

Avraham continued to speak for a little longer, but Kheti was stuck on the sixth day. Stuck on the sheer orderliness of the story.

"… And that is how my ancestors, A'dam and Havvah, came to be."

"So your daughter is named after this first woman?"

"She is. It is a name of great honor."

"That is a beautiful beginning." Kheti looked at Avraham's growing pile of woven papyrus. His own hands had slowed to a crawl as Kheti listened. His face warmed, and he picked up his pace. Papa would not mind him talking to Avraham as long as the work was completed. Papa insisted that Kheti be a good example to the slaves, for if he did not care to work diligently, why should the slaves?

"Do you know more of A'dam and Havvah?" Kheti asked.

Avraham looked sad as he completed yet another sheet. "Tragically, they rebelled against Elohim. Their rebellion had terrible consequences."

Maybe that was why Kheti had been enthralled by Avraham's words. He had described a perfect world. A world where there was beauty and true friendship between this god and his people, and between the people themselves.

"Elohim had placed A'dam and Havvah in a beautiful garden called Eden, somewhere near Babylon. They looked after the garden and walked and talked with Elohim himself." Avraham sighed. "If only they had not gone their own way, things would have been much better."

Kheti and Avraham worked together to move another stack of felt and papyrus.

"Elohim had given A'dam and Havvah absolute freedom, except for one thing," Avraham continued.

Kheti stopped working.

"Elohim had said, 'You are free to eat anything in the garden except the fruit of one tree, the fruit from the tree of the knowledge of good and evil. You must not eat that fruit, or you will die.'"

"What was so special about that fruit?" Kheti asked.

"I don't know. Maybe the fruit itself wasn't special. Maybe it was simply a test of whether they would trust Elohim, or go their own way. Maybe Elohim wanted them to choose to love and trust, and not be forced to follow him because there was no other choice."

Was that why it was so much easier for Kheti to obey his father than his mother? His mother tried to command his obedience, but Kheti respected and loved his father enough to want to obey.

"Now the snake was the craftiest of all the animals Elohim had made, and he came to Havvah and said, 'Did Elohim really say that you must not eat any fruit in the garden?'"

"It wasn't any fruit. It was just one fruit." Kheti forced himself to keep working when all he wanted to do was sit and listen.

"And Havvah knew that, for she said, 'No, we can eat the fruit in the garden, but we cannot eat the fruit from the tree in the middle of the garden, and we cannot touch it, or we will die.'"

Kheti frowned. He didn't remember any command about not touching the fruit.

"'You will not die,' the snake said, 'for Elohim knows that when you eat it your eyes will be opened, and you will be like Elohim himself, knowing the difference between good and evil.'"

Avraham continued to recount the pain and suffering that resulted when they ate the fruit, and shared stories about A'dam and Havvah's banishment from the garden. The murder of Abel. The confusion of languages. Of pride and evil. Of rescue and promises.

"Time to rest." Papa's voice broke into the account of Avraham's burial in the cave of Machpelah. Kheti blinked. He'd been so absorbed that he hadn't even noticed his hunger. His stomach rumbled, and he went to fetch their meal.

Kheti had never known such stories. Stories that not only drew a listener in but also called him beyond himself. Stories that weren't only about evil, but about life and love. Stories that might just change someone's life.

CHAPTER ELEVEN

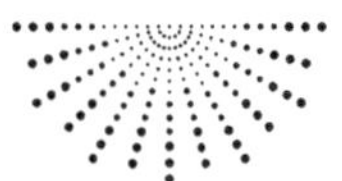

Kheti watched as Pentu hitched the oxen then attached the plow. After checking that everything was set up correctly, Pentu clicked his tongue to set the oxen moving. The plow dug into the earth, exposing the rich, black soil. Yosef's little sister would lead the oxen in straight rows while the rest of them planted the barley.

It was a family custom to come early with a mud statuette of the god Osiris, which they would plant among the barley as a prayer to avoid bad luck and to ensure a good crop. This year, Papa had shocked them by saying that he would no longer follow this custom. Pentu had been furious and presumably had done it on his own, for the libation utensils and incense sticks were in the center of the half-plowed field. The statuette would be buried under them. Kheti was relieved to see them. A farmer was vulnerable to disasters big and small.

Kheti had brought the seed ready for planting and untangled the bags they used to sow the seeds while he waited for Iset, Pentu's wife. She came over and handed him the baby, knowing Kheti couldn't resist taking a moment to hold him. Little Hepu clasped his hands together, looking like an old man. Kheti couldn't help laughing, but there was work to do, so he set the baby on a mat under a tree and left him in Havvah's keeping. Then he went back to Iset and tied the bag of seed around her shoulder and across her back and to her left wrist.

"Not too heavy?" he asked.

She shook her head, eyes down. Kheti barely knew Iset because she usually did housework when he and Tia visited, and only helped at planting and harvest. She hadn't grown up in the area—Pentu had met her when he'd taken grain to market.

Avraham took a heavier sack. Kheti and Yosef would follow him to cover the seed. As they started, Kheti couldn't help doing another check of the sky. Nothing darkened it, and the river sparkled in the sunshine. If they didn't still have the lingering marks from the gnat bites on their faces, arms, and feet, he could almost imagine he'd dreamed the blood, frogs, and gnats. He looked at the earth in front of his feet, which proved it hadn't been a dream. The flesh of the frogs buried in the fields had rotted and promised a good harvest, but their tiny bones were still visible.

The workers hoisted their tools and started down their assigned rows, gently pushing the soil back over the seed Avraham and Iset had scattered.

"Yosef," Kheti asked. "Do you think the plagues will continue?"

Yosef paused to look across at him. "They haven't achieved what they were meant to achieve."

That's what Kheti had been afraid of. Mosheh said the Hebrews were only asking to go away for a short time to worship their god, but that didn't make sense. Why would a people leave, then return to slavery? Was that why Pharaoh refused to let them go, because he assumed they would flee?

If Egypt lost the slaves, Kheti's family would also lose much of their workforce. No help in the fields and none in the house. Their lives would be hard indeed.

Papa treated their slaves well, but Pentu didn't follow their father's lead. Once Papa was gone, things would likely deteriorate fast. Given Pentu seldom listened to their father, he certainly wouldn't listen to a younger brother insisting he temper his harshness.

Talking to Yosef had shown Kheti his own ignorance about how it felt to be a slave. How it would feel to measure every word in case it led to trouble. It stung that Yosef didn't trust him because he was Egyptian. If only Kheti could live in a world where people were measured by their character and not by whether they were male or female, young or old, slave or free. Even Nanny only talked to him because she'd been pushed aside as increasingly irrelevant in Egyptian society as she became older and more infirm. Yet she had raised kings.

"Could you tell me what your god's purpose is with these plagues?" Kheti asked quietly.

Yosef bit his lip. "All I can say is that God has promised Pharaoh will eventually agree to Mosheh's requests. All of them." He clenched his jaw. "I cannot tell you more."

And as much as Kheti wanted to know more, he wouldn't force it out of Yosef's lips. He wouldn't become one of the oppressors for the sake of information. Kheti desired Avraham and Yosef's trust, but his position as the master's son made that almost impossible.

Kheti and Yosef continued down the row, pushing the plowed furrows shut. Pentu had almost completed the first field, and he'd take a break before moving to the second field.

"Where did Mosheh go after he fled from Egypt?" Kheti asked.

Yosef paused for a long moment. "I can tell you a little, but you must not speak of these things to others."

"May I speak of them to my father?"

"My father trusts yours, so yes, but no one else."

Kheti would have liked to talk to Tia too, but that would have to wait until she was a little older. She was usually at home with Mama, and discretion was not Mama's strength.

Yosef paused for a long moment before speaking. "When Mosheh fled from Egypt, he eventually came to the wilderness area where the Midianites dwelt. The Midianites are related to us through Avraham's third wife, Keturah."

Kheti remembered the mention of Keturah and her many sons. Avraham had sent them away from his heir, Yitzchaq.

"Mosheh sat down by a well, and the seven daughters of Jethro, a priest of Midian, came to water their father's flock."

Many Egyptians didn't like sheep and preferred to leave the shepherding to slaves. Kheti didn't mind them, although they did smell. Avraham had told his father the reason the Hebrews lived in Goshen was because they'd been shepherds, and the Egyptians had wanted them as far away as possible.

Yosef matched his story to the rhythm of covering the seeds in his row.

"Some other shepherds came and tried to push in ahead of the women at the well, but Mosheh came to the rescue. When the girls returned early from watering the flocks, their father asked why, then he asked why they hadn't invited their Egyptian rescuer home to eat with the family."

"Egyptian?" Kheti asked. "Mosheh wasn't Egyptian."

"Maybe his accent and clothes made him seem Egyptian."

And Mosheh probably had the pride of a palace-raised Egyptian, but that wasn't something Yosef would say.

"Mosheh stayed with the family and eventually married Jethro's daughter, Zipporah, and had two sons."

In Nanny's stories of Mosheh, she'd never mentioned a family. Maybe Mosheh kept it quiet—the easiest way for someone to put pressure on him would be to harm his family.

"So Mosheh had a quiet life all those years?" Kheti asked as they finished their rows. He stretched up to the sky before touching his toes. There'd be blisters on his hands tonight after the first day of this seasonal work.

"I've never heard anything about most of those years, but just before Mosheh returned to Egypt, he met Elohim while herding sheep."

Met Elohim? How did one meet a god?

Yosef sneezed. "When Mosheh came to Mount Horeb, he saw a curious thing, a bush in flames which never burned up."

"What do you mean, it never burned up?" Kheti asked.

They both turned to go up the next row. "That's the question Mosheh asked, so he went closer to see why the bush wasn't being consumed. As he approached, a voice called his name."

Now it was a talking bush!

"'Here I am,' Mosheh said. Then Elohim said to him, 'Do not come any closer. Take off your sandals, for the place where you are standing is holy ground.' Once Mosheh had taken off his sandals, Elohim said, 'I am the God of Avraham, the God of Yitzchaq, the God of Yaakov. I have seen the misery of my people—'" Yosef flushed and finished with a stumble, "'And I am concerned about them—'"

Yosef turned abruptly and went to get some water.

There was obviously more to this story … more which presumably related to this purpose that Yosef was reticent to talk about. The more Kheti heard about Mosheh, the more he wanted to know. A man with whom even the magicians could not compete. A man who dared to speak to Pharaoh as though he was an equal.

Who might know more? Nanny? Maybe. She had hinted that she had visited Mosheh, and that she'd continue to do so. Her heart must be divided between these two men she had raised.

CHAPTER TWELVE

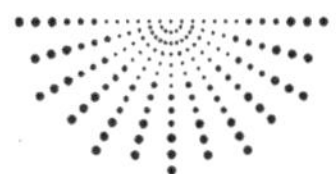

It was a breathlessly hot morning and Kheti and his father had worked late the evening before tying down and covering the last of the season's papyrus for delivery to the capital.

"Go for a swim before you leave," Papa said, checking the ropes on the load.

Kheti called for Tia, and the two of them set off. Kheti had taken Tia a few times lately, and she had now progressed to paddling along.

The lake was dark blue, shot with flecks of gold. Pentu must have had a restless night with the heat too, for he was already swimming in the deeper water.

"Come on." Tia dropped her few things on the shore and ran into the water. Kheti ran in after her and dove toward the bottom, letting the water wash away the sweat and dirt of the past days. All the fields had been planted with barley. Pentu would wait awhile until he planted the wheat. They'd had some light rain, and Kheti looked forward to the first flush of green shoots.

Kheti floated along on his back, kicking his feet and enjoying the feel of the breeze blowing over his exposed skin. Was Avraham right, that this world was not created by Ra and his fellow gods, but by the Hebrew god, this Elohim? The Egyptian creation story began with the same chaos, but there were several versions of how people came to be. Something to do with an egg or people coming from the tears of the god. Did having multiple versions mean it was simply a manmade story? Ever since he'd listened to Avraham tell their version of the creation myth, Kheti had been noticing the details around him. How every leaf shape and color was different. How each bird was also unique in size, shape, color, and song.

"Help me do that." Tia's voice punctuated his pondering.

Kheti stood upright. "It's not difficult, but you have to learn to trust that the water will hold you up."

"I tried just now, but I'm scared to put my head back in case I go under the water."

"Relax and stretch out on the top of the water."

She'd almost stretched out when she bent in her middle and clutched at him. "I can't. I keep thinking I'm going to sink."

"How about I keep my hands under your back?"

She managed a few moments, before she sat up again, spluttering in her panic. "I keep thinking you'll take your hands away."

Trust, so hard, even in a simple thing. How could he help Tia?

"I promise that I will not take my hands away until you let me," Kheti said. "Look up at the sky and count the clouds."

She took a deep breath and tried again.

"Relax and keep your body straight on the top of the water. You sink every time you bend in the middle or lift your head."

The tension was still in her face, but she gradually relaxed as she discovered she didn't sink and could breathe normally.

"How many clouds?" he asked.

Tia counted them, a new skill for her, as their father believed she should be able to count, even if most girls couldn't.

"You can take one hand away, and see if I can still float."

Kheti removed one hand.

"I can't tell the difference. What happens if you remove both?"

He did so.

"Am I floating?"

"You certainly are, all by yourself. Like you're a duck."

Her smile spread from ear to ear.

Pentu turned and swam toward them. Once he was close, he stood and flipped his wet hair out of his eyes. "What are you doing?"

"Kheti is teaching me to float." Tia sat up with a splash.

"Ouch." Pentu slapped his neck.

There was a buzz and a sting on Kheti's shoulder. He slapped the fly and it fell into the water. But another fly soon replaced it. "We've got to get home. Hurry!"

"Is it another plague?" Tia gasped as they plowed through the shallows.

Pentu swore.

"Let's get home first," Kheti said. "Grab your things and cover your head."

While Tia swathed her head, Kheti flapped his arms to keep the biting creatures off her. They looked like flies, and every moment there were more of them. He jogged on the spot which seemed to keep them off his legs.

"Run," Kheti said, tugging her along. Pentu had already sprinted off.

They ran, sandals slapping the ground and arms moving in a desperate attempt to avoid more fiery bites. As they came to their stables, the donkeys and oxen's cries were loud and high with panic.

"Go and help Mama," Kheti said to Tia, as he dashed for the stable.

Papa was trying to untie the first donkey, but it was swinging its head in an attempt to dislodge the flies attacking the softer skin around its eyelids and ears.

Kheti dashed forward. "How can I help?"

"They'll have to go back to the lake again, but I don't know how we can get them there safely."

One of the oxen let out a deep bellow while the other rubbed its muzzle along the nearest wall.

"Do you think they'll remember how the water helped last time?" Kheti asked.

"Maybe."

"It's worth a try." Kheti grabbed a head covering from the wall and wound it around his ears. The flies had already proved they could bite through his clothing, but only if they had time to settle. He didn't intend to give them time.

Between them, Kheti and his father got the first two donkeys untied, then got out of the way as the animals shot back out of their stalls. Kheti and his father stumbled out into the main courtyard, just as Pentu arrived, now wearing clothes that covered him more fully.

"Are Iset and Hepu all right?" Papa asked.

"They'll manage," Pentu said. "The doors and windows are closed, and we killed all the flies inside."

Presumably the bangs and crashes Kheti could now hear were the result of the same actions in the main house.

Kheti released the other donkeys, and they immediately headed straight for the lake at an uneven gallop, Pentu running in their wake.

"Kheti?" Papa called. "Please go and check on Avraham and his family."

"Do you still think we should go to the capital?"

His father looked at the oxen. "They'll probably be just as comfortable walking as remaining here. It's whether you and Yosef can handle it."

Kheti laughed. "We'll just have to keep moving."

A swarm of flies created a mini cloud above his head, their

buzzing irritating. Kheti clapped his hands together, and two flies fell to the ground. A shriek came from the house, and Kheti grinned as he walked toward Avraham's. Being away from his mother sounded like a good option at the moment.

Kheti marched rapidly toward Avraham's, accompanied by his circling entourage. If he slowed down at all, they descended in a stinging horde. He swung his arms.

Yosef was coming out of his doorway, and he turned and called goodbye to his parents and siblings. The two youngest waved from the window.

Kheti squinted at them. Something wasn't right. Why weren't the children's arms covered? The children's tender skin would be easy prey for the flies. Kheti continued walking until he stood in front of Yosef.

Yosef looked at him and frowned. "What's wrong?"

Wrong. What did he mean, what was wrong? But wait, something was different. Kheti shook his head. The buzzing was gone. He looked warily overhead. The flies were gone. Turning back he spotted them, hanging in a cloud near the front wall of Avraham's property. What was going on?

"Aren't the biting flies here?" Kheti turned back toward Yosef who was staring at him as if he'd lost his mind.

"What biting flies?" Yosef asked.

"The ones that arrived a little while ago. Pentu has had to take the donkeys down to the lake again."

Yosef's brow wrinkled. "There haven't been any flies here."

"Hmm." Kheti waved at the children. Was the plague somehow only affecting certain areas? Or was he now overly sensitive, and there wasn't a plague at all? "Come with me," he said, striding back toward the waiting flies.

Yosef followed.

As they approached the wall, the too-familiar buzz vibrated through the air. "Ready?" Kheti stepped through the gate. As though waiting for him, the flies gave a series of enraged buzzes and descended on them.

"Ouch." Yosef slapped his leg, and a fly dropped to the ground. "Back through the gate, quick."

They went through the gate, and once again, the flies did not accompany them. "It's like there is some sort of barrier protecting your house," Kheti said in confusion.

"Does your father still want us to deliver the papyrus?" Yosef asked.

Kheti nodded. "And he's keen for us to get the latest news."

Nanny might be able to shed light on the situation, if he could find her, and if she hadn't been debilitated by the fly stings.

CHAPTER THIRTEEN

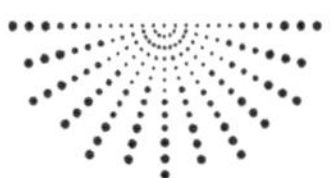

Almost every house Kheti and Yosef passed on their journey was shuttered, and few people were out and about. Those who were ignored them as they dealt with their own biting and stinging clouds of torment.

The temple doors were closed. He and Yosef hurried past and quickly sold the papyrus. Then Kheti went looking for Nanny while Yosef looked for a place to stay overnight. Nanny wasn't in her usual spot, which was no surprise as the whole courtyard was full of flies trapped within its high walls. Kheti went over to ask at the stables. The slaves in the stables pointed toward the roof of the neighboring building.

Kheti found the stairs and walked up. As his head cleared the top, the breeze lifted his hair and blew off some of the flies. Nanny, her head swathed in cloths, turned at his footsteps, and shaded her eyes to see who it was.

"You've come back, boy," she said with a broad, gap-toothed grin.

"Clever idea." Kheti pointed at the basin of water in which her feet were submerged.

"I have to keep these pesky flies off somehow, and they won't give me a slave to fan me all day."

Presumably all the slaves were fanning Pharaoh and his family. These four plagues would only mildly inconvenience people like them. It was the farmers and ordinary people who suffered most.

"Ouch," Kheti said as a fly breached his defenses and stung his ear. The bites were like fiery darts and swelled to itchy welts on tender areas. "We've just delivered the last papyrus of the season."

She snorted. "The priests aren't writing much nowadays. First Pharaoh demanded they come up with solutions to the plagues, and now that they've admitted they can't, they fear losing their jobs or worse." She gave a gleeful belly laugh. "Not exactly conditions for peaceful contemplation."

Once, many years ago, Kheti had heard a priest read a scroll in a singsong voice. The scroll talked of Pharaoh's mighty deeds. Would anyone make a scroll telling of Pharaoh's stubborn pride and the resulting pain for his people? Or would all mention of such things be absent, and the scrolls only contain a sanitized version of Pharaoh's reign, one that ignored the trials and focused on the triumphs?

"Those were steep stairs," Kheti said as he handed her a gift of dried fruit.

"And you want to know how I climbed them?" She winked at him. "I didn't. I was carried up, and they'll have to carry me every day, because it turns out this is a better place for me than down in the courtyard."

The breeze was better, but Kheti wasn't sure that was what she meant.

She looked around as if to check they were alone, then pointed toward a hole in the far corner.

It looked like a perfectly ordinary hole, probably for drainage. Certainly nothing to get excited about.

"What is it?" he asked.

"I don't know what its original use was, but—" She put one gnarled finger to her lips. "If Mosheh is speaking to Pharaoh, I can hear every word."

"And did you hear him when he spoke about the flies?"

She bobbed her head up and down, startling several flies that were too close. They flew off with an indignant buzz and settled on the parapet in front of them, awaiting their chance to return once she and Kheti forgot to be alert.

"Not directly. It was a stiflingly hot day, and I got some of the stablehands to carry me up to catch the breeze. They hadn't been gone long when I heard two men's voices as clearly as if they were next to me. I went to investigate and discovered the hole. The voices said they'd been down at the river when they witnessed Mosheh confront Pharaoh again and say, 'This is what the Lord says, "Let my people go, so they may worship me. If you do not let my people go, I will send swarms of flies on you and your officials, on your people and into your houses. The houses of the Egyptians will be full of flies; even the ground will be covered with them. But on that day, I will deal differently with the land of Goshen, where my people live. No swarms of flies will be there—"'"

"That's true," Kheti said. "I went to my neighbors' house to help them deal with the flies and discovered they didn't even know about the problem. The flies stopped at the borders of their property like they'd run into a wall. How does their god do it?"

"I have no idea. Are you expecting me to know the mind of a god, and a foreign one at that?" Nanny shifted her feet in the basin and water sloshed over the side. "But we do know why their god has done this."

"Why?" Kheti said, stamping his feet to get the flies off them. He was tired of not being able to sit still.

"Apparently Mosheh's god said, 'From tomorrow, when the flies come, there will be no swarms in Goshen, so that you will know that I, the Lord, am in this land. I will make a distinction between my people and your people.'"

"What, you again?" A man's voice echoed up the pipe.

"Pharaoh," Nanny hissed, cocking her head to hear better.

Kheti squatted against the parapet so he wouldn't miss anything. His skin tingled. He never thought he'd ever get to hear Pharaoh speak. Pharaoh was a constant in his life, like the Nile. Kheti had grown up expecting him to stand between the gods and any problems in their land.

"Go, sacrifice to your god here in the land," Pharaoh said.

"That would not be right," a second man's voice said.

"Mosheh," Nanny murmured.

"The sacrifices we offer Adonai our God would be detestable to the Egyptians. And if we offer sacrifices that are detestable in their eyes, will the Egyptians not stone us? We must take a three-day journey into the wilderness to offer sacrifices to our God, as he commands us."

There was a long pause, and then Pharaoh said, "I will let you go to offer sacrifices to your god in the wilderness, but you must not go very far. Now pray for me."

Kheti's eyes widened. The great and mighty Pharaoh was asking Mosheh to pray for him? Did he recognize that Mosheh's god was more powerful than himself and the gods of Egypt? Kheti's mother said Pharaoh was divine, one of the mediators between the gods and men, but now it seemed Mosheh and Aharon were more powerful. Were they too more than human?

Mosheh answered, "As soon as I leave you, I will pray to the Lord, and tomorrow the flies will leave Pharaoh and his officials and his people. Only let Pharaoh be sure that he does not act deceitfully again by not letting the people go to offer sacrifices to the Lord."

They heard the scuff of sandals below then silence. Kheti stood and moved closer to Nanny.

"Pharoah is saying all the right things," Nanny whispered, "but he always was quick to agree with people." She shook her head. "Like most of us, he runs from conflict. But if he is pushed into a corner? He'll strike like a cobra."

Pharaoh didn't sound like someone Kheti wanted to be around. Ever since he was a child, he'd been taught that Pharaoh was the closest being to the gods. Some even believed pharaohs were gods come to earth. They expected a pharaoh to be different, separate, above the things that haunt ordinary men. To be able to solve the problems of the land. This Pharaoh was looking less and less divine and more and more like an ordinary man. Kheti was disappointed to discover the image he'd had of Pharaoh was only common metal not the gold he'd imagined, but if others had believed he was divine, what might they do when they discovered he wasn't? Tension knotted in Kheti's belly.

"Do you think there will be more plagues?" Kheti asked.

"I'm afraid I do." Nanny clicked her tongue. "I don't know how many more, but at least as many as we've already experienced. I'd like to think Pharaoh won't keep hardening his heart, but he's always been stubborn, even as a young boy. Yet how can he outlast this god of Mosheh's?"

The tension in Kheti's belly spread to his back and neck. Looking back at the blood and frogs and gnats and now the flies, it wasn't hard to imagine this as a war, a war they were all a part of, whether they wanted to be or not. A war with a series of battles meticulously planned and carried out.

Someone was coming up the stairs behind them. Yosef's head appeared, and he said, "Master, I've found a place to stay."

Nanny fixed a stern gaze on Kheti. "Make sure you come again."

"I don't know when I will next visit, but whenever I do, I'll look for you."

"I'll be right here," she said, and he knew she was thinking of her listening post. She might no longer have the right to be near Pharaoh, but she'd found a way to be part of the action.

CHAPTER FOURTEEN

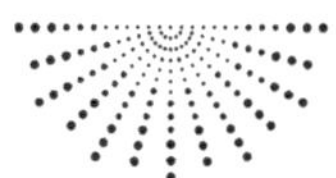

"I'll get you something to eat," Yosef said in the room Kheti had rented for the night. Normally, if they needed to stay overnight, they'd have brought their own food, but flies would have ruined anything they brought with them.

"No." Kheti rose from his seat on his sleeping mat. "Let's go together. It's too stuffy in here with the doors and windows closed."

It had taken them a long time to pursue and kill every fly in the room. They'd lined them all up along the floor but lost count at two hundred. Outside, they'd be surrounded by flies, but could avoid the worst of the stings as long as they kept moving.

The flies outside were worse than ever, clouds of them hovering anywhere there were people and especially wherever there were people attempting to cook. A delicious scent of roasting meat filled Kheti's nostrils, but he gagged when they found the stall. Flies swarmed over the meat waiting to be cooked, and descended again the minute it was cooked.

"We can't possibly eat meat," he said to Yosef. "It will have to be bread."

They found a clay oven, but even as each round of bread was

removed from the oven, the flies were faster. He watched a child race to beat the flies, but the only way to eat the bread was to ingest the flies too.

"I brought this bag," Yosef said, holding it up. "If we work together, we might be able to keep the flies off the bread until we get the bread in the bag."

"We'll try," Kheti said. "If we don't do something, there will be nothing to eat." His stomach grumbled in protest.

They moved to the front of the line, and Yosef tugged a square of cloth out of the bag. He handed it to Kheti, who took it and flapped it to keep the flies from polluting the bread. The baker looked at them, and when Kheti nodded, he slid his paddle under the bread and brought it out of the oven. Kheti frantically flapped the cloth and Yosef somehow managed to open the bag just enough to hide the bread and deny the flies entry.

"Another please," Kheti said.

They repeated the process, and Kheti paid for the bread and a tiny jar of herbs soaking in olive oil.

On the way back toward their room, they looked for other food, but everything was spoiled by flies.

"We'll have to make do with what we have," Kheti said with a shudder.

Once back in their room, they set about killing flies to join the line on the floor. They had it down to a fine art. Slap, slap, slap.

By the time they had eliminated the flies, their bread was no longer warm. Kheti divided one of the loaves. He was hungry enough to eat the whole lot, but they'd need more in the morning.

Yosef paused and closed his eyes before he ate. His lips moved but no sound came. Was he praying? How did the Hebrews speak to their god?

Yosef opened his eyes, and together they dipped their bread in the scented oil. Even without any accompaniments, the bread was good. Kheti was thankful that Yosef had come up with a plan to keep their food from being spoiled.

After the meal, Kheti found the stuffiness of the room oppressive. Normally windows were left fully open but if he opened the shutters he'd only get a mouthful or two of fresh air before the room filled with flies again.

Yosef paced up and down the room, muttering what Kheti assumed were prayers. When he'd finished, Kheti gestured him over.

"Do you have any more stories of your people?" Kheti asked. Stories, any stories, would be a distraction.

"There are always more stories."

"Any about plagues?" Kheti asked. It would be interesting to hear how others had coped with such occurrences.

"There are accounts of judgments."

Judgments seemed to characterize this god. Why then did Yosef and his family seem so loyal to him? But then, the god they talked of also walked with his people. A warmth filled Kheti's chest. A god who treated his followers more like family than subjects was surely unique.

Yosef sat cross-legged on the floor. "Many years ago, there was a descendent of A'dam and Havvah."

"Was this before Avraham?"

"Before Avraham, probably long before," Yosef said. "After A'dam and Havvah rebelled against Elohim, they were cast out of Elohim's garden. They had children, and their children had children, and many, many generations passed."

In his mind, Kheti could picture the long line of men and women with the same craggy faces as Avraham and his family.

"Each generation ignored Elohim and did what was right in their own eyes," Yosef continued. "The world became an evil and perilous place. Elohim looked down on the earth he had made, and he was grieved that he had created people."

The more Kheti heard of this Elohim, the more real he became.

"Yet there was one man who still followed Elohim," Yosef continued. "His name was Noach."

"Ah, the name of your little brother."

Yosef nodded. "The original Noach was a righteous man who walked with Elohim."

Kheti didn't know what "righteous" meant, but he was embarrassed to display his ignorance. How did you walk with a god that couldn't be seen or heard? Whatever it meant, it was clear that Noach was one man Elohim approved of.

"Elohim told Noach that he would judge the world by sending a flood that would cover all the land and all the mountains in the whole world."

The River Nile flooded every year, but most of the time there was a limit to how far the waters would spread across the land. Kheti shivered. If the river should one day forget its boundaries and cover everything, that would be terrifying.

"Elohim told Noach that if he wanted to be saved, he must build a huge boat that would save himself and his family."

"And did he build such a boat?" Kheti asked.

Yosef nodded. "He was given the design by Elohim himself. Elohim told Noach to build the boat big enough for at least one pair of every kind of animal, for any living creature outside the boat would die."

Kheti gave a low whistle. "The boat must have been simply enormous."

"Three hundred cubits long, fifty cubits wide, and thirty cubits high, and it had three levels of decks."

Kheti pictured the fields that they'd planted recently. The boat was longer than three of them.

"And it took many years to build," Yosef said.

Kheti gave a wry smile. "What did the neighbors think?"

"They probably thought Noach was mad. The boat would have

been bigger than anything anyone had seen, and there may not have been any water close by to float it on. They must have pestered him with questions."

"But would anyone have believed what Noach said?"

"Probably not," Yosef said. "After all, lots of people don't believe Elohim's signs now."

Kheti raised his head to look directly at Yosef. Avraham had said that many of the Hebrews hadn't believed Mosheh at first. Hadn't believed Elohim had really met him. Hadn't believed Elohim had commanded Mosheh to speak to Pharaoh. Mosheh had proven he acted with Elohim's authority by doing miracles. A staff turned into a snake. A hand that became leprous and then whole again when Mosheh put it under his cloak. And the third? The third sign was that a jug containing water from the Nile became blood. Yet even with these three miracles, many of the Hebrews still didn't believe. They'd doubted Elohim when life became harder, and they blamed Mosheh for causing their pain.

Were Kheti and his family and neighbors any different? They'd seen more than three miracles, but did they believe? Yes, they believed that the Hebrews' god was powerful, but was that enough? Did this god want something from them, or was he simply intent on wiping them out?

"At last, the boat was finished," Yosef continued. "Elohim told Noach and his family to prepare provisions for themselves and all the animals."

"How were they to find all the animals?" Kheti asked. "It would take more years than the length of their lives."

Yosef chuckled. "Elohim had things under control. Once the boat was provisioned, Elohim sent all the animals onto the boat himself."

Kheti's mouth fell open.

"Once the animals were on the boat, Elohim commanded Noach to get on the boat with his entire family." Yosef indicated on his fingers. "Noach, his wife, his three sons and their wives. Eight people in total. Then Elohim closed the door of the boat."

"And?"

"And it started to rain, and it rained and it poured. The ground itself opened up and released vast amounts of water. The water rose and rose."

It was hard to imagine. Kheti felt suddenly cold. It must have been terrible for the people outside as the water rose deeper and deeper. Had they beaten on the outside of the boat or had they simply run for high ground?

"The rain continued for forty days and forty nights until the flood covered even the highest mountain."

Yosef didn't say it, but he didn't need to. Every creature outside that boat must have died. Did Elohim have death in store for all the Egyptians?

"The waters flooded the earth for over one hundred and fifty days. Then Elohim allowed the waters to recede."

It would have taken a long, long time for the earth to dry out. Papa's farmland was always soggy for a good while after the river went back into its normal course.

"When it was dry enough, Noach and his family left the boat. Noach made an altar of stones and sacrificed some of the extra animals to Elohim as a thank you for saving them."

Kheti had never seen his family sacrifice to thank the gods. Their sacrifices were more about placating the gods so disaster didn't fall on them.

"And Elohim put a rainbow in the sky as a sign of promise. Elohim said, 'Never again will I curse the ground because of humans, even though every inclination of the human heart is evil from childhood. And never again will I destroy all living creatures, as I have done.'"

Kheti leaned forward. "And has he kept that promise?"

Yosef, looking remarkably like his father, fixed his gaze on Kheti. "Elohim always keeps his promises."

Always? Well so far, he hadn't kept his promises to the original Avraham. Avraham's descendants still didn't have their own land, and Pharaoh wasn't likely to let them go. Even if he did, other people lived in the land of Canaan. Fierce people, people who wouldn't leave without a fight. And so far, Mosheh and his people hadn't seemed the kind of people to do much fighting. They were a nation of servants and shepherds, not warriors.

CHAPTER FIFTEEN

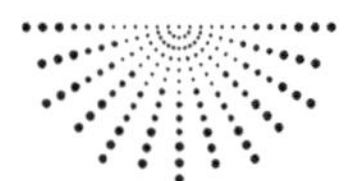

Several days after Kheti and Yosef arrived home, Kheti was washing his arms after a day in the fields. Mud ran off his arms into the drain below. He rubbed his arms and then rinsed them again. The welts from the fly bites had almost faded.

"Young master!" Avraham called from behind him. He sounded worried.

Kheti flicked the water off and turned to see Avraham hurrying toward him. Tension stiffened Kheti's neck. What was the matter?

"Is your father around?" Avraham asked.

"He's still in the stable," Kheti said and leaned toward the entrance to call him.

His father came out, blinking in the late afternoon sunshine. "Avraham?"

"Another plague is coming."

Kheti's stomach cramped. A messenger must have come. Kheti had asked previously about how Avraham was getting his information, but Avraham had been vague about the details.

"Tell us," Papa said.

"This time, Elohim will strike the livestock," Avraham said.

The blood drained from Papa's face, and he staggered to a log against the wall and sat down. "All the livestock?"

"Horses, donkeys, camels, cattle, sheep, and goats."

"And what about your livestock?" Kheti said. Would the Hebrews be protected again or had that protection been a one-off?

"The plague will not attack ours," Avraham said.

"Let me think," Kheti's father said, head in hands.

Kheti sat down and placed a hand on Papa's back. The first four plagues had been painful, but they hadn't struck directly at the livestock. But if all their livestock died, it would be a blow Kheti couldn't see past.

Papa's head came up. "We need to separate the livestock so the plague doesn't spread."

Avraham cleared his throat. "Do you think it would make a difference if your animals were at my place?"

Kheti's father put his head on one side. "It's a good thought, but I don't know. Will your god judge based on location or whether the animals belong to you?"

Avraham pursed his lips and thought for a long moment. "He usually looks at the heart."

"What do you mean?" Kheti asked.

"I mean that he is more concerned about our motives and attitudes than our actions. Some people do the right things, but their heart is far from God." Avraham paused again. "They do something because it is a ritual or even a just-in-case-but-I-really-don't-believe-it. They don't really love and respect Elohim."

Kheti had done many just-in-case rituals in his life. He feared the consequences of not making the proscribed offerings. And he feared what others would say if he didn't participate. To be Egyptian was to follow the Egyptian gods. If you didn't, you were choosing to step outside the community. No one willingly chose to be an outsider.

Kheti had never thought about love and respect in relation to the gods. He'd never even considered that a human could love a god. Lust, perhaps, as many of their images were designed to inspire such a desire. But love? No. He'd never loved any of the gods. It was all about fear. His family feared they would suffer if they didn't make the offering—suffer physically or suffer through the failure of their businesses. People made their offerings to prevent flood and drought and famine.

"This god of yours—what do you call him?" Papa asked, standing up.

"I always called him Adonai, which means Lord, or Elohim, which can mean simply 'God' but also carries the deeper meaning of living and mighty one, but Elohim has revealed a new name to Mosheh."

"And that is?" Kheti asked.

Avraham shook his head. "It is too precious to say."

How could a name be too precious to say?

"Kheti, I'll move the donkeys and our oxen to Avraham's place." Papa looked at Avraham. "Can you ask Yosef to move the sheep?"

Avraham nodded.

Then Papa shifted his gaze to Kheti. "Can you go to the fields and ask Pentu to stop plowing and bring the oxen across to join the others?"

A feeling of dread settled in Kheti's belly. "What if he won't bring them?"

"Go and try. We don't know if it will work, but I believe it is the only way to save them, to throw ourselves on El-Elohim's mercy." The name of the Hebrew god, with its strange syllables, trembled on Papa's lips.

It was worth a try, but Pentu was a stubborn man. Hardworking —he had been plowing since before dawn—but stubborn.

Kheti set off and found that Pentu had already completed plowing half the field. The rich smell of the earth filled Kheti's nostrils.

When Pentu saw Kheti, he pulled the oxen to a halt and turned towards his brother.

"Avraham says another plague is coming, and it will strike down our livestock."

A muscle flicked in Pentu's jaw. "May they and their god be cursed."

Kheti was reminded of Pharaoh's stubbornness, his hard heart. Had Pentu not witnessed enough to realize that Mosheh's god would not take no for an answer? If Pharaoh had listened the first time Mosheh had made his demand, could they have avoided all these horrors?

"The Hebrews will be protected again," Kheti said.

"Curse the lot of them."

In his mind, Kheti saw Avraham and Yosef and little Havvah's faces. "It's not their fault they're being protected."

Pentu spat. "Watch out you don't become a slave lover."

"I'm not a slave lover," Kheti mumbled, the sourness of shame in his mouth. "Father wants us to take the livestock to Avraham's place in case they can be saved."

"Once the slaves get their dirty hands on our stock, what's the guarantee that they'll return them?" Pentu cracked the whip in his hand and the oxen surged forward again. "No. We should be safe out here. There is no other stock nearby. I can camp out with them until the plague passes."

It might work if this plague was a conventional one that passed from animal to animal, but Kheti wasn't sure it would be. It could just as well be some sort of divine visitation which didn't follow the normal rules, like the blood, frogs, gnats, and flies.

Pentu clicked his tongue to encourage the oxen and turned his back on Kheti. So that was that. His brother would trust his own wisdom rather than their father's. So be it. There was no guarantee that taking the livestock across the creek to where the Hebrews lived would work either, but Papa had to try something.

Kheti trudged back toward their farm. Papa was crossing the creek from Avraham's, and he walked slowly up the slope toward Kheti. "Why don't we spend the day working on the boat that was ordered," he said.

Kheti headed for the shade of the largest tree in the yard. Every season of the year was different, and he'd never made up his mind which he preferred. It took much longer to build a single boat than it did to make paper, but the satisfaction was also much greater.

* * *

"Kheti, could you please carry some food out to your brother? I've made some of his favorites," Mama said, handing Kheti a fresh loaf of bread.

Pentu was camping out in the fields just as he said he would and Mama had insisted she'd provide Pentu's meals as though she doubted Iset looked after him properly.

Kheti glanced over the selection of things Mama had laid out. It would take two trips to carry that much. His mother conveyed her love for her firstborn, Pentu, by lavishing him with things. A stab of jealousy jabbed Kheti in the midriff. She'd never been interested in him.

As a child, Kheti had striven for his mother's attention, but it made no difference whether he was good or bad. He'd slowly learned there was no use longing for what she'd never give.

Kheti went to find a large basket to carry the first load of bread, herbs, dried fruit, nuts, and curds. As Kheti came back into the room, Papa entered. His face was pale and strained, and his arms and legs still damp from washing. "It's started."

"What's started?" Mother said.

Had she really not paid attention to what was occurring around them? She'd railed against the gnats and biting flies and her thirst, but if a plague didn't physically inconvenience her, it was as if it didn't exist.

"Half of our immediate neighbors' sheep died overnight, and some of their cattle. The farm next to them has lost their camels, more than half their donkeys, and many of their goats."

Kheti dropped the basket on the floor.

As if reading Kheti's mind, Papa said, "I don't know about ours because I can't risk carrying the disease toward them."

"And what is the disease, Father?" Tia asked.

"The neighbors said something about diarrhea and shortness of breath."

It could be anything, and it probably wouldn't matter what anyone did. If Elohim decreed livestock would die, they would die.

Papa glanced at the things laid out for Pentu. "You'd better go and check on your brother. Whatever you do, don't go anywhere near him. Leave the food at the edge of the field."

Kheti nodded, picked up the basket, and loaded it with food. He'd have to come back for the water. Yosef could help him, as they'd have to carry water for the oxen.

Pentu waved enthusiastically as he approached. Kheti wanted to believe it was because Pentu was pleased to see him, but it was more likely that his brother was feeling a little lonely and his belly was rumbling.

Kheti removed the food from the basket and then took the basket and moved away as Pentu approached. Pentu grabbed the bread and stuffed it into his mouth. Kheti waited until the first of Pentu's hunger was sated.

"Nothing wrong with the oxen," Pentu said, his voice loud enough to carry the distance between them. "Told you so. Just have to keep them away from other animals."

Kheti hoped Pentu was right, but he was considerably less confident than his brother. Elohim didn't seem likely to be limited by people's precautions and plans.

"Tell me the news," Pentu said, selecting a cucumber and some garlic.

Kheti told him about what was happening with the neighbors.

"And has anything happened to Father's livestock?"

"We don't know."

Maybe something would, maybe something wouldn't. The other plagues had all lasted between three and seven days. If this plague had started last night, they still had several days to go. Several days in which anything could happen.

"I'll need plenty of water for the oxen."

"Yosef and I will be back," Kheti said. He got up from where he was squatting and set off back home. He'd call out to Yosef on the way. Without donkeys to carry the water, he and Yosef would have to pull the small cart themselves.

* * *

As Kheti and Yosef approached the field on the third day, Kheti could see that things had changed. Both the oxen were sprawled on the ground and Pentu's face was lined with strain. Papa had told Kheti not to go close to Pentu, but it was obvious Pentu needed help.

"Stay here," Kheti said to Yosef as he put down the shaft of the cart and ran forward. Even at twenty paces from the oxen, the sound of labored breathing filled the air. Pentu looked up, his face white and drawn. The ox beside Pentu shuddered with every breath.

"Help me stand him," Pentu said.

Kheti grabbed the rope and pulled while Pentu slapped its rump and urged the ox to stand. Pentu yelled and swore, and the ox finally stumbled to its feet. It stood there, head down and swaying, then let loose a stream of feces. Pentu swore again as he jumped out of range.

Kheti cleared his throat. "How long have they been like this?"

"Since the middle of the night," Pentu snapped.

Kheti was not about to remind Pentu that only yesterday Pentu had again boasted that his isolation plan had succeeded. His boasts had turned to taunts against the Hebrews' god, but Kheti had been too afraid to stand up to him. Too afraid to warn Pentu against taunting Elohim. Shame filled Kheti's mouth. Maybe this could have been avoided if Pentu had not taken his defiant stand.

Underneath Kheti's hand, the ox burned with fever and its skin was dry and flaky. Kheti looked up to where Yosef still waited. He signaled for Yosef to leave the baskets and water jars on the edge of the field and indicated the second ox with his chin.

"That one's not as bad," Pentu said.

Yet. Kheti would not be surprised if they lost both animals by nightfall. This first one certainly wasn't going to be on its feet for long.

"I'll stay here," Pentu said. "You check the other."

Kheti crossed to the second animal and placed his hand on it. The skin was less hot, but its chest heaved. He slapped its rump and shouted, and it still had the energy to surge to its feet. He took the rope and led it forward a few steps. If he could reach the side of the field, he could talk with Yosef, who'd finished unloading the supplies and was waiting for instructions.

"Yosef," he called.

Yosef came forward, but Kheti held up his hand. "Don't come any closer."

Yosef halted. Kheti's decision to assist meant he'd now be stuck out in the field with Pentu for as long as this plague lasted. It couldn't be helped. Papa wouldn't blame him for helping Pentu.

"Can you go and find someone else to take the cart home? I'll have to stay. We'll need more water and wood for the fire." If the oxen died, they'd have to be burned.

Yosef nodded. Behind them, Pentu gave a cry of rage. Kheti

turned. Pentu was pummeling the ox, who'd slumped in a lifeless pile on the ground. By the looks of Kheti's ox, it wouldn't be far behind.

CHAPTER SIXTEEN

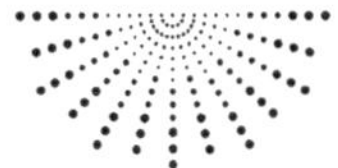

Kheti hammered the last stake in the ground, allowing the donkeys to be outside while tethered in a limited circle. He straightened. "Papa, your plan worked."

Papa was silent for a long moment. "I don't think it had anything to do with my plan. Elohim showed mercy."

A beaming Avraham had been the first to announce the plague had passed, and their livestock hadn't even sickened. Perhaps even Avraham had doubted and was relieved that none had died under his care. Not that Papa would have blamed him.

"Yosef and Havvah are coming over to look after the farm. A messenger came this morning and asked all livestock owners to assemble at the market this morning. I want you to come with me."

"Won't Pentu be angry if you take me?"

Papa sighed. "Pentu is angry at a lot of things, but sometimes we show anger to others when it's ourselves we're truly angry at."

* * *

here was a platform set up at the market, and a scribe was seated with a scroll of papyrus. Kheti hid a grin as he noticed it was slightly pink. He knew exactly where that had come from.

What was Pharaoh up to?

Kheti and his father joined the end of a queue.

"What is the scribe here for?" his father asked their neighbor in front of them.

"I think we might find out when we reach that tree," the man said, pointing ahead.

Under the tree was a man dressed in linen with a band on his upper arm denoting he was a man of status in Pharaoh's household. A group of Papa's fellow farmers were gathered around him, listening to whatever he had to say.

It was warm in the sun, and Kheti mopped his forehead with his forearm. It was a relief to only hear the buzzing of an occasional normal-sized fly. At long last, the itching bites had disappeared. Things were back to normal, but Avraham predicted more plagues to come. How many more could Egypt handle?

Kheti and his father slowly approached the tree, and now Kheti could hear what Pharaoh's man was saying. "Pharaoh wants a record of how many of your animals died. You need to say how many male and female of each animal."

Beside him, Kheti's father frowned. Was the information to be the basis of a new tax? Or had so many of Pharaoh's stock died that he was looking to build up his own flocks and herds?

"And Pharaoh also wants you to report on how many of your Hebrew slaves' livestock were lost."

The men ahead murmured among themselves, and he heard the first. "None of the slaves' stock," and then another and another. Each was shaking their head.

The line continued to move until he and Papa finally made it to the front. There were still three farmers before them, but already Kheti could see the scroll. One column was for the Hebrews' livestock, and there was not a single notation in that column. The other columns were full of figures.

"Three female donkeys. Two male donkeys. Twenty female sheep and two rams. One female camel and three male oxen, four female," the man at the front of the queue listed for the scribe.

How could these families manage with such large losses?

The next two farmers had similar losses and third farmer's voice cracked as he said, "Thirty ewes, two rams, and five female goats."

He'd lost the majority of his flock. Poor man.

Finally, Papa and Kheti stood in front of the scribe. Kheti's father lowered his voice. With such heavy losses among the neighbors, it was almost embarrassing to admit they'd only lost a single pair of oxen.

Kheti looked more closely at the figures. It was a grim toll. There was not a single farm without major losses.

His father nudged Kheti. "We can go home after I ask if these records are being taken all over Egypt or just here." Papa headed over to the man with the arm band.

He was back almost immediately. "Yes, the scribes are traveling to the whole of Egypt. Pharaoh wants to know the losses and if the Hebrews truly are being protected."

But would proof make any difference? Pharaoh was stubborn, but it wasn't just Pharaoh. Pentu's anger also lingered. Yet was Kheti any better? He might not be angrily opposed to this god, but he was staying neutral. Perhaps Elohim was only for the Hebrews and was planning to simply wipe out the Egyptians, one cruel knife cut at a time.

* * *

*P*entu had the surviving pair of oxen ready to go in the field, as Kheti's family were once again sowing seed—this time, wheat.

His father had volunteered to be Iset's partner, and her shoulders relaxed immediately. What had she been afraid of? Kheti glanced across at his brother, who was looking in the opposite direction. Kheti knew little of the ways between men and women, but he admired how little Papa allowed Mama to rile him. He could be gently firm, but seemed to know that being authoritarian would only make Mama more determined to go her own way.

Kheti dropped the seed in the ground, and Yosef covered it up before they moved down the row. He told Yosef about their trip to the market.

"My parents wondered if you would like to come to our home to offer thanks for the protection of your animals." Yosef flushed. "We would have liked to invite your father also, but—"

Yosef didn't need to complete the sentence. It would be easier to ask only one than have their invitation scorned by Kheti's mother. Mother would forbid Kheti to go if she knew, so it would be better if he didn't ask permission.

"I'd be happy to come."

Yosef grinned and then dropped his gaze before he could see Kheti's grin in response.

Could Kheti and Yosef ever be friends? Or was friendship between a free man and a slave impossible? Like it seemed impossible for Kheti to ever know Elohim. What god would welcome the people who had been slave masters of the people he loved?

* * *

*K*heti had told Papa where he was going, and Papa agreed that if Mama asked, he'd say Kheti had gone to run an errand and would be back before bedtime.

Yosef welcomed Kheti at the door and led him into the simple mud brick main room. A curtain separated off another room, and it was likely that this main room also functioned as a bedroom for Yosef and his siblings each night. Kheti's face warmed. His home had rooms to spare.

"We are privileged to have you come to our home," Avraham said, as he offered Kheti the best position at the low table. Kheti lowered himself to the floor where they were seated on a mat woven from the outer layer of papyrus.

Avraham held up a large flat bread and spoke some words in Hebrew—a blessing, perhaps? And then broke the bread apart, giving Kheti the first piece. "Welcome," Avraham murmured. "Welcome."

Kheti had never been in a Hebrew's home. Did they even eat what Egyptians ate? He watched what the others did. Each took a mouthful of bread and then laid it down. Perhaps the breaking of the bread was ceremonial.

Sara and Havvah rose and went out the back of the home to the open kitchen area. They soon returned with more bread, some sort of curds sprinkled with fresh herbs, and chopped garlic and onions and cucumber in what looked like a yogurt sauce.

Yosef offered Kheti the basket of bread, then served his mother and Havvah. Egyptians also served the guests first, but it was unexpected to see the womenfolk served next. In his home, his mother and sister were served last, and meals were mostly silent. Here the family spoke about their day.

"You would normally speak in Hebrew, wouldn't you?" Kheti asked.

"Yes, but that wouldn't be polite to you as our guest," Sara said.

There was a rat-a-tat-tat on the door, and Avraham looked at Yosef. "Can you please go and see who that is?"

Yosef got up, and soon they heard the murmur of voices speaking Hebrew.

Yosef came back. "Abba, he will only give his message to you."

Kheti's heart started to gallop. Who would be visiting at this hour?

CHAPTER SEVENTEEN

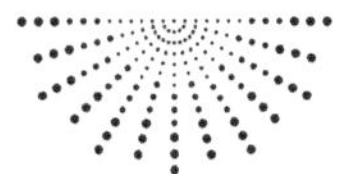

Kheti looked around the table. There was no conversation, no laughter, no eating. Everyone was waiting for Avraham to return.

The door closed and footsteps came toward them. Avraham entered the room and said, "Another plague is coming."

Gloom draped over Kheti like a dark cloth. "What is it to be this time?"

"Boils," Avraham said.

Kheti wasn't sure if he should rejoice that their livestock might live or despair at the pain ahead. He'd had one boil as a small child and had never forgotten the hot pain. Boils at plague magnitude would be nothing but miserable.

"Tell us what happened with Mosheh and Pharaoh," Yosef pleaded.

Avraham sat down. "When Mosheh and Aharon went in to speak with Pharaoh this time, they threw handfuls of soot from a furnace into the air. That soot became fine dust and now festering boils will break out all over the land."

"Just on us Egyptians?" Kheti asked.

"And on your animals, I'm not sure if the Hebrews will be exempt, but that seems to be the pattern now," Avraham said. He reached out his hand and took Sara's hand in his. "I imagine there is still time to do what I wanted to do tonight. Of course, we want to spend time thanking Elohim for his protection of the livestock, but first, let's think about what these signs are teaching us."

Kheti looked at the others. Was this kind of discussion normal in their family?

"We always take time to focus on Elohim after the evening meal," Avraham said. "Sometimes we tell a story about him, and we always end in prayer."

Avraham took a moment to smile at each family member. "So many of our people have almost forgotten Elohim, and we did not want that to happen in our family. It is all too easy to drift away and stop trusting our maker. So that is why we take this time each day." He looked at Noach. "What have we been learning?"

Noach frowned. "Elohim is powerful and mighty."

"Indeed he is," Sara said, drawing Noach close to her side, where he snuggled in.

"So powerful that he can arrange all creation to his own commands," Yosef said.

Indeed. Elohim would speak through Mosheh, and a plague began. Likewise, he'd turn it off whenever he wanted. It was awe-inspiring.

"And he can protect us," Havvah said, face flushing. "He loves and cares for us."

Kheti had certainly learned that Elohim saw and protected his people, although he did have questions about why Elohim allowed them to be slaves in the first place.

"Yet he doesn't work as we expect," Sara said. "If I were Elohim, which I'm not, and I'm glad I'm not, I'd have given us our land in Avraham's generation. What was the purpose in waiting four hundred years?"

Avraham looked at his children. "Does anyone remember what Elohim told Avraham?"

First Yosef shook his head, then Havvah. Young Noach joined the general head shaking.

Avraham settled himself into a more comfortable position. "Back when Avraham was still learning to trust Elohim, before Yitzchaq was born, Avraham had a vision. In it, Elohim told him the people in Canaan were not yet evil enough to be judged. Avraham's descendants would have to wait more than four hundred years before Elohim would fulfill his promises and give them the land."

"But it's four hundred years now," Yosef said.

"Exactly, my son, exactly. The time is here."

There was a long silence. Avraham had told Kheti that his ancestor had been promised he'd become a great nation, a nation that would bless the whole world. Had that time now come? As yet the Hebrews had no land of their own and no king, but they had become numerous. No wonder Pharaoh was afraid of them. Did he know of these prophecies? Prophecies that would mean the end of all that had been familiar for Kheti and his family. If the slaves left, they would not be able to manage the farm and the papyrus business. They'd have to choose to let some of the land lie fallow, and they'd all have to get used to being considerably poorer.

"And what will happen to the people in Canaan, Abba?" Havvah asked.

"Elohim will bring judgment and destruction on them," Avraham said in a hushed voice. "They have had more than four hundred years to repent, but they have not taken the opportunity. Instead, they have become more and more wicked."

Kheti gnawed his lip.

Avraham turned to him. "Feel free to ask any questions you have. I know that most of this is new to you and rather strange."

Strange was an understatement, but the stories helped. They

rooted this in the everyday instead of the esoteric ramblings of the magicians and priests. The utterances of the magicians were designed to make things mysterious.

"You mentioned *repent*. I am unfamiliar with the word," Kheti said.

"Havvah, do you remember how I explained the word to you?" Avraham asked.

She sat up straight. "Repentance means to stop going one way and to turn around and go in the opposite way. Like this." She walked her fingers across the table, then back again.

"And can you still apply it to our journey following Elohim?" Avraham asked.

She nodded. "We need to stop going our own way and stop trying to be in charge and turn to follow Elohim and do things his way."

"Good girl," Avraham said. Havvah flushed at his praise.

"But how does someone know Elohim's way?" Kheti asked.

"Do you remember the stories I told you?" Avraham asked.

Kheti nodded.

"Well, if you reflect on every story, you will see a model of either the wrong way to follow Elohim or the right way. In fact, you and your father demonstrated the right way when you put your livestock at our place."

Kheti and Papa had cast themselves on Elohim's mercy, but Pentu had insisted on trusting himself, and his oxen had died. It was a sobering thought.

"It takes a lifetime to learn to trust Elohim, but the more we choose to trust him, the easier it becomes," Avraham said as Noach came and sat in his father's lap. "We must remember how Elohim was trustworthy last time and choose to trust him again."

"Abba," Havvah said. "You haven't told us what you've been learning through the signs."

He ruffled her hair. "There is much to learn. I am learning to trust that Elohim always has a plan. He raised up Mosheh to speak to Pharaoh, but he took eighty years to do it. It gives me hope that Elohim might still have things for me to do."

Avraham looked across at Kheti. "I have also been pondering why Elohim has sent five plagues instead of using one almighty disaster. Maybe, just maybe, it is because his plan is far bigger than rescuing us. Maybe it includes Egyptians and other people too. People like you and your family."

Kheti's skin goose bumped. Could Elohim see him? He'd always known he was the lesser son in a family of no special importance. Anyone who was someone wanted to live in the capital where the glory of Pharaoh might fall on them. Living in Goshen, next to the despised Hebrews, was considered vastly inferior. Even his mother's sister wouldn't come here to visit.

"Kheti, it is our custom to talk to Elohim in the morning and in the evening," Avraham continued. "We usually thank him for his goodness to us and ask him to provide for our needs, but this evening I think we will just thank him. You may join in, of course, but you are also free to just listen." Avraham looked at his children. "We will pray so Kheti can understand."

"I don't know if I can pray if I don't do it in Hebrew," Havvah said.

"Do your best, sweetheart. We want Kheti to understand."

Avraham lifted his hands and the others followed. Kheti didn't know what to do, so he kept his hands on his knees. It would be terrible to do the wrong thing. Maybe Elohim only allowed his own people to pray to him. A god who could turn the river to blood and call up frogs out of its depths could snuff Kheti's life out even more easily.

"Gracious and loving Elohim, we thank you for your kindness in sparing not only our livestock but Master Hepu's," Avraham said. "Thank you that he trusted you, and you showed mercy."

Yosef continued. "Elohim, we thank you that we belong to

Kheti's family and not to another, harsher family. Thank you that you have sent Mosheh to res—" He coughed. "To us."

Kheti had expected Avraham and Yosef to pray, but when Sara spoke up, his eyes widened. A woman praying aloud. He'd never heard of such a thing. He was so busy being shocked he didn't listen to what she said.

Havvah spoke next. "Elohim—" She said a word or two in Hebrew. "Abba, I don't know if I can do it."

"A few short words should be enough. It gets easier if you practice."

She cleared her throat. "Thank you." She paused. "Thank you for bringing Master Kheti here for our meal. Thank you that you love us." Her voice trailed off and then she finished with something more in Hebrew. Perhaps a traditional ending.

Sara took Noach's hand, and he took his father's. Yosef and Havvah also linked hands and Yosef held his hand out to Kheti. What was happening now?

"We always sing a prayer at the end," Avraham said.

Kheti took the offered hands as Yosef's family started to sing. The music was solemn but joyful at the same time. He'd ask Avraham what the words meant later, but for now it didn't matter. For now it felt as though he belonged in this family circle. Avraham and Papa had a lot in common. If this family had not been slaves, Papa and Avraham would have been good friends.

CHAPTER EIGHTEEN

Kheti woke up during the night. His back was throbbing, and there were lines of fire along his legs and neck and across his chest. He rolled off his sleeping mat and nearly screamed when he stood. The boils, for that is what they must be, were even on the soles of his feet. He listened in the darkness for sounds of pain from his parents or Tia, relieved to hear nothing but the call of an owl. Kheti tentatively tested whether he could walk on his heels. Finding that he could, Kheti went and found a bucket of water and a large cloth which he thoroughly soaked and carried back to his sleeping mat to drape over his body. The coolness of the water temporarily lessened the heat radiating from the boils. He drifted into a doze, but soon was awakened again and again as he tossed and turned, trying to find a more comfortable position.

During the first two plagues, Kheti had begun to wonder if they were a private battle between Mosheh and Pharaoh. Then he'd begun to consider the plagues as a battle between Mosheh and the magicians. Some sort of power struggle. But now he could see the battle was on a higher plane, between Elohim and the gods of

Egypt, and so far the winners were all on Elohim's side, although total victory was still a long way off. If Elohim won on behalf of the Hebrews, the Egyptians would pay a high price.

At daybreak Kheti cracked open an eye. Somewhere he could hear Tia crying. He got out of bed and walked awkwardly on his heels to the front of the house. Tia was lying on her side and sobbing.

He sat down. So far, no boils were getting in the way of that task.

"Where is the worst pain, Tia?" he asked.

"I don't know," she wailed. "My nose, my ears." Slowly, and with many groans, she rolled over on her other side.

Kheti could see why she was crying. Huge swollen pustules were all over her face and neck. A particularly nasty one was oozing on her cheek.

"A wet cloth helps. Do you want to try that?" Kheti asked.

"Anything; I'll try anything. I've barely had any sleep." Tia sniffed.

Lack of sleep would make anyone disgruntled, but he'd never seen Tia like this. She was usually all sunshine and laughter. Someone must go and check on baby Hepu, for he would not understand why he was in pain.

Kheti hobbled over to the bucket and poured some water into another container. He found a clean cloth and returned to Tia, spilling the water twice on the way. After wetting the cloth, he handed it to her. She put it over her head and gently patted her cheeks with the tail ends.

"If the papyrus tanks were still full, I'd get back in the water," she said.

"I've already thought of the lake, but we couldn't walk that far," Kheti said. "At least, I couldn't. Have you got boils on the bottoms of your feet?"

"Could you have a look?"

He looked, but apart from two between her toes, the soles were clear.

"Mother's being quiet," Kheti said.

"Oh, she wasn't during the night," Tia said. "She made Papa get up a few times."

As though their father knew they were discussing him, he came out of his room, finger on his lips. If their mother was asleep, they'd all benefit if she remained that way. Papa hobbled over to them, his face pale and drawn with exhaustion. He rubbed his left shoulder and then grimaced as his hand touched a painful spot. "Let's eat something before we check the animals."

Kheti had forgotten about the animals. How would they handle an outbreak of boils? He'd have to watch out that he wasn't kicked this morning.

He could hear Sara and Havvah clattering around in the outside kitchen. He looked out the nearest window. They seemed to be moving around as normal. No wincing, no groans, and no hobbling. Protected again. If Havvah saw it as a sign of Elohim's love for them, then maybe Elohim hated the Egyptians.

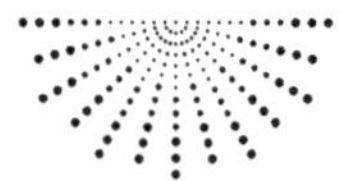

"You can't keep away," Nanny said as Kheti and Yosef found her on her rooftop seat.

Kheti had breathed a sigh of relief to see her hunched figure in the usual place. He'd been concerned about her as several elderly neighbors had succumbed to the pain of the boils, and there'd have been more deaths if the plague hadn't ended. This time everyone had taken many days to recover, and he could still see scar marks across Nanny's forehead and cheeks.

"If you'd come yesterday, you would have missed me. I didn't bounce back as quickly this time. I had a fever for several days and was too tired to get out of bed."

Kheti squatted down next to her. "My parents found it hard, too." Papa still seemed exhausted, and Kheti had asked Avraham to keep a special eye on him and to shield him from some of the heavier tasks.

"We weren't the only ones having a hard time. The magicians had such bad cases that they couldn't even stand." Nanny cackled. "I would have liked to see that, but I couldn't stand either. The boils were all over the soles of my feet and even between my toes. I'd have starved to death if Mosheh hadn't sent someone to help me."

"How did he know about you?" Yosef asked.

"Oh, I've seen him several times. Mosheh hasn't forgotten me. Not like some others." She didn't mention any names, but it had been obvious from the beginning that Pharaoh and the other princes and princesses had neglected their former nanny.

"Mosheh sent me food I could actually swallow. He also sent someone to help lift me and bathe my wounds."

Having done the same task for Tia, Kheti knew it wasn't a pleasant task.

Nanny shook her head. "I never expected foreigners would care for me better than my own people." She fastened her eagle-like stare on Kheti. "What are you back here for?"

"I wanted to see you," Kheti said.

Her cheeks flushed. "Fine-sounding words, but you have more to do with your time than visit an old woman. Have you got a girl here?"

Kheti shook his head. Despite his mother's urging in the last few years, he hadn't found anyone who interested him. Recently, he hadn't had time for anything more than enduring one plague after another. Besides which, with his growing doubts about the gods he'd served all his life, what family would accept him?

"Father wanted us to find out what's happening," Kheti said. "To see if Pharaoh has relented yet."

Papa had been so desperate for news that he'd asked Kheti and Yosef to leave the afternoon before. They'd stayed at an inn just outside the capital and been on their way again early.

"Ha!" Nanny said. "Pharaoh hasn't been inconvenienced that much. Yes, the gnats and boils and flies weren't fun, but he has pools of water and slaves aplenty to look after him. He lost lots of livestock, but it's not as if he actually farms himself. He is far removed from the pain and stench and daily toil. It will take much worse to hurt him."

Meanwhile, the ordinary Egyptians endured much because of one man's stubbornness. Although, even if Pharaoh hadn't been stubborn, there were plenty of others, like Pentu and Mother, who were still screaming in defiance. As each blow fell, it made them more stubborn rather than more compliant. Strange, for it was the same blow falling on each.

They stayed with Nanny all day, but Mosheh did not come to speak to Pharaoh. After some discussion, Kheti and Yosef stayed the night, bunking down in the corner of the Nanny's home.

* * *

"Not again!" A loud voice reverberated up the pipe.

Kheti and Yosef had returned to the rooftop at sunrise the next day, and now the sun was high in the sky. Kheti had been about to give up when he heard Pharaoh's voice.

"We are tired of you coming with your predictions of gloom," Pharaoh snarled.

Kheti, Yosef, and Nanny strained to listen.

"The solution is easy," Mosheh said. It must be Mosheh, because Aharon had a lower voice.

"This is what the Lord, the God of the Hebrews says: 'Let my people go, so that they might worship me.'"

The refrain was so familiar now that Kheti could have delivered the line himself, like a blacksmith's hammer-blow on metal that was already hard and unyielding.

"If you do not let my people go," Mosheh continued as he voiced Elohim's message, "I will send the full force of my plagues against you."

Full force? Kheti swallowed. Had Elohim only been playing up to this point? It hadn't felt like it to Kheti. *Pharaoh, listen and yield.*

Why, oh why, wouldn't he listen? Must Egypt be wiped out for this man's pride? Kheti's neighbors? His own family?

"So that you, and your officials, and all the people of Egypt will know there is no one like me in all the earth." Mosheh's voice was a clarion call, and Kheti's heart rose with it. "For by now I could have stretched out my hand and struck you and your people with a plague that would have wiped you off the earth."

Avraham had said Elohim could have done one massive plague rather than a slower approach. A shiver of terror rippled down Kheti's back.

"But I have raised you up for this very purpose," Mosheh continued. "That I might show you my power and that my name might be proclaimed in all the earth."

Kheti muttered the line again out loud. He must relay the words correctly to his waiting family and anyone else who would listen.

"Yet you still set yourself against my people and will not let them go. Therefore, at this time tomorrow, I will send the worst hailstorm that has ever fallen on Egypt, from the day it was founded until now."

Kheti had seen hail before. From the tiny pea-sized lumps that he'd loved to dance around in as a child, to lumps big enough to cut the skin and leave painful bruises.

"Give an order to all your people to bring in their livestock and everything you have in the field into a place of shelter, because the hail will fall on every person and animal that has not been brought in. Every living creature left outside in the fields will die."

Kheti stared at Nanny, a stabbing pain twisting his gut. Hail that could kill people and livestock would be terrifying.

Her face was pale, and she was shaking. "Such a foolish boy," she muttered. "When will he learn?"

"I need to get home as fast as possible," Kheti said. "I must warn our family and our neighbors."

Nanny reached across and patted his cheek. "Well done. A wise man fears this god and acts on every word that comes out of his mouth."

Had she finally conceded Kheti was a man? He didn't have time to rejoice in her changed opinion.

"Please, please make sure you're not outside tomorrow," he said.

She chuckled, the color back in her cheeks. "Don't you worry about me. I am no fool. You go and make sure your family and livestock are safe."

Kheti rose and ran down the stairs from the rooftop. He hoped that Yosef was ready for a long run, because a run it would need to be.

* * *

Once Kheti and Yosef were out of the capital, they settled into a steady lope. There was a lot of distance to cover before dark. Kheti did not doubt his father would listen to the warnings, but what about Pentu? They'd also need time to warn their neighbors. This plague was one that everyone could avoid if they simply listened.

Kheti groaned. No, he was wrong. They could only avoid loss of life. The worst hailstorm Egypt had ever seen would smash into their crops. Pentu's carefully tended barley would bear the brunt of this storm, although the wheat should survive because it was not yet above the ground. *Oh, Elohim, soften Pentu's heart.* His first private prayer to Elohim was tentative, like a flickering oil lamp flame. Did Elohim appreciate these prayers in the same way as Kheti would be excited to hear Hepu's first words? Or might Elohim zap him with a lightning bolt for speaking without elaborate rituals first? Kheti looked nervously at the sky.

"I must have a rest," Yosef said, gasping.

Kheti jogged to the shade of the nearest tree. Its shade was negligible but better than standing out in the blazing sun. Chests heaving, they leaned forward, hands on knees until their breathing slowed. Then they straightened, and Kheti took a slow mouthful from the water bag, allowing the water to swish around his mouth. He spat out that first mouthful to clear the dust that coated his mouth. Then took another mouthful. Beside him, Yosef was doing the same.

"Pity Papa doesn't have a horse," Kheti said.

"Yes, oxen and donkeys aren't fast enough," Yosef said.

"If we can keep going, we should make it by early evening." Kheti secured the water bag across his back and took off running again.

Tomorrow, while the storm raged, he and Yosef would be stiff and sore. But their soreness would be well-earned, not like the pain from biting insects.

"Let's run to the top of that hill, then rest again," Yosef said.

Kheti shielded his eyes with his hand to measure the distance, then looked down at the dusty road in front of them. It was better not to think of how far they still had to run.

As they settled into a rhythm, Kheti rehearsed Mosheh's words. The words were easy to remember. He grimaced. Probably designed that way. The first three plagues struck the Hebrews and Egyptians alike, and from the fourth, Elohim had put his hands—if a god had hands—around the Hebrews. Kheti could picture an enormous hand curved protectively around his people. Assuring them that they were safe and secure. Assuring them they were loved. Kheti longed to be within the shelter of that hand. Within the shelter of a god who was powerful yet loved his people. Avraham believed Elohim was kind and compassionate. No one could ever claim that Ra or Sekhmet were compassionate or merciful. Looking back, Kheti had spent a lot of energy placating them, never sure whether they would hear or capriciously snuff him out.

Kheti's foot slipped on a stone and he stumbled.

"Not so far now," Yosef panted as the road began to wind upwards. "I am looking forward to that next mouthful of water."

Every mouthful had become precious.

"Do you think those thieves will be around?" Yosef asked.

"If I was them, I'd run away. They probably still think it was you who conjured up the gnats."

"This time we could just yell, 'We can't stop, anyone outside will be pounded to death by huge hail.'"

"That's a plan." Kheti took a few more breaths before adding. "There's no need to tell them the storm won't strike until tomorrow."

Yosef managed a laugh. "No need at all."

They had their rest on the top of the hill and then set the next goal, a tumble of rocks ahead.

Kheti let the downward slope carry him forward. He didn't want to fixate on how hot it was, or how tired he felt, or how much he'd like a cool drink and a swim in his lake. It was better to think about Mosheh. The line that kept reverberating inside his head was, "But I have raised you up for this very purpose, that I might show you my power and that my name might be proclaimed in all the earth."

These plagues were indeed signs, as Avraham called them. Signs of who Elohim was. Signs of his purposes for the world. Signs written across the sky, saying, "Here I am. I am great. I am in charge of all of creation. You must listen to me." And like the sunrise and sunset every day, there would be people who noticed and people who didn't bother to look up and marvel at the unique beauty.

As a child, Kheti had loved to look at bugs and beetles, but Pentu was always on to the next thing. Kheti and Tia were more like their father. They reflected on life rather than squeezing out the last drop for their own benefit. These signs gave Kheti a chance to decide if he was merely going to get angry, to ignore them and simply endure, or stand back and admire the god who had such control of nature. The god who could bend nature to his will and display his character.

* * *

*A*head, what had seemed impossibly far was now visible. Kheti took a deep breath. "Almost there."

They ran into the yard and headed for the outbuildings where his father was most likely to be working. Before they reached the first building, Papa emerged, blinking in the late afternoon sun, followed by Avraham.

"Another plague is coming," Kheti wheezed. "Hail to kill all living things left outside."

Avraham didn't have to be told. He headed for the house and reappeared in minimal time with pomegranate juice. Kheti's mouth watered at the sight of its ruby-red color. Papa waited until Kheti and Yosef had drunk the juice before saying, "Tell us more."

Kheti gathered his thoughts together and then repeated the words he'd heard Mosheh say. When he'd finished, his father's shoulders slumped before he looked over at Avraham. "The donkeys and oxen are easy enough, but we will have to work out how to pen the sheep and goats under cover."

They started to talk among themselves. Kheti interrupted. "I will go and find Pentu and let him know."

"And can you ask him to help us?" Papa said.

Kheti had done enough running. He strolled along and checked Pentu's home. Iset said her husband was swimming at the lake. Good. Kheti would be more than happy to have a quick plunge to wash all the dust and sweat off his body.

As usual, Pentu was swimming up and down in the middle of the lake. Kheti waded in and then dove under the water, letting it wash him clean. Nothing beat this coolness on a hot day. He struck out on a line to intercept Pentu, using his frog stroke. Overhead an eagle screamed as it soared, climbing ever higher.

Pentu stopped swimming and trod water. "What do you want?"

"Father has sent me to ask you to come up to the main house. Another plague is coming."

Pentu scowled. "How many more are there going to be?"

"I don't know, but they'll continue until Pharaoh lets the Hebrews go."

"He'll never do that. I wouldn't, in his place."

That was what Kheti was afraid of. That his brother would follow Pharaoh rather than their father.

"Pharaoh will never admit this god is greater than himself," Pentu said.

Nanny would call that a sign that Pharaoh was a boy and not a man. Kheti had always accepted that pharaohs were divine—they certainly behaved as if they believed it—but all the previous pharaohs now lay in their graves. The outward trappings of their tombs might be glorious, but he now believed that inside the sarcophagi was rotting flesh, just like any one of their humble subjects. No longer speaking. No longer thinking. No longer loving. No longer doing anything at all.

"What's this one to be?" Pentu asked as he began to swim slowly toward the shore.

"Hail. Hail bigger than Egypt has ever seen. Hail that will kill any living thing left outside."

"So Father wants help penning the sheep and goats?"

"Yes." Their feet touched the shallow bottom and they waded to shore, water streaming off their bodies.

Pentu's gaze focused on the barley, which was coming into its head of grain. "And our barley?"

Kheti sighed. "We can only pray."

"Pray!" Pentu snorted. "I'll pray and make offerings, and you'd do well to join me. Perhaps the gods have been wanting us to show our reliance on them."

Perhaps, but Kheti had his doubts whether the gods existed at all. He and Pentu headed home ready to make the best preparations they could for the inevitable disaster.

CHAPTER TWENTY

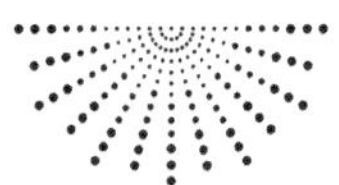

"Look at that," Kheti's father said, pointing out of the front of the shed.

Huge black clouds edged in dark green billowed on the skyline. Lightning flickered through them, and a deep rumbling shook the ground.

"Not long now." Papa rubbed his left shoulder. "I'm glad Tia agreed to go with Sara and Havvah."

Papa had tried to persuade his mother to go as well, but she'd stared him down and eventually said she'd go to Pentu and Iset's place instead. Rather than leave the main house empty, Avraham and Yosef had volunteered to either stay in the main house or help with the livestock. As they could have escaped the plague altogether, their decision had deeply touched his father.

The sheep and goats were crammed into the semi-darkness of the two main sheds.

"We've prepared the house as best we can," Papa said. "Kheti, you and Yosef go into the other shed. We should be able to call or signal between the sheds if necessary. The main thing is to keep the animals from panicking."

They'd seen occasional bad storms. Kheti could remember one that snapped trees in half like they were twigs and others that left mounds of hail. If this was to be the worst storm in Egypt's history, he doubted that shouting between the sheds would be possible.

"Avraham." His father cleared his throat. "Would you be willing to pray for us?"

Avraham stood up straighter. "I would be delighted to do so." He raised his hands. "Elohim, Creator of heaven and earth. Creator and controller of all storms. Thank you for giving us plenty of warning about the coming hail, so we could prepare. Thank you that there is enough space for all of us and for the animals."

There was plenty to be thankful for. Elohim could simply have sent the storm without any warning. Kheti or Tia or his parents might have been doing something outside and have lost their lives by simply being in the wrong place at the wrong time. Some of the sheep hadn't fit inside their sheds, but Avraham had driven them down to his place and the men had all been up late the night before building a temporary sheepfold.

"Protect us all and give us courage in the hours ahead. We know the barley will probably be destroyed, but if possible, please protect it too. Whatever happens, may we keep our eyes on you."

After a short silence his father said, "Kheti and Yosef, you'd better go now. The storm is almost here."

Outside, the air was heavy with menace. Kheti mopped his brow. Oh, for a breeze, but looking at the clouds, they'd soon have far too much wind.

A sudden flurry of wind picked up the fallen leaves under the trees and flung them into the air. Kheti tasted dust, and the animals stomped and bleated behind him.

"Look!" Yosef pointed as they reached the second shed's doors.

In the distance, the land disappeared under a gray blanket, and Kheti heard the first howl of the approaching onslaught. The trees were still visible in front of the storm, bent over like people bowing before a pharaonic procession.

"Time to close the doors," Kheti called. He'd been delaying because of the sultry heat, but it was better to be dripping sweat than leave it too late. If the doors were closed, the sheep had nowhere to run. Already the sheep and goats were restless, sensing the approaching storm.

Straining, Kheti and Yosef pushed the seldom-used doors closed and dropped the crossbar into place.

Yosef ran to the window to look. "It's close."

"Come away from the window," Kheti said. They closed all the wooden shutters too. Inside, the only sound was the shuffling of the sheep and the occasional bad-tempered bleat. They didn't like being shut in any more than he did.

A roar came from outside, and the storm was upon them with a shriek. The hail thudded against the building as though the gods were hurling rocks from a vast height. In the gloom, Kheti could only see the pale blur of Yosef's face and the whites of his eyes. He yelled Yosef's name, wanting the comfort of his voice, but it was as if he hadn't yelled at all. Nothing could be heard above the storm.

The sheep stirred and surged against Kheti's legs. He reached down and stroked the head of the nearest, trying to communicate calm.

Something crashed outside, and the animals trembled as they pressed against his legs. If they pressed too close, they'd sense Kheti's fear. He was trusting themselves and the animals would be safe if they remained inside, but what if the roof caved in? There were no trees near the shed, but there were large trees near the house. Would they still be standing after this storm of all storms?

Crack! A flash through the gaps around the window illuminated Yosef's face, eyes wide and his hand clutching the wool of the nearest sheep. Was he now regretting his offer to stay?

The rumble of the thunder followed close on the heels of the flash. The storm was right overhead. Thud, thud, thud. The drum of hail strikes was unrelenting. Nothing like the hail Kheti had loved to heap in piles as a child.

The thuds and cracks and flashes and rumbles continued until they pounded him into a stupor.

* * *

"*Y*oung master," Yosef called.

Kheti jumped as he opened his eyes and looked around in the gloom.

"I think the storm has passed," Yosef said, pushing through the flock.

Kheti shook his head to clear it and together they went to the window and levered it open. A slither of hail cascaded into the shed.

Peering out, Kheti gasped. The ice was piled up above the bottom ledge of the window and the ground was glistening white as far as the eye could see. Each hailstone was a jagged mass of smaller stones stuck together. He reached into the pile near the window and tugged one out. He held it up beside Yosef's head. They were the same size. He shuddered. Death would have been instantaneous.

Yosef indicated the door. "We won't be able to get out that way."

If they opened the doors now the sheep would likely panic and dash out to be smothered by ice higher than themselves.

"We need to get to that window." Kheti pointed across the shed. "See if our fathers are all right."

They pushed their way through the flock on ground slick with droppings. Kheti wrinkled his nose at the pungent smell of so many animals in close proximity.

137

This time, Kheti and Yosef were prepared for the ice coming in the window and they kept their feet well out of the way. Kheti leaned out the window and cupped his hands around his mouth. "Father, are you okay?" he yelled.

There was an answering shout. The window on the other shed also opened, and Avraham's head peered out. "We're fine," he called. "And the sheep are all unharmed." He turned his back to them, presumably while Papa spoke with him, and then called across to them. "We'll stay here until the hail melts."

"I'll climb out the window and have a look around."

Papa's head appeared at the window too. "Be careful, Son. It will be slippery." He laughed. "And colder than you've ever felt before."

Yosef helped Kheti out the window at the front, but he soon drew back. "It's too cold," he said. "That's not going to work."

"Can you stand on the windowsill?"

Kheti clambered onto the windowsill and stretched up as high as possible. "Uh-oh."

"What's wrong?" Yosef asked from near his feet.

"The ice is piled up on the roof. I'll need to get up there and push it off. Can't risk the roof collapsing."

"Let me get you something to push it off the roof with," Yosef said.

Kheti balanced on the windowsill until Yosef handed him a long rake. He swung the rake onto the roof and hauled himself up with a grunt. He worked from the edge and pushed the hailstones off the lip of the roof. Then he moved up the roof and pushed some more.

"Do you need help?" Yosef called.

"Let me clear a bigger space first," Kheti answered as he continued to push the hail off the roof. He didn't need to do all of it, just enough to reduce the overall weight. The ice was already steaming as it melted in the hot sun. Kheti stood and stretched his back and looked around. Their barley was buried to the height of the grain. It would not have survived. He pivoted slowly. One of the crashes they'd heard was a huge branch that had fallen off the tree next to the house. One corner of the house would have to be rebuilt. The tree looked odd, its leaves shredded and only a few tattered remnants of green fluttering in the breeze. As yet, there was no sign of anything dead, but there wouldn't be. Anything dead would be revealed only when the waist-high piles of ice melted.

Kheti looked over to the other shed where Avraham had followed his lead and was sending a cascade of ice off the roof-edge.

Yosef had found another implement and clambered up to join Kheti. Pushing the ice off the roof gave them something to do while they waited.

Something bright waved off to one side, and he put his hand up to shade his eyes. Pentu was up on their roof waving some sort of cloth. Kheti waved back, hoping he managed to convey that they were all safe.

They remained up on the roof when they had finished. Yosef took a knobbly hailstone and sucked it. "At least we won't get thirsty."

And they'd put food aside too. The sheep seemed content for the moment, as there was plenty of hay.

"Thank you, Yosef, for being here," Kheti said.

Yosef laughed. "It's a story I'll be able to tell my grandchildren."

Such a light-hearted response might be possible for those protected by Elohim, but these plagues were no light-hearted matter for the Egyptians. Kheti dreaded seeing the devastation hidden by the ice. How many of the people he grew up with had ignored the warnings and left their animals outside? Even worse, how many had stayed outside themselves?

Kheti loved Egypt. He loved its river and its moods. He loved the rhythms of its seasons. He loved its wildlife and growing up in a place where he could swim and sail and enjoy life along the way. It hurt to watch Egypt being devastated because Pharaoh refused to humble himself before Elohim. If the barley was destroyed throughout the land, there'd be little bread or beer in the year ahead. It was almost the season to harvest the flax to make rope. That too would have been destroyed. Was this the plague that would finally cause Pharaoh to submit, or would they be forced to endure more?

CHAPTER TWENTY-ONE

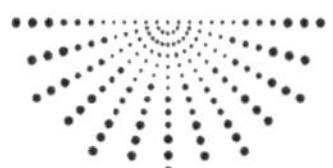

Kheti followed his father across the flat area between the sheds and the house. Their feet squelched with every step as the melting hail had turned the dirt into a quagmire. The late afternoon sun glinted off the hailstones that remained in shaded areas.

"Let's try again to reach the house and see how much damage is there," Papa said.

One corner was definitely damaged by the fallen tree branch, but as Kheti scanned the rest of the house, he breathed a sigh of relief. The rest seemed undamaged, so they could go and collect Tia and his mother. Much as his mother said she adored Pentu, she had a low tolerance for being around a young child. She'd had little to do with raising her own children, using a succession of Hebrew nannies to do the job.

Kheti hadn't thought much about those women in years. Just as he grew attached to one nanny, she'd leave and there'd be a new one. Did his mother fear their influence over them, or had no one been willing to work for her for long?

Kheti and his father reached the front door and used the water stored outside the door to wash their feet thoroughly before stepping inside.

"I'll look at the damaged corner," his father said. "Could you please check the rest of the house?"

Kheti went from room to room. There was occasional water leakage near the windows, but nothing serious. As he exited the back door toward the outside kitchen, he gasped. The hail had smashed the kitchen roof, which hung down like a broken stalk of wheat. They'd need to do a full rebuild. Since the kitchen had no walls, the wind must have howled beneath the roof and ripped it off. He headed back inside to report.

"This corner isn't too bad," his father said. "The branch covered the hole it made and prevented the hail from getting in. We can get it fixed fairly quickly. Could you ask Avraham and Yosef to come and help and send Tia home? Then go and let your mother know the state of things."

His mother would make up her own mind as to whether she'd return home or stay where she was.

The first message was soon delivered, and Kheti headed for Pentu's home. Pentu was standing on the edge of what had been his barley fields, head bent and hands clenched. Beyond him there was barely a single stalk still standing. Those standing were broken and bent. There would be no barley harvest.

Pentu reached down and picked up a clod of earth and yelled as he hurled it at the sky. Kheti waited a few moments before calling his name. Pentu turned and glared at Kheti as though he'd been responsible for the hail. "What do you want?"

"Father sent me to see how the house weathered the storm and to talk to Mother."

"See for yourself." Pentu gestured toward the house.

Pentu had taken great care in building this house for himself and Iset when they were married. Now his pride and joy looked rough where it had once been smooth. All along the lip of the roof, there were craters and dents where the hail had slammed into the house.

"Any leaks?"

Pentu shook his head. "It's well built."

Kheti blew out a breath. One less job to do, but there would still be a long list. He left Pentu looking over the pitiful remains of the barley and went to find his mother. She was waiting at the door as though she'd ordered a cart. "Good, you're here. Can I go home?"

Kheti told her the situation. She gave a decisive nod and gave him her small bag. She wasn't pleased when he insisted on going inside to give Hepu a hug first.

* * *

Kheti and his father worked all day, using the plentiful mud to plug the holes. The broken barley stalks made good straw to mix with the mud.

Havvah and Sara brought in food they made in the now-roofless kitchen, and Pentu and his family arrived to join the rest of the family. Once again, Kheti was thankful for his father's foresight in storing grain and olive oil. There was also plenty of garlic, onions, dried fruit, and nuts, but there wouldn't be fresh vegetables or fruit for some time.

They were only halfway through eating when Avraham came into the room. Kheti's father looked up. "Has another messenger arrived?"

Avraham nodded. "He's brought news from Pharaoh's palace."

Pentu grunted and kept eating, but Iset looked up, eyes bright.

"During the storm, Pharaoh summoned Mosheh and his brother, Aharon, and said, 'This time I've sinned,'" Avraham said.

Kheti blinked. Was Pharaoh finally admitting he'd been a fool? Surely not. But if his repentance was real, then the hail might be the final plague. Kheti's heart leaped for joy. Ah, repentance. Kheti had just learned that word, and this seemed a fitting place for it. To turn and follow. But would Pharaoh really follow Elohim?

"Do you think he means it?" Tia burst out. "Do you think the plagues are over?"

"I hope so, little miss," Avraham said.

"I doubt it," Pentu said. "These plagues have attacked many of our gods, but the greatest ones, Ra and Osiris, remain undefeated."

And Pharaoh had proved to be a man who changed with the wind. This way and that. That way and this.

Once Avraham was gone, Pentu snorted. "Pharaoh will never let them go."

"But that means … that means …" Iset's voice trailed off.

"Yes, it means that the plagues aren't over yet," their father said, his face gray.

"There's not much left to lose," Pentu said.

"I wish that was true," their father said. "There's always more to lose."

Fear settled in Kheti's belly. The first plagues had been painful and inconvenient, but now they were attacking Egyptians' lives and livelihoods. Their immediate future looked to be a hungry one. What other disasters were ahead, and would they live through them? And what if Elohim finally lost patience?

CHAPTER TWENTY-TWO

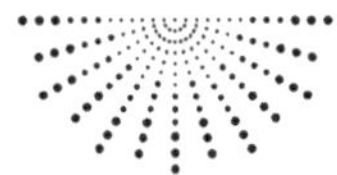

The next morning Kheti was eating with his family when there was a knocking on the door. Shortly afterwards, Havvah entered the room. "Master, it's one of your neighbors. They're asking for help to bury their livestock."

Papa got to his feet. "I'll go and talk with them. Please bring refreshment for the guests."

Havvah bobbed her head and headed to the back of the house.

Once she was gone, Papa said, "Kheti, join me."

Kheti followed. It wasn't one neighbor but a delegation. As his father went toward them, the oldest neighbor spoke up.

"Hepu, our remaining stock was all killed by the hail, and we need help dragging the carcasses to the pit we have dug. Would you loan us your donkeys and oxen?"

His father was silent for a moment. "I will also send my sons." Then he turned to Kheti. "Could you please go and ask Pentu to hitch up the oxen, and I'll get the donkeys ready?"

Kheti bowed to the older men and headed off. Pentu would be repairing some of the hail damage round his place.

When Kheti arrived, Pentu had just finished cutting a branch off a tree. Iset came out with a drink for him, and Pentu took a long swallow before squinting at Kheti. "Are you here to help?"

"Sadly not. The neighbors are requesting we assist them to bury their livestock and want us to use our donkeys and oxen to drag the carcasses."

Pentu swore. "As if we don't have enough work to do already."

"You know Father. He's always there for others."

And Papa was well-liked for it. Yes, some took advantage of him, but most respected him.

Pentu gulped down his drink then thrust the cup back at Iset. Still grumbling, he went to harness up the oxen. Kheti didn't point out that the only reason they had any livestock left was because their father had insisted they all were brought under cover. They might have some repairs to do, and they'd lost all their barley, but they still had stock to plow the fields and to breed. Not many Egyptians had as much, as most had ignored the warnings and left everything outside.

"I'll meet you on the way to the next farm," Kheti said. "I have to collect the donkeys." His spirits sank. It would be a depressing day.

The hail had been so deep that it had taken more than a day to fully melt. Even now, he could see the last remnants in dark corners where the sun did not penetrate. Pentu's barley fields looked even worse today, with the heads of grain lying half buried in the mud.

Kheti and Pentu approached their neighbor's property. The sheep and goats lay in crumpled heaps, blood crusted on each head and body. It was a massacre, as though an army had passed through wielding hammers.

"We dug the pit over there." The farmer pointed. "If you can bring the animals, we'll cover them over."

Kheti nodded, guilt swirling in his gut. He trudged over to the first pile of sheep and used rope to lasso their legs or horns. He clicked his tongue to move the donkeys forward, but they reared and wouldn't move. He went to their heads and settled them with the familiar tone of his voice, leading them forward with the carcasses sliding along on the ground behind them. At the edge of the pit, he untied the ropes and shoved the bodies over the edge.

After a few trips, Kheti worked out they could drag multiple animals each trip. The donkeys got used to their grisly burdens and no longer needed steadying.

By the middle of the day, they'd cleared one farmer's fields and snatched a break beneath a tree that did a poor job of providing shade as its leaves had been shredded by the hail. Kheti shielded his eyes and turned slowly in a circle. On every farm there were groups working to drag or carry carcasses to burial pits. He didn't dare to ask how many farmers had listened to the warnings. Not here, where he was standing amidst such devastation.

"Thank you for coming to help," the farmer said to Pentu. He sounded tired.

"Of course, of course," Pentu said as though it was his idea and he'd actually wanted to come.

"Only four farmers in the area still have stock, and two refused to help," the farmer said.

Four. Only four had listened. Everyone had received the warning—Father and Avraham had made sure of it. Many had also heard the official announcement at the market. Two warnings, and yet they'd ignored them. How was it that people who had gone through six plagues still didn't trust Elohim's word? Kheti sighed and stood, ready to move on the help others.

At the next farm, the women and children were standing in front of their home. Every face drooped, every shoulder slumped, every eye looked away. Without animals or barley, their future was uncertain.

Kheti urged the donkeys forward and trudged to get on with a job no one wanted to do. He'd prefer to be elsewhere, looking out over ripening crops and counting the harvest. A harvest that would not come this year.

Behind him, Kheti heard a bleat and then another. He turned his head as a small flock of sheep trotted out of the barn.

The farmer gave a grim smile. "My daughter insisted we cram as many sheep as could fit into the barn."

His daughter had probably given the family a future. Kheti looked at her with interest. She looked perfectly ordinary. Just a girl, a bit younger than himself, with curly dark hair and a shy smile. Yet this ordinary girl had not only had the sense to trust Elohim, but to lead her family in storing some of the sheep in a barn. Had the rest died because the family ran out of room, or because they'd overruled her?

What was the word that Avraham had used as he relayed the message from the capital? Pharaoh and his officials did not fear Elohim. Kheti assumed the word meant afraid, but that didn't seem right. He'd been afraid when he visited a temple as a child, but it had been a fear that made his stomach hurt. A fear that made him afraid of the dark, afraid of what might lurk in its shadows. A fear that made him want to curl up in a corner and block out the world. A fear that led to inaction.

Yet the fear that Mosheh talked about, in relation to Pharaoh, was a fear that should lead to action. A fear that meant the farmers should have taken God at his word and brought all living things inside. A fear that was more respect and awe. A respect that had prompted Kheti and his father and this girl and a few others—very few—to spring into action to protect their livestock, and remain inside themselves, away from the death that rained down from the heavens.

It was a respect that meant Kheti would have to go back to the capital and speak to Nanny. She seemed to be in touch with Mosheh and his family. She might know what the next plague would be and when it would strike. If at all possible, Kheti's family must be ready. Not only for their own sake, but for the sake of their neighbors.

CHAPTER TWENTY-THREE

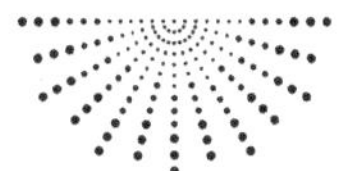

Cleaning up after the hail took longer than Kheti had hoped. Pentu helped, but he also spent much time pacing around the field of wheat. With the barley destroyed, he was making daily offerings for the wheat's protection.

When Kheti finally approached their father about returning to the capital, Pentu accused him of trying to get out of work. Papa rebuked Pentu and let Kheti explain why he wanted to go, then gave him and Yosef permission.

"Avraham has passed on some of the messages he has received, but every time he does so, I see the war of loyalties on his face," Papa pointed out to Pentu. "Avraham hasn't told us everything, because he's loyal to his own people."

Kheti and Yosef trudged along the dusty road. Kheti was weary from days of burying their neighbors' animals and working to rebuild their kitchen. It felt like a long way to the capital, and he would have preferred not to walk, but Papa needed the donkeys and oxen for work. Papa would also been worried that any livestock might be a temptation too great for any Egyptian who no longer had livestock of their own. Even so, Kheti and Yosef had to scare off a few skinny youths who'd made a half-hearted attempt to beat them up and steal anything they might have. Yosef had simply shouted and waved his shepherd's staff, and they had backed off. Kheti had given them half their bread and left them wolfing it down.

"Come with me to see Nanny," Kheti said to Yosef and then added, "only if you want to, of course."

Yosef stared at him for a long moment and then said, "Will she be willing to talk in front of me?"

"It shouldn't be a problem. She was Mosheh's nanny when he was raised in the palace." And she was being looked after by the Hebrews, who were doing a better job than her own people.

The destruction in the capital was much more severe than in the Delta. Maybe it was because there were more houses clumped together. Collapsed roofs, broken tree branches, damaged statues and temples were everywhere. Kheti and Yosef hurried through the streets, weaving their way through piles of discarded building materials. They used the public fountain, cracked but still doing an adequate job at holding water, to sluice the dust off their bodies before they climbed the stairs to find Nanny.

Kheti introduced Yosef, and Nanny's gaze raked Yosef up and down. "Young man, welcome to my rooftop."

What was it about Yosef that immediately made Nanny call him a young man?

"Were you safe during the storm?" Kheti asked.

"Safe enough, apart from terrified out of my wits. Thankfully Mosheh sent a woman to stay with me." Nanny looked at Kheti. "Now sit down and tell me what happened with your farm."

Kheti lowered himself against the low wall, feeling the warmth of the mud bricks on his back.

"Yosef and I were able to warn people in time." A wave of sadness washed over him. "But few people heeded the warning."

Nanny shook her head. "They take their lead from Pharaoh. When will they learn?"

"We were all safe, but the barley and flax were wiped out, and a corner of the house and the kitchen were damaged. We've made the repairs." Building in mud brick meant repairs could be made quickly and easily. "We've spent several days helping neighbors bury their dead animals."

"Was anyone foolish enough to stay outside?" Nanny asked.

Yosef nodded. "At least ten in our area."

Only the deaf and blind could have avoided seeing that a major storm was coming, but some had thought they had nothing to worry about. Bile rose in Kheti's throat. The bodies had been pulverized by the force of the hail.

"Many died here," Nanny said. "They won't learn that when El Shaddai speaks, he means it."

"El Shaddai?" Kheti asked.

"It means, 'God almighty' or 'God of heaven,'" Yosef said.

Kheti wrinkled his brow. "You seem to have a lot of names for this god of yours."

"Maybe it's because he's so great. Each name describes part of his character," Yosef said.

"What other names do you have?"

"You know Elohim and Creator, but we also call him our Adonai, Lord God."

Creator was obvious, but this God could equally be called "plague-bringer."

"Enough of the Hebrew lesson," Nanny said. "Let me tell you what I know about why the storm ended. Of course, this time I wasn't here at my listening post. I didn't dare to leave my home until well after the last hailstone had melted away, but I heard via one of the magicians' apprentices." She winked at Kheti. "I was nanny to his mother."

She seemed to have been nanny to everyone. "And what happened?" Kheti asked.

"You're going to have to learn patience in life," she said.

She was still treating Kheti like a child, yet Yosef had been labeled a man. A young man, but still a man, even though he was a few moons younger than Kheti.

Nanny waited until she deemed Kheti and Yosef were paying enough attention before saying, "When Mosheh and Aharon arrived at the palace, Pharaoh said to them, 'This time I have sinned. Your god is in the right, and I and my people are in the wrong. Please pray to your god to take the hail away, for we have had enough thunder and hail. I will let you go. You don't have to stay any longer.'"

Nanny was giving them more details than Avraham had.

Kheti leaned forward. "Do you think he meant it?"

"The words sound good, but Pharaoh was ever apt to say whatever words would enable him to get his own way." She sighed. "The apprentice told me Mosheh said, 'When I have gone out of the city, I will spread out my hands in prayer to the Lord. The thunder will stop, and there will be no more hail, so you may know that the earth is the Lord's. But I know that you and your officials still do not fear Adonai.'"

"So there will be more plagues," Kheti said, heart heavy.

More plagues and more death and more destruction. Pharaoh's heart was as hard as the pit in a date. Seven plagues had left Kheti's beloved country on its knees. Would the Egyptians soon be on their faces eating dust?

"There will be more," Nanny said. "I talked to Mosheh yesterday. He said that El Shaddai had hardened the hearts of Pharaoh and his officials. These signs mean the Hebrews will be able to tell their children and grandchildren how El Shaddai dealt harshly with the Egyptians, in order for the whole world to know he is the Lord."

"Abba said these signs were as much for us as for the Egyptians,"

Yosef said, then flushed. "Not that you're like the other Egyptians."

Nanny reached forward and patted Yosef's cheek. "Recently, I've been ashamed of being Egyptian, so I'm happy to be included among the friends of your people."

It was easy for her to say. Nanny didn't seem to have any family around her anymore, or anyone else who cared. If she joined the Hebrews, no one would say much. But Kheti was a member of a family. A family already divided. Pentu and Mama had submitted to Father's leadership during the hailstorm, but would they have done so on their own? Probably not. Even if Pentu had brought his live-stock inside, it did not signal a change of attitude. Not really. Pentu still hated Mosheh's god, and it didn't cost him much to keep the animals and his family inside. But the loss of the barley had hard-ened his heart again. He was angry that all their work had gone to waste, and seeing the Hebrews being protected made him even angrier.

"Shh," Nanny said, finger on her lips. "Mosheh is back."

That's why she was here on the roof. After talking with Mosheh, she'd expected him to speak to Pharaoh again and had been listening for his footsteps.

Mosheh didn't waste any time. "This is what the Lord, the God of the Hebrews, says: 'How long will you refuse to humble yourself before me? Let my people go, so that they may worship me.'"

Let Pharaoh listen, Kheti's heart urged. *Don't let his pride destroy us all.* Was Kheti praying? If so, he wasn't sure who he was praying to. He doubted the gods of his childhood could hear, but would the Hebrews' god listen to an Egyptian? Kheti did not know. He would have to ask Avraham. Kheti might pray, but he didn't expect it to make any difference. A hard rock has no ears with which to listen and no heart with which to feel. Kheti crouched as still as a mouse hiding from a hawk, not wanting to miss a word, making sure he'd be able to repeat these words to Papa and the neighbors.

"If you refuse to let them go," Mosheh continued, "the Lord says,

'I will bring locusts into your country tomorrow. They will cover the face of the ground so it cannot be seen. They will devour what little you have left after the hail, including every tree growing in your fields. They will fill your houses and those of all your officials and all the Egyptians—something neither your parents nor your ancestors have ever seen from the day they settled in this land till now.'"

Kheti stared across at Yosef, eyes wide. He'd seen a locust plague before, and the horror was still etched on his mind—the sound of their hordes, the devastation they'd left behind. That plague had been bad enough, but now Mosheh was threatening another, like the hail, the worst that Egypt had ever seen.

No, no, no. Kheti's family would be wiped out. Losing the barley was bad enough, but now the wheat would be gone as well. Even the cool shade, which had increased as the leaves grew back after the hail, would be gone, and their livestock would be exposed to the full force of the sun. What good had their efforts been to save the livestock? Without any green things, the livestock would starve. A great weariness settled on Kheti's shoulders. He almost missed hearing Mosheh and Aharon leave Pharaoh's presence.

Yosef opened his mouth. "We must—"

Nanny held up her hand. Other voices were speaking. A murmuring grew in volume until one man said, "How long will Mosheh be a snare to us? Let the people go, so they may worship their god. Do you not realize Egypt is ruined?"

Beside him, Nanny gasped. Surely no one had ever dared complain against Pharaoh to his face before.

Kheti held his breath as the silence stretched out. Pharaoh could order this official's death. *Don't let him. Make him listen.*

"Bring back Mosheh and Aharon," Pharaoh thundered.

There was the sound of pounding feet as the messengers raced after Mosheh.

"I know you want to get home," Nanny said. "But you must wait to hear the rest."

Kheti nodded. He had no intention of leaving yet, but his heart was already preparing for that long, fast journey home. His father had said they could hire donkeys if needed, but there was no guarantee they'd find suitable animals and the search would waste valuable time. They'd run.

A door creaked open, and footsteps walked toward the end of the building where Pharaoh would be seated on his throne. A throne designed to intimidate but one that seemed a mockery in this fight between Pharaoh and Mosheh, between the multiple gods of Egypt and the single god of the Hebrews.

Almost before the footsteps had ceased, Pharaoh said, "Go, worship the lord your god, but tell me who will be going."

"We will go with our young and our old," Mosheh answered, his voice slow and clear. "With our sons and our daughters, and with our flocks and herds, because we are to celebrate a festival to the Lord."

"Your women and children cannot go, for clearly you are bent on evil," Pharaoh said. "No! Have only the men go and worship your god, since that's what you have been asking for."

There was a long silence. What was happening below Yosef, Kheti, and Nanny? Were the men looking at each other to see who would bend?

Let Pharaoh bend.

"Get out," Pharaoh snarled. "Get out."

There was a scuffling of feet as Pharaoh's officials rushed to obey their master and remove Mosheh and Aharon from his presence.

"Hurry," Nanny said. "You've got to get home. You will have to run as fast as the locusts can fly."

Kheti sprang to his feet, and he and Yosef rushed for the stairs. Overhead, the sky was a cloudless blue with not a hint of the previous storm or the storm to come.

CHAPTER TWENTY-FOUR

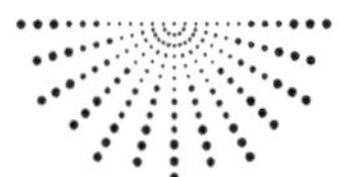

"Hurry, Yosef," Kheti croaked, his mouth as dry as the dust that filled the air. Dust kicked up by the steady wind that had been blowing from the east since they left Nanny's side. "We're almost there."

"Look," Yosef said, pointing. "Abba."

Kheti looked ahead. Sure enough, Avraham was coming toward them on a donkey, his long legs nearly dragging on the ground.

Keep running, Kheti urged himself. His breath whistled in his ears, and he forced himself to place one foot in front of another. He wanted nothing more than to lie down and sleep for a week.

At long last, Avraham reached them and dismounted from the donkey. "Tell me."

Yosef poured out the message while Kheti leaned his hands on his knees and took deep gulping breaths.

"I'll take the message to your father," Avraham said to Kheti. "He has already set up a way to get the word out, and he'll pass on the warning immediately. Get back to the main house as soon as you can. He'll need everyone's help."

Help to do what? There was no way they could cover the wheat. It wasn't nearly ready for harvest, so it wasn't as if they could bring in the grain early. Kheti stood up straight and took a few steps after Avraham. His feet faltered and he willed himself on. Step by determined step, his feet settled into the pace they'd maintained all the way from Nanny's rooftop. If he didn't focus on his tiredness, he could make it.

* * *

"Well done, Kheti and Yosef," Papa said as they staggered across the yard. "Seat yourself in the shade. Tia will make sure you get something to eat and drink."

Tia headed off at a run as Kheti sprawled on the grass Mosheh said would be eaten to the last mouthful, under a tree that would soon be leafless. He squinted up at branches bursting into new life after being pummeled by the hail. This was not a plague like the last one, when they could listen and obey and thus save themselves. This one would hit them no matter what they did. Fatigue dragged at every limb. It would be so much easier to lie down and give up, but they would fight. They had to fight.

Tia returned with dried figs and cool milk. Kheti sat up and drank the milk. Once his thirst was quenched, he ate the figs.

His father came over. "Tia, call your mother. We'll need everyone's help." Then his father turned around slowly, scanning the sky, before looking down at Kheti and Yosef. "We don't know how much time we have, but I hope someone has some ideas. It's possible nothing will work, but we must try. We are more fortunate than most, for we have good supplies of last year's grain, and it's stored out of harm's way."

Pentu joined them and after hearing the news said, "It will be difficult to scare the locusts away or kill them. The locusts will be in vast swarms, and they can munch plants far more quickly than we can get there to protect them. There are too few of us, and we'll be spread too thin."

"Maybe we should only aim to protect part of the crop," Papa said, as Mama and Tia came out of the house and walked toward them.

"Let's try to save all of it," Pentu said. "But pull back to that section there." He indicated the most productive area between the tree, well, and gate. "Only if we're losing the battle."

"Excellent plan," their father said. "Yosef, you often have good ideas. What are your thoughts?"

Pentu rolled his eyes, and Papa glared at him. "This is a bigger threat than we've faced before. We need every idea, and we'll choose the best ones. Some might not work, but at least we will have tried."

"Well," Yosef said, his face flushing as they all looked at him. "If we want to kill the locusts, we need to squash them or burn them. How do we do that?" He stood. "Our feet are too small to make much impact if we crush them."

"What if we threw a cloth? No, that's too soft—" Tia pursed her lips.

"Or a thick cloth to scoop them up and then jump on them," Havvah said.

"It's a good thought." Papa scratched his head. "The scoop will have to be light enough for you to keep using it over and over."

"There's some coarse linen in the storeroom," Tia said. "Shall Havvah and I go and see what we can work out?"

Papa nodded, and the two girls ran off. At least someone still had energy.

"That should cover squashing," Papa said. "Any other thoughts?"

"Smoke?" Yosef asked.

"Only if it can be done without setting the field on fire," Pentu said.

"There's lots of dried grass and flax around after the hail," Kheti said, getting to his feet.

"That won't be much use—it will burn too quickly. We'll need green branches like those up there." Pentu pointed above their heads.

"Don't you dare cut down my tree," Mama said.

Papa leaned across and touched her shoulder. "The locusts will eat every green thing they find. Better that the tree helps us keep the locusts off the wheat."

Mother tightened her lips and folded her arms.

"Abba is coming," Yosef said. "And the rest of the family."

Tia and Havvah came out of the shed with four poles and some lengths of cloth. Once Avraham and Sara arrived, Papa summarized what they'd already discussed.

"What shall I do?" said Kheti's mother.

"Why don't you and Sara work out which jobs you're best suited to?" his father said diplomatically.

"Men never think of food and drinks until they need them," Sara said. "Why don't we organize those?"

Kheti flashed a grateful smile toward Sara. She knew her mistress well. His mother would be of little use doing the physical tasks, and she wouldn't volunteer to look after baby Hepu.

Tia and Havvah were soon laughing as they worked out how to best make their linen scoop. Kheti envied their carefree attitudes. They had no concept of what famine would be like if they couldn't save some of the wheat. He glanced across at Papa. With each plague, the weight of responsibility seemed to weigh more heavily on him.

"We need to prepare the fuel so we can light it easily with a torch," Pentu said. "Yosef and Kheti, fetch the best leafy branches you have. About this long." He spread his arms apart. "Or a little shorter. They have to be light enough to wield for hours but not so small that they burn quickly." Pentu looked at his father and

Avraham with pursed lips. "Papa and Iset, could you collect the dead barley and flax to start the fires?"

Their father nodded. Did he appreciate not having to make all the decisions? Avraham and Pentu went to get the oxen and the cart. They would load the wood from plentiful piles stored at various points around the farm.

"Come on, Yosef," Kheti said. Even though Mosheh said the locusts would come tomorrow, he checked the sky yet again. It was clear with no indication that tomorrow would be anything but normal. No indication of the death and destruction to come. Strange to think of the desperate work they were doing in the belief that the locusts would come. All of them were now chained to the words spoken by Mosheh.

Pentu brought out the oxen and cart, clicked his tongue, and directed the oxen beneath the tree. "I'll park here for you to stand on the cart to reach the higher branches." He'd also brought an ax.

Kheti sprang onto the back of the cart. Looking into the tree, he selected the first branch. "Hold the end, Yosef, and I'll chop through the branch."

Yosef pulled down the branch, and Kheti gently cut a V in the branch before wielding his ax. Thwack, thwack, thwack. With one final cut, the branch was severed, and the main branch leapt back into position. Yosef laid the cut branch on the cart, then looked and found another suitable branch. It was difficult to gauge how many they'd need, but if most of the family were involved with creating smoke, they'd need multiple branches each.

They continued around the tree until they'd cut all the accessible branches and the tree looked as though it had a major haircut.

Pentu waved toward Kheti and Yosef. "Bring the branches, and put several beside each stack of firewood."

Avraham, Pentu, and Papa had made wood piles about five paces apart around the edges of the field. Kheti and Yosef did as Pentu had directed, then gathered with the others near one of the wood piles.

"What do you think about plowing a thin strip down the center of the field and building more fires there?" Papa asked. "That way, if we can only save one area, we're ready to withdraw from the bigger field."

Pentu gnawed at his lip. "I hate to do it."

"But it must be done," Papa said. "I doubt we have the manpower to save the whole field. We'll try, but we must be realistic."

Pentu scowled. He turned towards the oxen, unharnessed the cart, and connected a plow.

"Let's light one fire and work out how best to produce the smoke," Papa said to Kheti.

Kheti squatted down and placed some of the dead barley stalks against the jar of coals Sara had brought from the kitchen. The stalks caught. He put down the jar, cupped his hands around the stalks, and thrust them among the loosely packed dead flax. Blowing gently, he coaxed the flame to spread and fed more tinder to the hungry fire.

"We'll have to be faster than that," his father said. "Perhaps if we have some torches ready to go so we can light the grass more quickly."

They burned up a couple of branches before they learned how to create the most smoke. Kheti stretched and looked around again. The positioning of their fires was good if the wind continued to blow from the east, but who could guarantee the direction of the wind? And an eastern wind was unusual at this time of year.

"It's nearly sunset," Pentu said, his voice dripping with scorn. "And no sign of any locusts."

Their father looked across at Pentu, his expression solemn. "Don't think that means the locusts aren't coming." Papa scanned the sky. Pink-tinged clouds scudded across their line of sight. "I doubt they'll come at night, but we must be ready from sunrise. Kheti, would you sleep outside just in case?"

"In case they come at night?" Kheti asked.

Papa nodded. "I've never heard of locusts coming at night, but I've also never heard of many things that have happened in Egypt since the river turned to blood."

That was the situation for all of them. Farmers knew what was normal and occasionally encountered extreme events like fire or flood, but nothing had been normal since Mosheh had first confronted Pharaoh. Kheti would sleep outside and remain alert for the whirr of uncountable wings bringing disaster.

CHAPTER TWENTY-FIVE

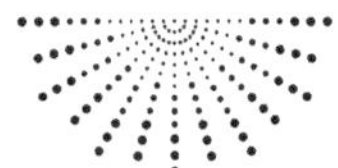

The wind blew all night. Kheti slept little and uneasily, getting up once to relight the fire which would supply the burning coals. In his dreams, he was pursued by biting hordes of insects. The buzz of a mosquito woke him at dawn, and he stood up stiffly and scanned the sky. What was that? His gaze shifted back to something that appeared out of place. Where the land met the sky, there was a pitch-black cloud and it was growing by the moment. Kheti sprinted for the house, skidded to a halt, and pounded on the main entrance.

"Father! I think they're coming."

Almost immediately, Papa yelled "Everyone up. Get to your posts."

The door opened. "What did you see?" Papa asked.

"A black cloud growing in size and coming our way."

"Get the fires going," Papa said. "Hurry! I'll fetch Yosef and Avraham."

Avraham's and Pentu's family had all slept in the main house, everyone dressed and ready to go. His father had said there might be no time to waste summoning people. As usual, he'd been right.

Kheti turned and ran toward the fields. The black cloud had already doubled in size. He grabbed the torches they'd prepared and placed them on the hot coals. They soon caught alight, and he raced toward the first of the piles of wood and dry grass. At the first one, he pushed the flaming torch into the center of the tinder. A tiny flame shivered into being and licked with greedy appetite at the dead flax. Kheti fed the flames until the fire produced some heat.

Yosef and Avraham arrived at a run and brought some of the pink papyrus to fan fires on the other side of the crop. Tia and Havvah hastily munched something as they approached.

"Over here, Havvah," Kheti called. "Keep this fire going while I go to the next."

The first smoke drifted across the field. Kheti and Yosef moved to the next.

"Spread out," Avraham yelled. "Don't light two fires next to each other yet."

Kheti didn't argue. It made sense. By the time he had the second fire going, they had been joined by Papa, Pentu and Iset, with Hepu fast asleep and tied on her back.

The second fire was blazing, and Kheti risked a glance at the sky and a quick look round the field. Half the fires were now flaming into action, but it was going to be a close race. They would not have had a chance if they had not made careful preparations.

"Listen to that," his father said with his hand cupped around his ear.

Kheti straightened and listened. The rapidly expanding black cloud now had an edge that pulsated with life, and a rustling crackle filled the air. Kheti swallowed and pain twisted his gut. Such tiny creatures, but creatures with insatiable appetites that took and took and left nothing.

"While the wind continues blowing from the east, we only need the green branches on the other side," Papa said.

Kheti looked down and scooped up the majority of the branches to transfer to the side closest to the danger. Beside him, Papa, Tia, and Havvah followed Kheti, and they raced around the field to drop them near the other fires.

"Make sure there are still a few scattered around the rest of the field," his father said. "Hurry. They're almost here." Already Papa was having to raise his voice to be heard.

Kheti scurried to carry out his father's commands, then dashed back to the fire on his side. Pentu would keep the more distant fires going and go for more wood if needed. Kheti and Yosef and Avraham would make the smoke. Kheti returned to the fire and placed the green branch and its leaves into the flames. For a moment, it looked like he'd dampened the fire, but then the fire belched out smoke. Carried by the wind, the smoke surged in, among, and over the young wheat plants.

"Water," Avraham shouted. "Damp leaves will produce more smoke."

Kheti should have thought of that. Was there even time? He looked at his father, who gave a curt nod. Kheti sprinted for the wagon. He'd put one large water container on top, then bring smaller containers to place nearer each fire.

Kheti slapped the nearest ox on its flank, and it threw its head back and let out a bellow. "Don't stage a rebellion now." The ox lowered its head and hauled the cart into motion.

The roar of the locust swarm was so loud that Kheti risked a look over his shoulder. What had once seemed black now gleamed yellowy-green in the remaining light. The swarm blotted out the sun, and the smoky gloom meant he could barely see the others tending their fires.

There wasn't time to wait for the oxen. Kheti would start the water running into the larger clay jar and carry two buckets out to the field first. He scooped water out of the water cistern, slopping some on the ground in his haste. When the buckets were full, he ran as smoothly as he could toward where the smoke producers waited.

The first locusts fluttered in and landed in the wheat. They didn't rest. They didn't hesitate. They simply opened their mouths and began to eat. More and more arrived, their wings whirring. Each locust as big as Kheti's longest finger.

Kheti placed the buckets close to the fire keepers, and Avraham and Yosef plunged the green branches in the water then into the fire. The fire sizzled and pungent smoke blew thickly across the field. The locusts didn't seem to notice. They just went on feasting.

Kheti ran back to the oxen. The water jar was nearly full. With much difficulty, he got the oxen turned in the correct direction. They shook their heads as though to get the whirring out of their ears. For once, their flesh was not part of the food on offer. The locusts were only interested in anything green.

The locusts still in the air seemed as big as birds. One crash-landed on Kheti's head, and barbed legs pulled at his hair. Ugh. He swiped it off, and it fell awkwardly on the ground. He stamped on it, and it squashed with a satisfying crunch. One hand on the near ox's back, Kheti strode forward.

Tia and Havvah were swooping on the locusts and scooping them up in their cloths. The cloths were already stained. The girls had obviously been hard at work, but was all their effort of any use? The cloud of locusts seemed endless, and the munching of their destructive eating blocked out everything else.

The bushes on the edge of the field were bent over with the weight of locusts and would soon be bare twigs. Underfoot, Kheti's sandals crushed a multitude of locusts, a moving carpet of color. Yet still they came.

He came to the buckets and refilled them. Avraham and Yosef barely glanced up. Their bodies streamed with sweat and their eyes were rimmed red.

Papa tapped Kheti on the shoulder. "Tell Pentu and Iset to give up and move closer," Papa yelled in his ear. "We might save this portion of the field, but we're too thinly spread."

Kheti nodded, too tired to speak, and headed for Pentu's end of the field. All he could see were several fires and two dark figures moving between them.

Pentu didn't argue, simply handed him some of the remaining branches. They all moved, heads down, toward the plowed section midway along the field. Kheti doused their branches in the water pots and watched the smoke from these fires join the rest.

"Who is that?" Papa's voice made Kheti jump.

Kheti peered through the smoke to where his father pointed. Two figures were walking toward them. Two skinny figures. Surely not adults.

"Go and see," Papa said.

Kheti passed his damp branch to his father and went to see who they were. It wasn't until he was close to them that he recognized their neighbors' daughter, the one who had hidden some of her father's sheep and goats inside before the hailstorm. Beside her was a young boy.

What he lacked in size, he didn't lack in confidence. "I'm Intef and this is my sister, Nophret. We came to help," Intef said and looked at his sister.

"Because you're the only ones doing anything," Nophret said. "Everyone else is just sitting there and watching the locusts devour everything in sight."

Kheti sighed. "I'm not sure that anything we're doing is helping."

He gestured for Nophret to help Tia and Havvah, and set Intef to scooping water and refilling the smaller buckets.

Back at the fire, Kheti worked with renewed vigor. Maybe they weren't achieving anything, but the fact that these two children had come to help spurred him on to try. Battling seemed the right thing to do. Much better than sitting and watching the destruction of their crops, their fruit trees, their papyrus, their prosperity. To watch the crops gifted by the Nile, all ravaged, food to a witless creature he could crush between finger and thumb.

Sweat trickled down Kheti's back and soaked the cloth around his waist. His body ached like he'd aged years since sunrise. How much longer could this go on? No doubt until Pharaoh gave in, and Elohim relented.

"Elohim, have mercy," he muttered. For if Elohim didn't have mercy, there'd be no food in all the land. Already Pharaoh's stubbornness had cost them the barley harvest and most of the land's livestock. Without the wheat and fruit and vegetables, they would all soon be as dead as their crops.

Elohim, have mercy.

The refrain echoed in his head. Without Elohim's mercy, they had nothing. Not one of their gods had done anything to counteract any of these disasters. Not Hapi, god of the River. Not Sekhmet, not Heket, not Hathor. None of the gods and goddesses he'd been taught to revere. Not only had they failed to help, but they had remained silent as well. Silent while the land they all supposedly protected had been all but annihilated without a single sword stroke.

Elohim, have mercy.

Yet still the locusts whirred overhead.

Intef appeared through the smoke and filled up the water pot next to Kheti. Kheti plunged his head cloth into the water and rubbed the cool water over his head and face. For a brief moment, his eyes stopped stinging, then he bent his back to the task. Plunge the green branch in the water, put it on the flames, wait for the leaves to begin to singe, then plunge them back into the water. Over and over, until his back and arms screamed in protest.

The smoke and the locusts cut Kheti off from all sight of the others. He was alone. Alone, battling in a situation that seemed unwinnable.

Elohim, unless you have mercy, we are lost. Our strength is too puny against this army of your creatures. You are creator. Only you can command them to leave. Only you can win this battle.

"Something's happening," Papa bawled in his ear.

Kheti jumped, having not heard Papa arrive.

They stood together for a brief moment. There was a sudden clearing of the smoke across the field, and Kheti held up his hand to test the wind. "The wind has changed direction." He grabbed the last few of the green branches he'd had to put in the water pot to protect them and crossed the plowed section to the fires on the other side.

Everyone followed.

What did the wind changing direction mean? The breeze strengthened to a west wind and blew against his hot skin. Kheti placed the wet leaves on the fire. Once again, a plume of smoke rose to cover the field.

The wind was no longer gentle. It tugged at his clothes. Beside him, Havvah struggled to hold onto her cloth scoop.

"Look," his father shouted.

Kheti squinted in the direction his father pointed. With a mighty whirring, the locusts lifted off. A gust of wind whipped them away. Like a blanket being peeled back, the ground was visible for the first time since the locusts had arrived.

Kheti cheered, but his cheer ended on a croak as he coughed. Sara appeared at his shoulder and handed him some milk. He swallowed, and the smooth coolness soothed his burning throat.

The field was a mess of dry stalks. Had anything been saved at all?

There!

Right in the middle, a dense clump of wheat still stood straight. If the wind had come any later, there would have been nothing.

Thank you, Elohim.

CHAPTER TWENTY-SIX

"It's devastating," Kheti said to Yosef. "How could such small creatures wreak so much havoc in so short a time?"

All around them were dry stalks of wheat, lying in twisted masses. Every tree held bare limbs to the sky. The land was yellow and brown and dusty.

Papa had sent Kheti and Yosef back to the city to find Nanny and any news that they could glean. Back home, the family were hand-carrying water to any plants that might still have life in them.

"What's that ahead?" Yosef asked.

Kheti squinted through the heat haze. Some sort of oxen-drawn cart was clearing the rise ahead. It was surrounded by straight-backed men riding donkeys.

"Someone important. Maybe we should get off the road, just in case." Kheti said remembering the bandits they'd encountered before.

Kheti and Yosef tugged on the donkeys' halters and drew off the road into the shelter of a tumble of rocks. Papa had insisted they take donkeys this time so they could return more quickly if they had to carry warning of another plague, but he had cautioned them to keep a lookout for robbers.

"They're Hebrews, not Egyptians," Yosef whispered as the cart drew close.

Kheti had been focused on the cart, not the men accompanying it. But Yosef was right. Why would Hebrews be traveling in these times? The only person he could think of was Mosheh himself, but whoever was on the cart was a woman. An old woman, partially hidden by a canopy.

The cart drew level. A voice called out, but they couldn't hear the words. The whole group stopped, and Kheti held his breath. Now what?

One of the men came over. "Hey, you two. She wants you."

Who wanted them? And was it safe?

Yosef talked in his language to the man and then said, "There's nothing to worry about."

Kheti followed him toward the cart.

"What are you doing here, boy?" said a familiar voice.

Nanny?

"We were coming to see you," Kheti said with a small bow.

Nanny chuckled. "Well this time, I've come to see you. Ride along with me."

They tied their donkeys to the back of the cart, and Nanny made a space for them to sit cross-legged on the floor. The cart moved forward with a jolt and continued in the direction they'd come from, back to Goshen.

"I suppose you want me to tell you where I'm going," she said.

Kheti nodded.

"Mosheh sent the cart to get me," she said. "He said he doesn't want me alone in the next plague."

Kheti shuddered. He would not have wanted to endure any of the plagues by himself. But what made the next one any worse to be alone?

Yosef leaned forward. "Do you know what the next plague will be?"

She shook her head. "All I know is that it will be a challenge to Ra, for Pharaoh claims to be a son of Ra."

Ra, lord of light and life, one of the greatest of the gods in the Egyptian pantheon. Was this to be a plague that brought death to people rather than livestock?

"If only Pharaoh would bend his knee," Nanny said. "But if he won't listen to his own officials, I fear he won't listen to anyone." She shrugged. "I tried, but he wouldn't even let me see him. Probably knew what I'd say and didn't want any criticism. Foolish boy."

Kheti glanced around. Calling Pharaoh a boy could get her killed, but it was unlikely that any Hebrew would report her. The Hebrews might have started as a divided people, but they'd unified over the last few plagues. They couldn't help but see their god was protecting them.

"I'm not sad to leave the capital," Nanny said. "There was no longer anything there for me."

It was no small thing for such an elderly woman to leave everything familiar and identify herself with a bunch of slaves. Did she know things Kheti was as yet unaware of?

* * *

Kheti filled the manger with hay for the donkeys. They'd spent days collecting the dried straw left by the hail and locusts and bundling it for the livestock. With the land already so battered by eight plagues, his father had stopped Pentu from burning the stubble and urged him to see if the livestock would eat it.

"The stubble doesn't taste too bad, does it?" Kheti stroked the donkey's shoulder. He hurried out to the well and brought water to the stock inside the barn before filling the outside troughs for the sheep and goats. They were corralled in the yard because Papa didn't dare leave them out of sight. Raiding parties had been stealing any livestock they could find.

Although it was early, heat already radiated off the earth. Pentu, Iset, and the baby were coming toward the house. Baby Hepu flapped his hand and smiled a toothy grin. Kheti waved in reply.

And suddenly it was dark.

Pitch-black, as though someone had extinguished the sun as easily as pinching out the wick of an oil lamp.

Iset screamed, and Hepu let out a terrified wail.

Kheti froze, the sound of his heartbeat loud in his ears. He was out in the middle of the yard, with nothing to hang on to. Nothing to give him any sense of right or left, up or down. This was no ordinary darkness. It was darkness without any pinpoint of light at all. No stars, no lamps, nothing. Only blackness and terror.

"Pentu, Iset, are you there?" His voice didn't sound like his, and embarrassment surged as he heard the wobble of fear.

There was no answer. Kheti took a tentative step and bumped into an animal that leapt away with a bleat. He dropped to his knees and felt the squish of excrement beneath his hand. No matter. It was better than the dizziness of trying to stay upright when there were no clues as to which way was up. He crawled forward, the ground hard beneath his hands and knees.

His nephew had stopped wailing and was quiet, but sounds were hard to pinpoint. He crawled forward and called again. "Pentu, Iset."

"We're here," Pentu said. "We'll aim to reach the house."

"Crawl," Kheti shouted. If they didn't, they risked a fall.

There was a pause and then Pentu swore loud and long. He too must have found the droppings. They'd need a wash if and when they reached the house. In darkness this thick, they might miss it altogether. Kheti crawled further forward, hoping to intercept the trio. He called again. Pentu answered, much closer this time.

"I'll wait here," Kheti said. "Try and find me."

He concentrated on listening. Soon he heard breathing. "Pentu, I'm here. Reach out your hand." A hand struck him on the side of his head.

"Iset, are you there too?" Kheti asked.

"I am." Her voice shook.

Kheti understood her fear. It was as if Ra had died. "Where's Hepu?"

"Clinging to my back. He won't let go."

"You're alright, little man. We won't leave you." Kheti wasn't sure who he was assuring. Even though the others were right next to him, Kheti couldn't see them. "We need to find the others."

"Are you even sure what direction the house is?" Pentu asked.

"I have tried not to deviate from my route, but I don't know if I succeeded," Kheti said. "Why don't we yell together, to make sure we can find the house."

They took a deep breath and yelled, "Papa!"

Their voices were swallowed up by the darkness as though they'd dropped a stone into thick mud. "Again. Let's count this time, so we yell together. One. Two. Three."

"Papa!"

There was an answering holler.

"What direction was that from?" Pentu asked. "I couldn't tell, and it sounded like it was well off to the side."

Kheti took a deep breath. None of them knew how long this darkness would last. It must be the ninth plague, for it was indeed an attack on Ra. He'd been raised to believe that Ra controlled the path of the sun across the sky. Without the sun, all living things would die.

There was a faint smudge of something pale to the side. "I can see your clothes, Iset. Maybe we could see if someone stood at the front door and waved a piece of linen. Let's try."

"Can you hear us, Papa?" Kheti sat on his haunches with his

hands cupped around his mouth. The smell of sheep droppings assaulted his nostrils.

"Yes."

"Ask Tia to wave some linen to help us see."

"Do you think he heard?" Iset said from somewhere close.

"There," Kheti said. "Did you see it?"

"No," Iset said. "I must be pointing the wrong way." She shuffled around and bumped into Kheti. Eventually they were all able to see the pale smudge ahead of them.

"We're coming," Kheti called.

"Not too fast," Iset said.

"Whose foot is this?" Kheti asked.

"Mine," Pentu growled. "Shall I lead?"

They followed in a line. Kheti let Iset and Hepu go in the middle, and he grasped her foot. Tia guided them the last part by yelling and waving her cloth.

Kheti couldn't help hugging Tia when they arrived. Being out in the dark had been unsettling.

"Poo," she said. "You stink."

Better stinking like sheep droppings than being lost alone in Elohim's darkness.

CHAPTER TWENTY-SEVEN

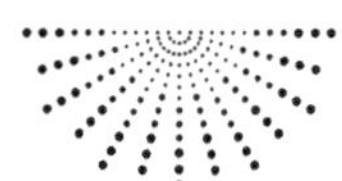

"When is that troubler of Egypt going to stop sending these plagues?" Kheti's mother's words sliced through the darkness.

They were the first words spoken in an age. In this total darkness, each moment dragged, and it was hard to summon the energy to speak. How much time had passed? There was nothing to distinguish night and day. No glimmer of stars, no sliver of the new moon, no sunrise or sunset. They simply sat or slept.

"You sound like Pharaoh," his father said.

"And what if I do?" Mama said, voice hard. "He is my ruler."

How could she remain so loyal after Pharaoh's stubbornness had cost their once-great nation so much? Pharaoh was supposed to preserve and bring harmony, yet all they had was total chaos.

"If Pharaoh had listened to Mosheh when the river turned to blood, our nation would not have been brought to its knees," Papa answered.

Kheti admired his father's patience.

"Why should Pharaoh listen to a nobody?" Pentu said mockingly. "Mosheh belongs to a nation of slaves."

"His people might be slaves, son, but Mosheh was raised and educated in the palace. He is far above any of us," Papa said with quiet dignity.

Pentu snorted. He rated Hebrews well below the value of the prized oxen.

Avraham's family was out there, a family that Kheti couldn't help comparing to his own. A united family, a laughing family, a family who worked hard and loved each other. Kheti loved his sister and loved and respected his father, but as for the rest? It was complicated. He would say he loved them because they were his family, but they also puzzled and frustrated him. His mother was never content, forever believing she had married beneath herself. Pentu was like her. He treated people as a means to achieve his own ambitions. If Kheti ever had a family, he'd model it after Avraham's.

Yet it wasn't just that Avraham and Sara were fine people, but that they were united in love and respect for their god. Not duty. Their god who had answered their cries for rescue. Their god who was making good on promises given to their ancestors rather than remaining still and silent while they suffered. Their god who placed a wall around them to protect them from harm. Kheti had never sensed any personal care from the gods of Egypt. They were far removed from the affairs of men. Scary beings who must be placated or else disaster would strike.

"If Mosheh was raised in the palace as you say, he ought to show gratitude for all we gave him and not bring these disasters upon us," Mother said.

Kheti nearly burst out with a bitter laugh. Mosheh couldn't possibly win in her eyes. Yet Mosheh had been entirely consistent through all these months. He'd repeated the same request every time. "The God of the Hebrews says, 'Let his people go.'" And Pharaoh had been equally consistent in saying, "No, no, no."

"Dear," Papa said. "Elohim has been remarkably forbearing this whole time. He could have wiped us all out with the first plague, but he's given us nine opportunities to submit."

"Pharaoh will never submit," Pentu said, his tone short. "And I'm entirely in agreement."

"Son." Papa's voice was low and even. "I fear what will happen as a result of such stubbornness. Elohim has demonstrated his power over and over. He has shown that the gods of Egypt are powerless."

"How dare you say such things?" Pentu said, anger reverberating with every word.

"I dare, because it is true." Papa sighed as though it pained him to say these things. "The Egyptian gods did not protect the Nile or prevent the gnats or flies or boils. They did not protect the livestock or our crops, and now there is no light. If Elohim doesn't allow the sun to rise again, we will all die here in the darkness. Ra is impotent. Elohim holds all things in his mighty hands."

There was a long silence, a silence filled with tension. Even though Kheti couldn't see anyone's faces, he could picture the expressions on each. His father's sad and troubled, his brother's angry, and his mother's bewildered but determined. Tia and Iset would be looking from one to another, not sure whom to support.

Kheti had known his father's views had been changing, but it was a surprise to hear how far he'd moved. Just months ago, the entire family had trusted the Egyptian gods. All of them had only known the Egyptian gods and the various ceremonies and ways to worship each of those gods. Even though each temple was different and each god was responsible for different areas of life, Kheti hadn't found it confusing. It was simply the way things were. He'd absorbed the complexities in his early childhood. Of course, they'd known the Hebrews worshiped a different god, but Kheti and his family had never considered Elohim had anything to do with them.

"Time for a little something to eat," his mother said in a toobright voice. "Tia, the food's near you, I think."

It wasn't an easy thing to hand out food in total darkness, but they managed to pass around some bread and dried figs. Kheti knew his father was worried about their future. They had saved a tiny section of their wheat, but none of their neighbors had anything. The locusts had eaten the wheat and vegetables, and the hail had destroyed the barley. Many families had lost most of their animals as well.

If only Avraham would come. He might know if and when this would end. None of the plagues had lasted more than a few days because each time Pharaoh had begged for the end of the plague and each time, Elohim had obliged. What if Pharaoh hardened his heart further and did not submit? If the darkness lasted much longer, the new growth on the trees would wither.

"What's that?" Tia said.

Kheti opened his eyes to the same darkness that had enveloped them since yesterday, or maybe since two days ago. He was losing track and sometimes he didn't even know if he'd slept or if he was the only one still alive in Egypt. He shivered.

"What are you seeing, Tia?" Kheti asked.

"A flickering, over there," Tia said.

"That doesn't help me. I have no idea which way to look." Tension rippled along Kheti's arms.

"Follow me then," she said.

Kheti heard the swish of Tia's clothes as she passed by and he crawled after her. She bumped into something and he was able to work out that they must be crawling toward the front entrance. Now he could see what she'd seen. A faint glow. Perhaps a lamp. At the entrance, Kheti used the wall to help him stand. The lamp, if that was what it was, moved forward. Maybe someone was coming at last.

The lamp moved from side to side as it crossed the yard and there was the startled bleating of sheep. Finally the light approached. Avraham! Kheti could see the flash of his teeth and the gleam of the whites of his eyes.

"Are we glad to see you," Kheti said.

"I'm sorry I took so long to come. When I tried earlier, the lamp kept blowing out."

Kheti couldn't take his eyes off the glow of the light. It made him feel safe. "Do you have news?"

"I do," Avraham said. "A messenger arrived a short while ago. He had a great deal of difficulty traveling from the capital."

The messenger would have had to rely solely on his animals, and not his own eyes and senses. It would have been terrifying to not know if he might fall over a cliff or into the river.

"How long will your light last?" Kheti said as they walked back into the house.

Avraham showed Kheti the pot in his other hand. "I brought extra oil."

Good because Mother and Tia would want to get more food and water. They were fast running out of the supplies they'd had close at hand when the darkness descended. There'd been no accessible stores of oil in the house because most people didn't use lamps, they simply went to bed when it was dark.

"Thank you for coming, Avraham," Papa said when they all were together again. "I know it must have been frightening to come to join us.

"Elohim is my light," Avraham said. "He helped me not to be afraid."

"What's it like for you?" Kheti asked.

"We have light as normal but there is a wall of darkness separating us from you."

"Can you see the sun?"

"It's hard to describe. There is day and night, and we could see the moon and stars last night. Looking anywhere else, it is like everything disappears."

"And when will it end?" his mother asked, failing to hide the strain in her voice.

"The messenger didn't know." Avraham set down the lamp in the middle and all of them huddled close. Already the fear, that Avraham would take the lamp and leave, gripped Kheti.

"Soon after the darkness fell, Pharaoh summoned Mosheh and said, 'Go, worship your god. Even your women and children may go with you; only leave your flocks and herds behind.'"

"So Pharaoh gave in," Pentu said.

"Not exactly," Papa said. "He's still trying to have his way— Mosheh wants the Hebrews to be allowed to leave with their livestock."

"Pharaoh wouldn't be foolish enough to let them do that." Pentu talked as though Avraham wasn't present.

"What did Mosheh say?" Tia leaned forward.

"He said, 'You must allow us to have sacrifices and burnt offerings to present to the Lord our God. Our livestock too must go with us; not a hoof is to be left behind. We have to use some of them in worshiping the Lord our God. Until we get there, we will not know what we are to use to worship the Lord.'"

"It's obviously a lie," Pentu said. "Mosheh would never return."

Kheti agreed with Pentu, but there must be a reason that Elohim kept making a lesser demand rather than simply saying, "Let my people go." Maybe it was to make it easier for Pharaoh to submit.

"Then what happened?" Iset asked, gently rocking little Hepu.

"Pharaoh said, 'Get out of my sight! Make sure you do not appear before me again. The day you see my face, you will die.' And Mosheh said, 'Just as you say. I will never appear before you again.'"

Fear gripped Kheti's throat. "What happens if Pharaoh doesn't relent? Will we be left in the dark?"

"Pharaoh has always relented … eventually. Surely he'll do it again," Iset asked. "Won't he?"

Kheti didn't know. By now, Mosheh would know that Pharaoh's words couldn't be relied upon. Pharaoh had claimed he'd let the Hebrews go many times already, and had gone back on his word each time. Pharaoh had even claimed he had sinned and that the Hebrews' God was in the right, yet he'd backtracked again the minute the hail had stopped. When Kheti had lied as a child, his father had walloped him so hard he couldn't sit down for a week. Presumably Nanny hadn't been allowed to take such liberties with a future Pharaoh.

* * *

"I can see." Tia screamed, her voice held a tinge of hysteria. "Wake up, everyone. The sun is back."

Kheti groaned, as she shook him, "Wake up."

"I'm awake," he mumbled. He opened his eyes, but closed them again as the flood of light half-blinded him. Kheti covered his eyes with his hand, cracking his fingers apart to allow his eyes to adjust. They had eaten their previous meal in the dark and huddled together in the darkness to sleep.

Once his eyes had adjusted, he leapt to his feet. "Come on," he said to Tia.

They bounded outside and stood barefoot with their faces to the sun. Miraculous. The light and warmth raised his spirits. Gratefulness welled up in him.

"Praise be to Ra," Pentu said. "He has won and brought the sun back."

Kheti wanted to disagree, to say that Ra's hands had proved tied, but fear sealed his mouth.

"Do you really think so?" Tia asked. "I would have thought that to win he'd either have prevented the darkness falling or solved the problem immediately. Not wait three days."

Well done, Tia. She'd not been cowed by fear. Kheti tasted the all too familiar sourness of shame.

"Would you defend the slave god and spit in the face of our

ancestors?" Pentu turned his back on them. "Stupid girl. I thought you had more sense than that."

"At least have the politeness to stand and face me when you insult me," Tia said.

Pentu moved away as if he hadn't heard.

Tia had courage. Courage that said the right thing even if she was mocked. How did someone gain that sort of courage?

CHAPTER TWENTY-EIGHT

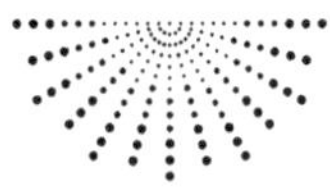

"Kheti, come with me. I've just seen a messenger arrive at Avraham's." Papa emptied a bucket of water into the sheep trough.

They'd spent many days working hard to keep the animals alive on the barley straw. The grass was finally recovering from the onslaught of the locusts, and there were new leaves on the trees, but they feared letting the sheep out into the fields too early.

Ever since the sun had returned, his father had been worrying about the next plague. He was sure there would be at least one more, and that any plague to come would be the worst yet. Kheti tried not to think about what could be worse than what they'd already experienced.

They set off down the hill and across the little waterway. Before they reached Avraham's, the messenger departed in a cloud of dust as if in a desperate hurry.

Avraham was talking rapidly as they approached his home. Then Yosef dashed out the back. Something was definitely going on. Something urgent.

"Avraham," Kheti's father called.

There was silence for a long moment and then Avraham appeared in the doorway. "I was about to come and see you. Tonight there will be another sign." He clenched his fists. "A terrible night is coming."

Kheti held his breath. Heart thumping. What could be worse than what they'd experienced already?

"Adonai will come tonight at midnight, and the firstborn livestock will die."

Kheti let out the breath he'd been holding. That wasn't as bad as he'd expected.

"And?" His father's gaze was fixed on Avraham.

Avraham took a deep breath.

"And he will strike down all the firstborn sons."

The breath caught in Kheti's throat.

His father grabbed the doorpost, knees sagging. "All of them?' His words came out in a croak. "Pentu and little Hepu?"

Avraham nodded. "You're not the oldest son, are you?"

Papa shook his head. "My older brother died years ago." He straightened and clutched Avraham's tunic. "Is there no way we can escape?"

"We have been told what we need to do, but I don't know if it applies to Egyptians," Avraham said.

"What is it?" Papa cried, clutching Avraham's arm. "What do we need to do?"

"We've been told to choose a one-year old male goat or sheep. It must be slaughtered, and the blood drained in a basin. Then we must use hyssop to paint the lintels of our door, above and on either side."

The bleat of an animal could be heard. Yosef returned, leading a pure white lamb.

"The sacrifice must be perfect," Avraham said. "No blemishes. No lameness. The very best of the flock."

"We can do that," Kheti's father said. "What else?"

"The meat must be roasted and entirely consumed tonight and the whole family must stay in the home all night. "

Havvah appeared around the corner of the house with some herbs in her hands. Kheti had tried them once, but their bitterness had made him spit them out.

Avraham ticked off a list on his fingers. "You must also bake bread without yeast and eat bitter herbs."

"Is that all?" Kheti asked.

"Those are the main directives. Adonai has given us instructions for the future. This will be a lasting festival for us. Our new year. We are to tell the stories of these ten signs to our children and their children."

Ten signs. Then this was the end. But what kind of end would it be?

"Kheti, my mind is not as clear as yours," Papa said, his voice urgent. "Repeat the instructions. We must get them right. We must."

Kheti went over the instructions twice more as he and his father hurried back up the hill.

"Kheti, you go choose the animal," Papa said. "I will speak with your mother."

But would she listen? Would she realize that she and Papa must present a unified opinion or Pentu would not heed them? Although there was no guarantee Pentu would believe even if his parents were united. And if Pentu chose to go his own way, he would be dead by midnight. Worse, he'd take little Hepu with him. Kheti's throat narrowed.

His father turned to Kheti. "Pray! And not to Ra."

"Do you think Elohim listens to Egyptians?"

"I think he looks at our hearts, not our skin," Papa said. "There will be Hebrews who won't listen, and there may be other Egyptians who will. All we can do is cry out for mercy."

* * *

*K*heti walked toward the flock. The first one-year old had a blemish over its eye, another had a limp, and another had some sort of running sore. He noted it to deal with later.

There was one that looked spotless. Kheti gently approached it and shooed it toward a corner. It flicked its ears and made a break for freedom, but he grabbed it on the way past. It bawled in protest, but Kheti ignored it, flipped it on its side, and tied its feet. Then he looked for a second animal. Papa could make the final choice.

Kheti tucked one lamb under each arm and walked toward the house. Inside, the sound of raised voices indicated things might not be going well.

"If I'd known you'd become a lover of the slaves' god, I never would have married you," Mother said as Kheti reached the door.

Papa emerged from the inner room, face reddening when he saw Kheti.

Kheti looked away. "I've chosen two possible animals, Papa."

"Good lad. I'll have a quick look, then we'll go to your brother's place. He must be warned before it is too late. There is still time."

* * *

*A*s they walked toward Pentu's house, Kheti glanced across at his father. His face was drawn, and he rubbed his left shoulder as though he'd strained it. These months had aged him faster than Kheti would have thought possible.

"I am sorry you heard that, Kheti," Papa said quietly.

"Mother does not mean what she says. She is simply afraid." Kheti spoke in a rush, wanting to comfort his father, but failing to fill his voice with conviction.

Papa paused for a long moment, as though he was making a

decision. "Perhaps, but her fear runs deep. You know how she likes to talk about her priestly ancestors?"

Kheti did. Mama claimed her ancestry whenever she wanted to claim superiority. Even after all these years, she still despised farming.

Papa was puffing a little with exertion, so Kheti slowed down his pace, almost imperceptibly, to make it easier for him to keep up.

"Yosef told you the story of the man he was named after," Papa said. "What do you remember?"

"The original Yosef was sold into slavery in Canaan and worked for Potiphar before being thrown into prison." The story had been a vivid one. "He became second to Pharaoh when he interpreted Pharaoh's dream and helped him prepare Egypt to face a famine and Yosef had a huge influence on Egyptians of his generation."

Papa looked at Kheti. "And did Yosef follow Elohim?"

Kheti nodded. "And he wasn't afraid to talk about him."

His father glanced across at him. "I think you can guess what happened. Your mother's ancestors listened to Yosef and turned to follow his God."

Kheti whistled. "So they stopped being priests?"

Papa nodded. "Her family went from one of great influence and power to ordinary farmers, and she lays the blame on Yosef and his descendants."

"And now she's worried about you doing the same."

Papa rubbed his shoulder again. "She doesn't want anyone in this family to have anything to do with Elohim."

Kheti had often pondered about Mama's superior attitude toward her neighbors and deep hatred of the Hebrews, but never guessed her reason was so personal. He wasn't sure how he felt now that he knew. Excited, perhaps, and somewhat comforted to think that many generations ago, his ancestors had followed Elohim.

Pentu was planting onions. He stopped work as they

approached and mopped the sweat off his forehead. "You look grim."

"We have reason to be," Papa said. "There is going to be another plague, probably the last."

Pentu spat. "What has their god conjured up this time?"

Pentu made Elohim sound like a wandering entertainer providing amusement to the lower classes. Even if Pentu didn't want to submit to Elohim, did he not at least have some reverence?

"Son, it will be no laughing matter. The hail and locusts were bad enough, but this one will strike the oldest sons."

Pentu blinked.

"If you do not follow Elohim's instructions, you and Hepu will both be struck down at midnight."

Pentu laid down his hoe and put his hands on his hips. "Let me guess the real reason. I bet this god will demand great amounts of gold from us to save our lives."

"No," Papa said sadly. "He is not at all like you suppose."

"Since when did you become such an expert?" Pentu snapped.

It was a reasonable question. It almost sounded like Papa had made the decision to follow the Hebrew god for himself. But how did a person follow this god? As far as Kheti knew, Elohim had no temples, no priests, no rituals. If Papa had decided to follow Elohim, what would that mean for them all?

Papa's face was sad. "There are no experts. Elohim is far beyond anyone's understanding."

Pentu kicked a clod of earth. "Mother is not going to be happy with you."

No, she was not. It wouldn't surprise Kheti if she became more outwardly religious to demonstrate her disagreement with Papa's decision. Papa was in for a rough time.

"You must listen," Papa's voice pleaded. "There's not much time."

Pentu scowled and folded his arms.

"At midnight tonight, Elohim will come and strike down the

firstborn sons of all who do not follow his instructions."

Pentu's eyes widened, and he swiped the sweat that glistened on his upper lip.

"That means you and Hepu. The only way we can be saved is if each family chooses a perfect one-year old male lamb or goat, kills it, and paints the blood on the lintels of the door. We will roast the lamb and eat it with unleavened bread and bitter herbs, and we must not leave the house until daybreak."

"Is that all?" Pentu said. "It seems too easy."

"Easy or not, I am not going to argue," Papa said. "We've already chosen our lamb. Please come and stay overnight with us."

"And what guarantee do you have that this will work?" Pentu asked.

"Have you so quickly forgotten the plague of hail? Those of us who obeyed Elohim were saved."

"What guarantee?" Pentu said again.

"I'm not sure there is one," Papa said. "The instructions were for the Hebrews, but just like during the plague of hail, I intend to do all I can to show Elohim I am trusting him."

Pentu spat on the ground. "Have you no pride? You're an Egyptian, not a Hebrew slave."

Papa shook his head. "Stop thinking of them as slaves. Elohim could free them within the blink of an eye."

"Then why hasn't he done so?" Pentu asked. "Perhaps he isn't as powerful as you like to think."

A look of intense sadness crossed their father's face. "Elohim has given us a way to be saved. I beg you to take it."

Pentu snorted.

"At least think on it," Papa said. "To lose you and Hepu would be unbearable. We will go home and prepare, but you must join us by sunset."

No matter how much it would anger Pentu, Papa was sure to warn Iset as they passed by Pentu's place.

CHAPTER TWENTY-NINE

The sun was dropping toward the horizon, but still Pentu did not come. Fear clutched Kheti as firmly as a crocodile's jaw. The smell of roast lamb wafted through the house. Kheti sniffed. If it wasn't for such a solemn event, he would have been looking forward to the evening meal.

All day, Father had been back and forth to the front of the property watching, watching, watching for Pentu, Iset, and Hepu. All day, he'd been disappointed. At each disappointment, his shoulders slumped further, and another worry line was added to his face.

"He's afraid, isn't he?" Tia said at Kheti's shoulder.

Kheti nodded, sorrow swirling in his gut. "He knows Pentu well."

And Pentu's pride would not let him submit. That didn't usually matter, but this time it mattered. Dying because of pride was one thing, but sacrificing Hepu as well would be a tragedy for all of them.

"What will Papa do?" Tia put her hand in the crook of his elbow.

"I don't know." Kheti's stomach ached. He would have to save Hepu somehow, but how? Pentu wasn't a fool. He must know they wouldn't give up easily. He'd be watching like a hawk for any attempt to go around his authority.

"I'm going back to Pentu's," Papa said as he passed. "I can't give up."

"Do you want me to come?" Kheti asked.

Papa shook his head. "He's less likely to bend if you are there. Besides which, you and Tia are needed here."

Needed to keep the meal preparations moving forward. Mother never cooked. As Avraham and Sara were busy with their own family, Tia had done most of the work after Kheti had killed and prepared the lamb.

Kheti watched Papa walk toward Pentu's, head low and feet plodding as though weary beyond all measure. *Elohim, keep him safe.*

"What's going on at Avraham and Sara's?" Tia asked, pointing with her chin.

Kheti shielded his eyes with his hand. Yosef was bringing in their small flock of sheep and confining them close to their home.

"They've been busy all day, washing and cleaning." Tia turned to him. "Like they're getting ready to move."

Move? Maybe they were. Maybe they too were expecting this to be the last plague. If it was, would they be leaving? Leaving and going where? The Hebrews had been in Egypt for more than four hundred years. If they had a home, it was as much here as anywhere else. Not that Egypt had been a welcoming place for them. No wonder their hearts longed for elsewhere.

"Can you look after things here?" Kheti asked.

"Of course," Tia said. "The lamb is nearly finished, and the bread and herbs are ready."

He kissed her on the forehead. "Thanks. I'll run down to Avraham's and see if I can find out what is going on." If Avraham and Yosef were willing to tell him. Sure, they each respected the other, but trust was difficult when Kheti belonged to those who'd enslaved them. In another time and place, he liked to think they'd have been friends.

Avraham's front door was firmly shut. Flies buzzed and walked their sticky feet through the lamb's blood still damp on the lintels. Kheti went round the back. Tia was right. A cart he hadn't known Avraham owned was neatly stacked with wooden boxes. Avraham and Yosef were busy fixing the frame to make a shaded covering for the top.

Yosef froze when he saw Kheti, pink staining his neck.

Kheti walked forward. "I wanted to check that you were okay and had everything you needed."

"Yes, thank you," Avraham said.

This was awkward. What would his father do if he were here? "Father also thinks this will be the last plague,"

"Yes," Avraham said, straightening and meeting his eye.

Kheti was sure Avraham and Yosef knew more than they'd admitted so far. There was a long silence and Avraham pursed his lips. Deciding if Kheti could be trusted?

"I know you will leave," Kheti said. "I heard Father telling Mother." His mother's anger had rung throughout the house. Life ahead would be a good deal harder for all of Egypt, as they'd all grown used to a huge slave force.

Avraham nodded. "Adonai has told us that Pharaoh will drive us out before sunrise tomorrow. We are to be prepared to leave immediately." He gestured to the cart.

"And will Pharaoh's son also die?" Kheti asked.

Avraham nodded. "Mosheh was told at the beginning that Pharaoh would harden his heart until Elohim battered him with this last terrible plague, the plague of the firstborn."

A wave of hatred rose in Kheti's throat. Hatred for a Pharaoh who valued his pride so highly but saw his people as expendable. If Papa couldn't convince Pentu to come to their home, both he and Hepu would die tonight. Pentu was old enough to choose, but Hepu would never know his future had been chosen for him. He should have a choice.

"Abba, the lamb is nearly ready," Havvah called from the doorway.

Kheti glanced beyond the house. In the distance, his father was toiling up the hill toward home. He was alone. Kheti sighed, despair heavy in his limbs.

"I must go. Pentu is still refusing to come to safety."

"You have killed the lamb then?" Yosef asked, his eyes bright.

Kheti nodded. "And put the blood over the door."

"You could come with us, you know," Avraham said. "You would be most welcome."

Kheti glanced up at their faces; Avraham serious but warm, Yosef eager for him to say yes, and Havvah alternating smiling and flushing. For one long moment he wanted to say yes, but he remembered Papa and the worry and fear creased his face. "I couldn't. I could never leave my family."

"Your papa is a good man," Avraham said. "All would be welcome."

Tears pricked his eyes. Kheti sniffed. Papa was a good man, but his mother wouldn't leave Egypt for all the treasures of Pharaoh. There was no point in even considering it.

"Keep safe," Kheti said as he turned to go.

"May Elohim shelter you under his wings," Avraham said.

The image was as warm as a hug.

Oh Elohim, have mercy on Hepu. Have mercy on my brother. He has often annoyed me, but he is the only brother I've got.

* * *

"I pleaded with him to come, for Hepu's sake, if not his own," Papa said as he and Kheti stood at the front door of their home. Papa's voice shook. "I even got on my knees and begged, but it was no use."

Kheti put his hand on his father's shoulder. If Kheti had thought Papa looked old before, he now looked worse. Ancient and gray and somehow shrunken, as though his energy was draining out of his feet.

The shadows outside were lengthening, and they stared at the sun as it dropped, a flaming ball of orange. The clouds were puffs of pink and gold as though to taunt them with their beauty.

Kheti's mouth went dry. "Elohim, have mercy."

His father gripped Kheti's arm as the orange sun slid out of sight. He bowed his head and a tear trickled into his beard.

His father pushed the front door closed with a creak just as Tia came toward them. "The meal is ready, Papa."

It would be almost impossible to swallow anything, but Kheti and Papa followed Tia. She'd spread the cloth on the floor and arranged cushions for everyone. At another time it would have been a meal to savor.

They sat, and Mama reached for the meat.

"No, dear," Papa said. "First we pray."

Mama pursed her lips but said nothing.

Papa raised his hands, and Kheti and Tia followed his example. The unfamiliar action felt right and proper, but Mama crossed her arms and stared at the wall. Even now, she was not going to bow her head. *Elohim have mercy.*

"Elohim, Creator of all. We are not worthy to call on your name, but we have seen your mercy. Mercy that has issued many timely warnings. Mercy that has spared us more than most."

Mama muttered something under her breath.

"We ask for your mercy tonight. Please change Pentu's heart and bring him and his family here soon. Please save little Hepu who has never had a chance to know you."

Kheti swallowed around the rock in his throat.

"Give Hepu a chance. Save us all." Papa lowered his hands. Taking up the first of the unleavened loaves, he tore it and handed it to Mother first, then to Kheti and finally Tia. "Take and eat, and remember all that has happened."

Kheti took a mouthful and thought back to all they'd gone through in the last moons. From the stench of the river turning to blood on that first day, to the feeling of the frogs beneath their feet, to the sting of biting gnats and flies. He'd always thought Papa a quiet man who simply did his work. He'd never considered Papa a leader, but the plagues had shown Papa's underlying strength as he stood up for what was right.

Tia handed Papa the meat.

"Thank you, daughter. You have done well."

Tia glowed under his praise, then passed the platter of meat to Mama, then Kheti. The still-warm meat was perfect, slightly crispy on the outside and juicy and moist inside. Kheti closed his eyes and enjoyed the rich taste.

His father choked. "I can't do this."

Kheti opened his eyes.

"I can't sit here without Pentu and Hepu."

"But we were told not to leave the house after sunset," Kheti said.

"I must risk it," Papa said. "Iset wanted to come, but Pentu insisted that they stay."

Bile rose in Kheti's throat. How dare Pentu play with his family's lives?

"Father, you're exhausted. Let me go," Kheti said, rising to his feet.

"No, son. We don't know what will happen if I leave the safety of home. I cannot risk you too."

"It's better that Kheti goes than we lose you," Mother said.

Kheti bit his lip to stop himself saying anything. His mother only had room in her heart for Pentu. He'd always been of lesser importance in her eyes. Maybe she was now realizing that she should have added her pleas to Papa's. Even if this whole threat was a hoax, it would have been better to play safe instead of risking two lives.

"No. Kheti is the future, and Pentu will not listen to him."

To Pentu, Kheti was merely a younger brother of lesser wisdom and importance. Someone to order about, not someone who might contribute anything worthwhile.

"Father, let me try." Kheti rose to his feet. "Or let's go together. You can talk to Pentu while I grab Hepu and run."

Kheti had seen Iset's desperation. She wouldn't protest.

"No, my son," Papa said. "But you can accompany me to the door."

Once Kheti and Papa were far enough away from the others, Papa stopped and turned. "I don't know what will happen." He swallowed. "I may not make it back."

The full moon illuminated the doorway under which they were standing.

"No!" Kheti said. "You must come back."

"I'll try, but we must face reality. They might not come, and Elohim might strike me down for going."

Fear clutched at Kheti. "Would he?"

"I don't know."

Kheti's blood pounded in his ears. Papa had always seemed to have all the answers, yet not in this important issue. How could Papa entrust himself to a being he couldn't know?

"Elohim judges the heart, but we must not make the mistake of bringing him down to our level," Papa said. "If he truly is God, then there will be much about him that we'll never comprehend." He gripped Kheti's shoulder. "Listen to me."

Kheti looked up into Papa's eyes. They were fixed on his with an intensity they seldom held.

"Son, if I don't make it, you must take Tia and Iset and anyone willing to go, and follow the Hebrews."

Kheti swallowed. "Why?"

"Because the Egyptian gods do not exist. I see this clearly now. There is nothing but wind echoing through our temples. If there was, they would have acted, if not for our sake, then to preserve their own reputations. We must follow Elohim. He is the only one worth following."

"Surely we can follow him here." The thought of leaving all that was familiar and going off into an unknown future was like a weight around Kheti's neck.

"We must follow where he leads."

Like the first Avraham. A man who'd followed Elohim though he'd never seen some of the promises fulfilled.

Papa turned to go. "I must go. Watch for my return but do not go out the door."

Kheti reached towards his father. If this was goodbye, then it should be a proper one. His father turned back, and Kheti hugged him. "Love you so much, Papa."

"Love you, too. You are a son to be proud of."

Kheti's eyes stung, and he hugged Papa fiercely. "I'll be praying."

"To Elohim?"

Kheti nodded. Where else did any of them have to turn?

CHAPTER THIRTY

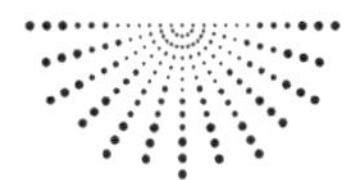

Kheti peered out the door. The full moon bathed the land in a silvery light. He strained his eyes toward Pentu's home, but there was no movement. No sound of voices and no indication of Papa returning.

Elohim, have mercy.

If Papa was coming, surely he'd be here by now. Tia had delivered the remainder of Kheti's meal while he remained near the window, but that had been finished long ago.

There! What was that? A pale blur of something. Kheti strained his eyes. The leaves danced and cast shadows on the silvered ground. There was definitely someone there.

"Papa," he called. "Is that you?"

Someone spoke but the voice was indistinct. Kheti ran to the door and opened it. Again he peered through the shadows. Papa, if it was Papa, was alone. His back was bowed, and he stumbled forward.

"Father," Kheti called again.

The figure stopped and leaned against a tree. He shifted his shoulder awkwardly and lowered a sack onto the ground. "Don't come out." Papa's voice was low but urgent. "Call Hepu."

Hepu! The sack on the ground moved and held out his arms to his grandfather.

"Call Hepu," Papa said again.

"Hepu," Kheti called. "Come this way. Come to Uncle Kheti."

Hepu turned in the moonlight and looked at Kheti. Kheti called again.

Elohim, help us.

Hepu reached out his hand for his grandfather, who kissed it, and then gently pushed him in the direction of the doorway. Hepu took a hesitant step toward Kheti.

Tia appeared at Kheti's elbow.

"Bring me a light," Kheti said in an undertone, his gaze locked on his nephew. "Hepu needs to see us clearly."

Tia hurried off. Kheti called Hepu again, but still he stood with his thumb in his mouth. Why wasn't Papa bringing him? Kheti peered toward the tree. Papa had slid to the ground. Fear gnawed at Kheti's gut. Was Papa alright?

"Hepu!" Kheti called again, trying to sound welcoming, not desperate.

Tia appeared, a clay lamp in her hand. The light flickered in the breeze.

"Shelter the flame and help me call Hepu," Kheti said.

They called together. Maybe a woman's voice would help. Hepu looked toward them and checked back with his grandfather, who waved him forward. Still Hepu hesitated, and Kheti stepped forward.

"Don't—"Papa held up his hand. "Don't come out." He moved, then crawled forward. Why was Papa crawling? Each forward movement was slow, forced, hesitant, as though he moved forward only by the strength of his will.

Tia gasped and Kheti gripped the doorposts. Something was wrong. Everything in him longed to dash out the door and help.

Papa reached Hepu and nudged him forward. Tia called again. At last, Hepu began to move forward. Closer and closer. Now they could see the glistening tracks of tears on Hepu's face. He had not left his mother easily.

Beside him, Tia opened her arms. Hepu toddled forward, grabbed her, and held on with a glad cry. "Mama," he said with a wail.

"She'll be here soon." Tia patted his back.

Kheti hoped she was right.

"Take him inside. I'll help Papa." It was obvious something was terribly wrong. Papa's face was shiny with sweat, and every so often he grimaced.

Tia picked up the still-crying Hepu and carried him back into the house. Kheti heard Mama give an exclamation of joy. He looked toward Papa. He was close now, the sound of his breaths loud in the quiet night air.

Kheti dropped down on his hands and knees and focused his gaze on his father's.

Come on, Papa. If Kheti could will him forward, he would. He'd dash out immediately if it wouldn't distress Papa even more. Papa moved one hand and the opposite leg.

Come on, Papa.

He was much closer.

"You're nearly here," Kheti said. "Well done."

Papa looked at Kheti then down at the ground again. He moved one more hand and one more leg.

"Only five more to go," Kheti said. Then Papa would be close enough for Kheti to haul him in.

Papa moaned and swayed back and forth. With a grunt he moved his other hand and then his leg. Kheti wrinkled his nose at the smell of sweat. Again Papa moved forward, and again he grunted. Had Papa broken a bone? Had Pentu beaten him? There were no visible signs of violence, but pain and strain were evident in every movement.

"Two more," Kheti urged.

Papa closed his eyes and moved. One, two.

Kheti reached out and hauled Papa into the doorway.

"Enough," Papa panted, collapsing as Kheti tried to move him further inside.

"Come, rest," Kheti urged, but his father resisted.

"Safe now." He indicated the blood-painted beams of the doorway above their heads. "Safe now. We can stay here."

"What's wrong, Papa?"

"Pain," Papa said. "Chest. Shoulder. Arm." Each word was an effort. "Hepu is safe?"

"Tia has him. She and Mama will look after him. Can I make you more comfortable?"

Papa nodded weakly. Kheti stood and gently turned Papa over, then used the bottom of his tunic to dab the sweat off Papa's face.

"Hard to breathe," Papa said, his face blueish-gray in the moonlight.

Kheti pulled Papa more upright, so he rested on Kheti's thigh. "Better?"

Papa nodded almost imperceptibly.

"Pentu refused to come?" Kheti asked.

"Mmm."

Hot anger throbbed in Kheti's chest. Pentu was a fool. Elohim had not asked anything unreasonable. Kheti had no idea why the lamb was important or why they had to follow such specific instructions, but the instructions hadn't been difficult.

If Pentu refused, how had Papa managed to convince him to allow Hepu to leave?

"Worried about Iset." Papa moaned again, sweat breaking out on his forehead. Kheti dabbed it off.

Panting, Papa said, "Iset begged me to take Hepu."

Ah. So Pentu had nothing to do with it. Papa was worried that Iset might pay the price for her action. There was no telling what Pentu would do at what he'd consider defiance of his wishes.

Elohim, have mercy.

Iset would have known the danger, yet she'd chosen to give Hepu a chance. Kheti was proud of her.

"Papa, you saved Hepu." Shame oozed into his heart. He should have overruled Papa and gone. Kheti smoothed back Papa's scant locks of hair. "Do you want me to get Mother?"

"No." Papa took a wheezing breath. "Just want to rest."

Papa's head was heavy on Kheti's thigh.

"You must go with the Hebrews." Papa clenched Kheti's hand. Another pain?

"I still don't understand why Elohim didn't just rescue the Hebrews with one plague," Kheti said. "Why drag it out?"

"For us," Papa said. "We needed ten plagues to come to know Elohim." He gasped. "And trust him." Papa frowned. "Don't you remember? You heard Mosheh say, 'So you may know there is no one like me in all the earth. I've raised you up so that my name might be proclaimed in all the earth.'" He took a few more breaths. "Ten plagues work much better than one."

Ten plagues over many moons meant the news had spread like ripples on the lake, throughout Egypt and maybe even beyond their borders. Egypt hosted visitors and merchants from many far-flung places. As a child, Kheti remembered being terrified at seeing black men from the south, and there were rumors Pharaoh had concubines with eyes of blue like the sky.

"Avraham said his people had much to learn." Papa's hand was clenched. "They doubted Mosheh when he first told them Elohim had sent him."

Papa rested for long moments and then said, "Look at how long it took us to trust Elohim. Most of our neighbors lost their livestock because they didn't learn that lesson."

The only people in the area who'd learned the lesson were the neighbors' daughter, Nophret, and her brother. Everyone else had ignored the warnings.

Kheti's shoulders relaxed as Papa quieted. Maybe the pain was lessening.

Suddenly Papa grabbed his hand, crushing it. "Look after them for me," he said through clenched teeth. Sweat was again on his brow.

"Who?"

"Tia—Iset—Hepu—" Each name choked out.

Panic began to dance in Kheti's stomach. "Papa, I can't." Tears flooded his eyes. "Don't leave me."

"Don't weep for me." Again Papa clasped Kheti's hand. "Weep for your brother and your mother." He was silent for a long moment. "Promise me."

Kheti dashed tears away.

"Promise me you'll take care of them."

"I promise." The weight of Kheti's promise settled heavily on him.

"And promise me you'll go with the Hebrews," Papa said.

Kheti paused. That was a much harder promise to make. "If I believe it's what's best for them all, I will go."

"I can trust you to do the right thing." Papa closed his eyes and took a shaky breath. "Proud of you." Two more shallow breaths. "Elohim will guide you."

"No, Papa. You and Elohim will guide me."

"Elohim will guide you," Papa repeated.

Kheti wished he was as certain as Papa was.

"Elohim," Papa moaned. "Elohim!" The sound of Papa's stressed panting was loud in the quiet night air. "Content to be here—" His breath came in short gasps, and he clutched his chest with one hand. "Under the blood."

Papa took a few more rattly breaths, then his face contorted, his hand lost its hold of Kheti's and fell to the ground with a thud.

"No. Papa. No!" Kheti threw himself onto his Papa's body. Sobs burst out. This wasn't the way it should have ended. He still needed Papa's wisdom, love, and support. How could Kheti possibly go it alone with all these people depending on him?

Footsteps ran toward him, and Kheti laid Papa gently on the ground and stood.

"What have you done?" Mother shrieked and pulled her hair. "What have you done?"

Kheti didn't answer. Couldn't answer. Mama was in no state to listen to anything he said. Her wails split the air, and Kheti jumped when Tia came up behind him and touched his shoulder. Hepu was on her hip, tear-stained cheek pressed tight to her neck, still sucking his thumb.

Kheti touched his hand to Hepu's cheek, then gave Tia a sideways hug, leaning down to say in her ear. "Papa's last thoughts were of us and Iset and Hepu."

"I knew he was unwell," Tia murmured. "He was often in pain."

Tia had been more aware than he had been. Looking back, Kheti recalled seeing Papa rubbing his shoulder but hadn't realized it was anything serious. Certainly not this serious. He shouldn't have let him go back to Pentu's. Shame curdled in his stomach. He was so much younger and stronger. Maybe Papa would have survived if Kheti had gone instead.

"Their god has taken everything from me," his mother hiccupped, her face covered in tears and her nose running. "I hate him. I hate him."

Kheti wasn't going to argue, but he did intend to set one thing straight. "Papa was not taken. He gave up his life to save Hepu. Papa knew it might cost his life and still he chose to do it."

Mother stared at him as though she'd suddenly noticed Kheti had grown up. Papa had shown Kheti the way to live. Now he intended to follow Papa's example. Tia squeezed Kheti's arm, and he looked down at her. Her eyes brimmed with tears, and she tightened her lips. She understood.

"We can't leave him here," Mother said. "It's disrespectful."

Papa would have preferred to continue to lie under the blood of the lamb that had died for Hepu, but Kheti would move the body for his mother's sake. "What about on your sleeping mat?"

Mama nodded and stood up. Kheti stooped and managed to drape Papa's body over his shoulders. The heavy weight of the body mirrored the weight in his heart. He straightened with a grunt and slowly followed Mother to the place she indicated. Once there, he lowered Papa gently onto the mat and arranged his limbs neatly.

Kheti swallowed the lump in his throat as he looked at Papa, all pain lines now smoothed from his face.

"Your brother can arrange for the priest in the morning," his mother said.

Did Mama still not understand? Without a miracle, Pentu would not be alive past midnight, and it must be nearly that now. Even Hepu was not yet safe. Hepu had not been safely in this house before sunset. If Elohim did not show mercy, there would be two more deaths before morning.

Elohim, please show mercy. We are not your people, but we ask you to extend your mercy over us as well. Save Hepu.

CHAPTER THIRTY-ONE

Someone pounded on their front door. Kheti groaned and remembered. Papa was dead, and he wouldn't be the only one. Last night, after his mother had ceased her weeping, Kheti had collapsed into bed and slept soundly. He had a vague impression of wailing during the night, but maybe it was the memory of his mother's cries.

The knocking came again. Kheti rubbed his eyes, grabbed his tunic, and threw it over his head. He ran toward the front door and threw it open. "Iset!"

"Is he safe?" Iset pushed into the room, hair matted, clothes torn, and with dark bruises on her face. "Is he safe?"

"Come and see." Kheti led her to Tia's room, where his mother had collapsed after hours of weeping.

At the entrance, Kheti held up his hand and they peeked in. Mama and Tia were sprawled messily and Hepu was lying between them, his face a healthy color, and a bubble of saliva at the corner of his mouth.

"He's alive," Iset whispered brokenly. "He's alive."

Kheti nodded. Too overcome to say anything and with more tears threatening to spill. Yes, Hepu lived because both his grandfather and mother had acted in faith. Faith in a God who could be trusted. A gush of gratitude bubbled up. "Praise be to Elohim."

"Yes, praise him," Iset murmured next to him.

Hepu opened his eyes. "Mama, Mama." He rolled over, scrambled onto all fours, and then clambered over Tia's legs.

Tia groaned and opened her eyes and looked at Iset. "What happened?"

"Not important now," Iset mumbled, her face flushing.

Anger surged through Kheti. Pentu's fists had happened.

"And Pentu?" Kheti asked gently in an undertone.

"He was struck down." Iset sniffed and wiped her hand across her face. "One moment he was alive, and the next he fell to the ground."

Hepu reached where his mother was standing. Iset bent down and hauled him into her arms, burying her face in his hair, and hugging him like she never wanted to let go.

The ache of missing Papa throbbed again like a toothache deep in Kheti's belly. It was going to be a heartbreaking day. And backbreaking—it would take all day to dig graves and bury Papa and Pentu. He'd better get onto it, for there was no one else to help. He turned to his sister-in-law.

"I will go and prepare the grave now. Do you want to come?"

Iset shook her head emphatically. "I've said my goodbyes."

* * *

Kheti collected the tools for digging and headed toward Pentu's home. No. He'd go via Avraham's place first. All was quiet as he approached, and the door was latched. The cart was gone. He unlatched the door, which opened with a creak, and looked around. The walls and shelves were completely bare. Kheti sighed. Everyone was gone. He could have used their help today. No. He would miss their help every day. There was no way he could run the farm now, not having lost half of their main workers. His head pounded. He wasn't ready for all the responsibility that had fallen on him. And as for following the Hebrews as Papa had urged, Kheti didn't see how it was possible.

Heavy in heart, Kheti turned to leave. Outside, cart tracks led east. Away from Egypt and toward Avraham's hoped-for future. Kheti swallowed the sorrow of more losses and plodded toward Pentu's home.

Inside, clothes and plates were scattered on the floor, and right in the center of the mess was Pentu, his eyes staring up at the ceiling, and his face set in shock.

Kheti stood there, numb, unable to process anything more. His brother was dead, yet Kheti felt nothing. They hadn't been close, but Pentu had always been around, like the clouds in the sky.

Kheti turned and went out to survey the remains of the wheat field. He walked over to the far side, which overlooked their lake. It seemed as good a spot as any. The earth was still soft on top, and the hoe sunk in easily.

Kheti was already sweating when he heard a sound behind him. He whirled around. Nophret and her little brother were behind him, holding hands on the edge of the field.

Nophret tugged Intef's hand, and he allowed himself to be led forward. "Umm," she said looking down at the ground. "Umm."

Kheti took a deep breath. More responsibility. "What's wrong?"

A tear trickled down her cheek. "Father's dead … and my older brother. They refused to listen. Refused to sacrifice a lamb."

"And your mother?" Kheti asked, leaning on his hoe.

"She's at home. Rocking back and forth."

It looked like Intef wasn't in any better state.

"Do you have any other family?"

Nophret shook her head. "Just us three. I don't know what to do."

"Have you got the strength to help me dig here?" Kheti asked. "Then I will go home and get my sister Tia to accompany us."

Tia was young, but Kheti wanted someone to accompany them, and Tia had proved to have plenty of common sense in recent days.

Nophret sat her brother under the nearest tree, and Kheti showed her how to move the dirt he loosened. Without a word, they worked together, silent with the enormity of what had happened. It took much more effort to dig the harder earth beneath the plowed surface.

"Not much more," Kheti said, wiping the sweat off his forehead with his arm.

They moved the last of the dirt.

"Take Intef for a walk down to the lake."

Nophret frowned at him.

"I will bury the body on my own."

She nodded, went over to the tree, and took her brother by the hand. Kheti waited for them to walk a little way before he returned to the house, bound Pentu's body, and used a sleeping mat to drag it to the grave. Mama would be furious that there'd been no ceremony, but there'd be many more irregularities in the coming days. Priests were often eldest sons. How many of them would still be alive?

Once he'd covered Pentu's body with earth, Kheti took a large rock and dragged it over to mark the head of the grave. Then he looked toward the lake. Nophret was urging her brother to paddle, but he simply stood there and stared at the other side.

Kheti looked up at the sky. "Elohim, it is me, Kheti son of Hepu. I am sorry that Pentu did not follow you. Help me to know what to do."

Kheti checked that Nophret couldn't hear him. "Papa said you'd guide me. I need your wisdom for what to do about Mama, Iset, Hepu, and Tia, and our neighbors too." As Kheti said each name it was as if a new rock settled on his shoulders. Elohim had better help because Kheti couldn't possibly do this himself.

CHAPTER THIRTY-TWO

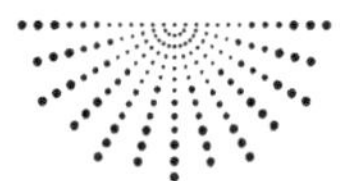

Kheti pushed open the door. Inside, Nophret's mother was curled up between two bodies lying stiffly on the floor where they'd fallen.

"Mama." Nophret ran forward, knelt, and put her arms around her mother. "Mama, Kheti has come."

Nophret's mother blinked at Kheti, her eyes unfocused. She needed help that was well beyond Kheti's abilities to provide. *Elohim, help.*

They'd judged it better for Nophret's brother, Intef, to stay with Iset and Hepu. Hepu didn't know why everyone was solemn around him. He'd woken giggling and playing with his toes. Hepu was the one most likely to help Intef.

"Nophret, come and choose a suitable place. Then I think you'd better stay with your mother. Tia and I will do the rest."

Nophret nodded and got to her feet, and they went outside together. He should leave someone inside with Nophret's mother, but he was scared to do so in case she did something unpredictable, either to herself or others. "Tia, could you stay near the window and keep checking on Nophret's mother? We'll choose a site, then

I'll call you."

"Did your father have a favorite spot?" Kheti asked Nophret.

Nophret pursed her lips. "Not Papa, but my brother loved those rocks over there." She pointed. "He could see the lake from there."

They'd all loved the lake.

"There's a little cave too."

Kheti looked at her with interest. "Could we use that?"

"It will still need some digging but not as much."

Kheti shouldered his hoe. "Show me."

Nophret headed for the rocks, and he followed. The cave was small but looked like a possibility. He stuck his hoe in the ground. It turned the earth on the floor of the cave. "This looks fine, and there are plenty of rocks to block up the entrance."

"It's the best spot," she said, brushing her eye with her finger. "I'll go back to Mama and send Tia up to join you."

Kheti watched her go. She still walked with the lack of self-consciousness of a girl, but the events of the night had flung her into adulthood. How was Nophret able to function when her mother and brother had shut down?

The sun was high in the sky before the bodies were laid in the grave and he and Nophret had finished blocking up the hole.

"Nophret, do you want to say anything?" Kheti asked.

She shook her head. "But could you pray?"

Who did Nophret want him to direct his prayers toward? Kheti would not pray to the gods of the dead, for they were no longer to be feared.

"But not to Anubis." Nophret nibbled her lip. "Do you know how to pray to the Hebrews' God?"

He nodded. "I'm learning."

"That will do," Nophret said. "I've been praying to him, but no matter how much I prayed, my father would not listen." Her voice shook. "I loved Papa, but he would not listen."

There had been too many like him.

"Avraham used to stand like this when he prayed." Kheti raised his hands with the palms facing heaven. Tia and Nophret copied him.

"Elohim, it is Kheti. Tia and Nophret are here too. We are sad. We are sad to see the destruction of our country, and we are sad to see that so many did not take you at your word. We ask you to look after our dead. We don't know how you do that, but you are great enough to do so."

Kheti's face warmed. Was he making a fool of himself? "We ask you to comfort us and give us wisdom about what to do next. We are young, and there are so many decisions to make. We want to follow you, but we don't know how. Help us. Thank you that you protect those who trust you."

"Thank you," Nophret murmured and then turned toward him. "I don't know what to do next."

He'd been half afraid and half hoping she'd turn to him. "Let me talk to my sister first."

Kheti and Tia walked out of Nophret's hearing. "Tia, do you think we should invite Nophret and her mother for tonight?"

"Mother won't be happy. She's never liked these neighbors."

He couldn't remember Mother talking to any of the neighbors once her more gregarious mother had died.

"We can't leave them here. Nophret's mother is in no state to be alone with her children."

Intef was also in deep shock and hadn't said one word to anyone.

"We still have to bury Father." Kheti's shoulders tensed at the thought. "There is no need for them to be part of it. It will probably be best if we can get Intef and his mother to nap first."

* * *

*K*heti finished wrapping Papa's body in linen. Once his mother had been convinced that Pentu really had died, she'd insisted the two be buried together and that Papa be buried in a papyrus boat. It was going to be a long, hot afternoon because the grave would have to be twice the length of Papa's body.

Kheti carried the boat, and then Papa's body to the cart and hitched up the oxen.

Kheti looked over at Tia and Iset, who were entertaining Hepu nearby. "Climb on, both of you, and please keep a firm hold on Hepu," Kheti said.

Each carried digging tools. Iset had made sure that they had water and bread and some dates. Mama had stayed at home.

When they reached the site, Kheti paced off the length of the boat and set out stones as markers. Then he bent his back to the task. Iset spent most of her time chasing Hepu, but Tia worked hard. Maybe the hard work helped her too. It prevented him thinking too much about what they'd lost and the decisions he'd have to make by tomorrow. If they were to follow the Hebrews, as his father had wanted them to do, they must leave soon.

* * *

"*I*s it done?" Mama asked.

Kheti nodded, weariness making every limb heavy.

"Go and wash." She wrinkled her nose.

Kheti dragged himself to the stored water and taking a hollow gourd, splashed water over himself. He gasped at the cold, but with the second and third dipperful, it cleared his head. He'd need a clear head for the discussion to come. At least Kheti planned for it to be a discussion. It might not be anything so calm.

215

Tia was waiting at the door. "Can I be there when you talk to Mother?"

He nodded. They must all be there, for this discussion might change the course of their lives.

Tia and Iset had prepared food. The bruises on Iset's face were darkening, and she winced whenever Hepu clambered over her. Tia had said Iset was covered in welts and bruises. Kheti was sorry. Sorry at the grief their family had brought her. Sorry he had ignored all the signs that his brother mistreated her, and sorry he had not acted to protect her.

Elohim had seen the suffering of his people and done much to protect and then rescue them. In his mercy, he'd sent many signs and warnings. Signs that the Egyptians had ignored again and again, clinging to the belief that their life beat to a rhythm set by gods who now proved powerless.

Kheti couldn't stay. The river might rise and fall until the day he went the way of all his ancestors, but Kheti would always know, deep down, that a greater God controlled the river, the harvest, the turn of the weather, their health, and even the breath in their bodies. The rhythms that had once sustained him were gone. To live while pretending he still believed would be to live a lie.

Avraham had talked of Elohim making the first people and planting them like new seeds in a beautiful garden. They were to obey Elohim's ways and flourish. Was this flourishing possible for him? Kheti would never find out if he stayed here.

Mother was in the front room, staring out toward Pentu's home and the burial place.

"Mother, we need to talk about the future," Kheti said.

"What future is there for us?" she said, voice dull as she turned to face him.

"Won't you sit down." He gestured toward the carpet.

"Your father's and Pentu's bodies aren't yet cold in the grave. I don't want to talk about this now."

Kheti felt much the same, but there was no time. A decision had to be made, whether they felt up to it or not.

His stomach lurched. "Mama, we must talk. Father made me promise that I would care for you all, but he wanted me to go with the Hebrews." The Hebrews had already left. They would be moving slowly with all those women, children, and livestock, but every day they were moving further away.

"With the Hebrews?" her voice rose, tinged with hysteria. "Why would anyone want to go with slaves?"

Kheti took a deep breath. He did not want to show his frustration. "They're not slaves anymore. They're free."

She snorted. "They'll always be slaves. At least here they had food to eat and places to live. Now they only have what they could carry, and no roof but the desert sun."

"I think Father had planned to go with them, if he could."

Mama sank to the carpet. "He'd have had to leave me behind. I would never abandon this country. Never follow Elohim. That god has taken everything."

Out of the corner of his eye, Kheti saw Tia wince. Mama still had two children, a daughter-in-law, and a grandson. Didn't they count for something? Anything?

What would Papa have done? He would probably have stayed here, hoping Mama would one day change her mind. But what would Papa have wanted for Kheti and Tia? Kheti pictured his father lying in the doorway, asking him to promise to follow the Hebrews, his body wracked in pain, but crystal clear in his mind that following the Hebrews was the way to hope.

"I want to go, but I must speak with the others. I promised Papa I would care for them."

"Do what you like. I don't care," Mama snapped. She stood and turned her back on him to again stare out the window.

He wasn't going to take her words to heart. Mama was scared to face a life without her husband and eldest son. He glanced at Tia and they left the room together. "Let's find Iset and Nophret and see what they want to do."

They gathered outside under the large fig tree, bright green with new growth. The three girls looked expectantly at him. He wished Papa was here to make the decisions.

"Papa made me promise to look after you, but he also wanted me to follow the Hebrews."

Iset frowned. "Leave Egypt?"

"That's right. Follow the Hebrews to know more of Elohim."

"Can we not worship Elohim here?" Tia asked.

"The Hebrews are gone," Kheti said. "Who would teach us?"

"Mother won't leave," Tia said tightly.

Kheti shook his head. "No, and it is also extremely unlikely that we would return." He looked around the little group. "I'm sorry that we have to make the decision so quickly, but it will be difficult to catch the Hebrews once they leave the borders of Egypt."

"So we'd need to leave by tomorrow or the day after," Nophret said.

Kheti hadn't expected her to join them, but his heart lifted at the thought. She could be a friend for Tia, but would Nophret's mother agree to come? Would Nophret leave if her family did not?

"Iset, you might prefer to return to your own family," Kheti said.

"No," Iset said. "They would not welcome me home. I must either stay with your mother or go with you."

Kheti straightened. "If you stay here, you would have a home and I would leave a portion of the stock."

"But there is no one to help me. No Hebrews, no menfolk. It would be impossible." Iset looked at him. "It's much too difficult a decision to make right now."

"Why don't we make the decision tomorrow morning," Kheti said. Iset nodded. "I'll start preparing."

"Shouldn't we be praying about this?" Nophret asked.

Kheti looked at her. "Do you think such a great God cares about our decisions?"

Nophret pointed to the ants marching in a line near her foot, carrying seeds back to their nest. "If he sustains the ants, then surely he cares for us?"

They knew so little of Elohim's ways.

"Nophret, would you be willing to pray?" he asked.

She flushed. "I'll try."

There, under the fig tree, they stood in a circle and raised their hands.

"Elohim, creator and sustainer." Nophret's voice shook, but she took a deep breath and continued. "You made the mighty river and the stars in the heavens and the trees and even the ants. We have seen your power over nature demonstrated right before our eyes. We want to know you, but we don't know whether we should stay or go. It's scary to go because we don't know where we're going and everything will be different."

They would be like Avraham of old. Yosef had said that turned out alright, not because Avraham was faithful, but because Elohim was faithful. Excitement churned in Kheti's belly alongside his fears. Elohim had promised Avraham to bless all the world through him. Maybe that included Egyptians too.

"We don't know if we'll be welcome, and we don't want to leave anyone behind," Nophret continued. "Please help Mama and Intef and Kheti's mother to choose to come with us. Give us wisdom." She stopped and a flush spread up her neck as she said in an undertone. "I don't know how to finish."

"I heard Avraham end with, 'Thank you great Creator of all,'" Tia said.

Nophret repeated the words and looked up at them all.

Kheti smiled at her. It was good not to be alone. Elohim was with him and these few. *Elohim, help us make the right decision.*

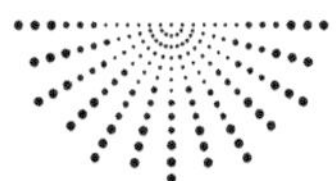

Kheti rolled out his sleeping mat and dropped onto it. His whole body ached with weariness. He'd spent the evening working by firelight to prepare the cart for a long trip. He still hadn't definitely made up his mind to go, for what son would leave his mother to fend for herself?

Tia had helped him rig up covers for shade, and they'd loaded up wheat and oil and jars of dried figs, dates, and raisins. The food wouldn't last long, but there was a limit as to how much they could take. If they overloaded the cart, then they wouldn't be able to travel faster than the carts they were chasing.

Kheti had also spent quite a while working out how to transform the cart into a shelter at night and deciding what tools to take. Flax rope and papyrus were essential. He'd give the rolls of papyrus to Mosheh and Aharon, perhaps they would want to keep a record of the trip.

Kheti sighed. If only there was another male relative his mother could stay with. Perhaps going would be a mistake. He wasn't simply planning a long trip. He was planning to leave everything they'd ever known to launch out into the unknown. There were no guarantees life would be better than here. The fact was life here had mostly been good. He'd never lacked for food or shelter. He'd loved boating on the river and swimming in the lake. Even during the plagues, Papa's wise preparations had ensured they'd weathered the disasters better than most.

Why should he exchange all he had for a path into the desert? And when they got there, it wasn't as if they were walking into an empty land. They would still have to go to war to claim what Elohim had promised to Avraham and his descendants.

Outside, an owl screeched. Some poor mouse was about to be a midnight snack.

Here in Egypt, Kheti knew the creatures and the seasons. He knew enough to continue the papyrus business, and he could train Tia and Iset to help him. Here, he could build a future for little Hepu, and perhaps even his own children. Here he could fulfill his promise to look after the women of the family and provide them with security. It would be hard, but he could do it.

He turned over. Nights should be for sleeping, but somehow he was too tired to actually sleep. He took deep breaths and willed himself to relax every part of his body, but still he lay awake, his mind racing.

Egypt might be destroyed, but at least here Kheti knew the challenges and had some idea how to overcome them. He sighed. But it would be almost impossible to learn more of Elohim in Egypt. Pharaoh would surely try and block all knowledge of the humiliations he'd suffered, and soon there would be no one willing to talk about what had happened.

Kheti linked his hands behind his head. He hadn't realized how easy his life had been. All he'd ever had to do was get up and do the work allocated by Papa. No decisions, no worrying about the harvests or if the annual inundation of the Nile was early or late or higher or lower than usual. A stab of grief pierced him. Papa, how he missed him. He'd always been there, faithful and steady and wise.

Now that the responsibilities Kheti had never had to pay much attention to had fallen on him, he lay here unable to sleep. Tossing and turning and wondering how he'd provide for them all. Iset might want to marry again, and Tia was close to marriageable age. How could he choose the right husbands for them?

These sorts of tasks weren't supposed to fall on him. They were the responsibilities of a father. If Papa wasn't around, they fell to the elder brother. He tightened his jaw. Pentu should have been here. The elder brother who'd been more determined to hold onto pride than bow his head and live. Fool! And that pride now meant that Iset and Hepu were Kheti's responsibility. Although, perhaps they felt safer now if Pentu had regularly beaten Iset. It wasn't a question he could ask.

It would be wonderful to have Nophret with them, but her mother and Intef would be a huge responsibility, especially if they never recovered from their grief. Kheti needed everyone to work together. He sighed. He hadn't even passed twenty summers, yet he was now responsible for seven people.

Elohim, I hate to bother you. We would really like to follow the Hebrews, but you know my mother will not go. Please change her heart. I do not feel it is right to leave her here on her own.

He felt a little foolish praying about such things. If Elohim had created the world and the stars and the hippopotamus, did he really have the time to bother with the concerns of someone such as himself? Nophret thought Elohim cared about small things, but was she right?

Kheti tossed and turned for a while longer, finally falling into a fitful sleep where he was pursued by dreams of Tia, Iset, and Nophret holding out their hands and weeping for him to help them. Behind them were many other shadowy hands. Pleading, pleading, pleading.

CHAPTER THIRTY-FOUR

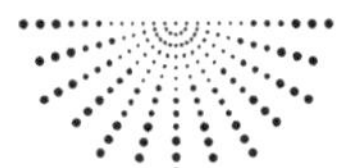

$\mathcal{K}$heti dropped the yoke on the necks of the oxen. He was ready to go, if that was the group decision. And it had to be a group decision. Papa hadn't known Nophret would become part of the group, but she was definitely one of them now. Now he didn't feel so alone in his journey of faith, for despite the opposition of her father and brother, Nophret had shown the faith of Avraham of old.

A sheep bleated, longing to get out of the barn. Kheti had shut them in last night, as he didn't want to waste precious time rounding up any they might take with them.

"Help!"

Kheti looked in the direction of the voice. Nophret and Tia were on a small cart trying to get the donkeys to obey. He'd intended to give them a driving lesson this morning, but the girls must have gone out early and collected the second, smaller cart, from Pentu's place and managed to hitch the donkeys up and get them this far.

He moved toward the cart.

"It's too narrow just here," Tia said to Kheti. "If you want the cart closer to the house, you'll have to do it yourself."

Kheti straightened his shoulders. He'd been considering these girls a burden, but they'd already proved themselves.

"Well done to get it this far." Kheti leapt onto the cart and showed them how to tell the donkeys know which way to go.

"Iset was still asleep when I came out," he said as they drew near to the house. "Please check on her and ask her to meet us under the tree."

Tia got down from the cart and headed inside.

Kheti glanced across at Nophret. "Will your mother come?"

She shrugged. "She doesn't seem to know who I am, but this place has too many bad memories." Nophret nibbled her lip. "Can someone fade away with grief?"

He shrugged. "Maybe."

"What about your mother?" Nophret asked.

Kheti sighed. That was the sticking point in this decision for him. Without her, Kheti would leave without a qualm, but a son couldn't just abandon his newly widowed mother.

"I've been praying Elohim would give you wisdom," Nophret said.

Mama and Pharaoh had a lot in common. Both had hardened their hearts. It had cost Pharaoh the respect of his people and the life of his own son. Not that the news had been confirmed, but Kheti doubted Pharaoh would have put lamb's blood on the palace door posts.

"Who's coming?" Nophret asked, indicating the road leading to the farm.

A small group of donkeys were moving quickly. A prickle of alarm ran up Kheti's arms. Bandits would be first to seize any opportunities during this time of grief and mass burials.

"Go into the house and bar the doors," he said.

Nophret's eyes widened, and she scampered toward the front

door. Kheti went to the cart, picked up his hoe, and walked to intercept the approaching people, making sure to keep a wall close by. Bandits had been kept in check for many years, but Papa had told him there'd been killings when he was a child.

Kheti's heart pounded as three people on donkeys approached, and he wiped his free hand on his tunic. If they turned out to be a threat, he couldn't fight off three. He peered through the dust. There was a woman in the middle. Maybe they weren't bandits, but who would come to visit them? Surely not more people wanting help. *Please, no.*

The donkeys reached him, and the woman hauled on the bridle. Dust swirled and one of the donkeys brayed.

"I presume you're Kheti," the woman said. "I'm your aunt."

Kheti didn't remember ever meeting her, but the resemblance to his mother was striking.

"Well, don't stare at me. Take me to your mother," she commanded, as though he were a slave. "And the donkeys need to be watered."

His aunt dismounted, handed him the bridles, and strode towards the house, calling out to announce her arrival.

Kheti watered the animals as instructed and left the two men to wait in the shade of a tree before entering the house. In the dim coolness inside, he could hear his mother's raised voice. "Kheti wants to go tearing off after the Hebrews. He has some mad scheme that he'll become one of them."

Kheti doubted it would be that easy.

"But surely he wouldn't stay with them?" his aunt said. "Not forever?"

"Oh, I think that is his intention," Mama said. She didn't sound happy about it and guilt stabbed him.

"But what about you? And Tia?" his aunt said.

"There is Iset as well, and little Hepu."

Mama might not mention Pentu, but at least she now recognized he was dead.

"He's young for that much responsibility."

"Pentu was used to responsibility," Mama answered her sister.

Pentu was older. It wasn't a fair comparison, but when had Mama ever been fair? Pentu was her golden boy, the child who could do no wrong. Named after a grand court official, he'd proved to be handsome and charismatic. Maybe one of the reasons Kheti wanted to leave was so he didn't have to face the disappointment in Mama's eyes. She would always wish Kheti had died and Pentu had lived.

"I don't suppose one can get a drink around here," his aunt said. "It was dusty on the road."

Mama clapped her hands as though expecting Sara to answer her summons. Tia hurried past Kheti with drinks on a tray and a selection of dried fruit.

"Well, sister, you ought to be proud," Kheti's aunt said. " Your daughter is beautiful. Just like you when you were her age."

Tia always hated to be praised for her beauty. She'd much prefer to be praised for her cooking ability, or weaving prowess. Things she'd worked hard to perfect.

"Sister, she mustn't be allowed to go off with Kheti. She could make a good marriage here." There was a long silence. "Although suitable matches might be a little hard to come by at the moment."

It was the first hint of how many might have died. Had his aunt lost a son? Kheti didn't even know if she had children.

Footsteps pattered across the floor toward him and Tia emerged from the room, her face flushed. "How dare she?" she muttered. "She appears out of nowhere and thinks she can dictate my life."

Kheti gave Tia a little hug. "Simmer down and let's listen. Then we'll continue our interrupted talk."

He still didn't know if the others wanted to stay or go. And he still didn't know what to do about their mother.

"What happened in your area?" Mama asked.

Kheti leaned forward.

"I'm not aware of any household in the area that didn't lose husbands or sons." His aunt sniffed. "Oh, sister dear, it is a terrible thing to lose a husband and a son in the same night."

"It is," his mother said, voice tight as she struggled for control. "The question is what we do now."

"That is why I've come. I suggest we combine our households. Either you come to live with me, or I come here."

Kheti's heart raced. *Elohim, is this your answer?*

"I am not sure I want to stay here." Mama sniffed. "Too many memories. You know."

"You always were more imaginative than me," his aunt said.

Mother started to cry, and Kheti sat waiting for his mother's decision.

* * *

Kheti first had to wait for Tia to prepare a room for their aunt. The servants who'd accompanied her were directed to the barn. Kheti waited with impatience in a patch of sunlight near the tree. They'd lost yet another day, but he was free to go, as long as the others wanted to go with him. Kheti looked around as they gathered and quickly updated them on Mama's decision.

"So the question is, do you want to go, or do you want to stay?" Kheti asked. "I make no promises that going will be easy. We are unlikely to be popular in the Hebrew camp."

"Going is our best chance to know more of Elohim." Nophret smiled with joy, her choice clear.

"I will go wherever you go," Tia said.

Kheti looked across at Iset. She had the hardest choice. To go with them or to stay with Mama and have a much higher chance of remarrying.

"I will go," Iset said. "We belong together."

The tension eased out of Kheti's shoulders. *Thank you, Elohim.*

"We'll leave at dawn. Nophret, we'll prepare a comfortable spot on the cart for your mother and Intef. Do you think you can manage to drive?"

Nophret nodded.

"Tia, I'll get you to drive the other cart with Iset and Hepu," Kheti said. "I'll walk behind with the sheep we are taking."

Leaving at dawn would give them time to say their goodbyes.

CHAPTER THIRTY-FIVE

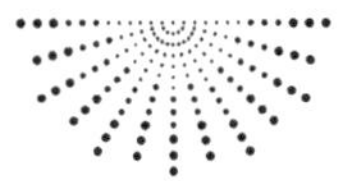

"Kheti, what is that?" Nophret asked.

Kheti, Nophret, and Tia stood on a slight rise, looking in the direction they expected to find the Hebrews.

"It looks like fire, but it's tall, like the tallest tree," Tia said. "What could be burning?"

"I once saw lightning strike a tree, but it burned down quickly. This has been burning for ages. I think I saw it last night." Kheti rubbed his eyes. The fire, if that was what it was, was still there. "It's a mystery and one we'll have to wait to solve. We'll set off again at daybreak."

They turned back toward the carts. On the first night, Kheti had worked out they could park the carts next to each other and place woven flax mats on the ground underneath them for a comfortable nights' rest. He slept further away, next to the livestock. On the second evening, Intef had surprised him by walking over to the sheep and spending the night close to them. If Intef could help with the sheep, it would lighten Kheti's load.

Kheti took his sleeping mat off the cart. "Goodnight, aunty," Kheti called to Nophret's mother, but she didn't answer. She didn't eat much, and Nophret was worried she was simply going to fade away. Intef walked with him over to the sheep, reaching over to give the closest one a friendly scratch. Maybe Intef was going to be all right. This morning, the tiniest of smiles had crossed Intef's face when Hepu had picked a flower and given it to him.

Kheti spread out his mat near where the oxen and donkeys were tethered and curled up under his cloak. Above him, a shooting star shot across the sky. If he turned his head, Kheti could glimpse the mysterious orange glow far ahead of them. He fell asleep to the munching and snuffling from the animals.

An animal stamped its foot, and Kheti woke, shivering in the chill of dawn. He stood up and rubbed his arms. The sun had just risen, and the streaks of cloud were stained with pink.

He arose and checked the animals.

Tia soon joined him and they took the sheep down to the river and watered them. Then did the same with the larger stock.

* * *

"Kheti, will you pray for us as we go?" Nophret asked.

She asked him to pray every morning. The first two mornings, Kheti had struggled to find the words, but it was getting easier.

Nophret's mother was already lying on the cart. They stood in a semi-circle around her and raised their hands. "Elohim, good morning," Kheti said. "Thank you for the good sleep and that we are safe. Thank you for the beautiful weather. Thank you that the animals are all healthy, and we are making good progress. Help us to catch up soon with the main camp." Kheti turned to the others. "Does anyone else want to pray?"

Nophret opened her mouth. "We praise you for the magnificence of the sky each night. It's like you painted it. Thank you for

230

your kindness in making our way smooth, and help us not to grumble when harder times come."

Nophret's prayers were full of praise. She talked to Elohim like he was close to her, not far away as Kheti thought of him. When Nophret and Intef had first come, Kheti had seen them as yet another burden. Now, he was more thankful every day that they'd come.

Kheti and Nophret hitched up the oxen and donkeys and set off. The fire ahead had disappeared at dawn, but there now seemed to be a tall column of smoke or cloud traveling in the same direction. Yet there'd been no rain and the ground ahead was firm, although it had been flattened and traversed by a vast host.

* * *

"Kheti, there's someone else camping in that grove of trees," Tia said. "Should we sneak past?"

He pursed his lips. "No, better talk to them. They might have news."

They'd been skirting past villages because Kheti didn't want anyone seeing their group only had one man to protect the women.

"I'll go." Kheti picked up a heavy stick and used it as a staff.

As Kheti approached, he called out a greeting. A woman with two children hiding behind her skirts peered out at him, and a man answered his greeting. They seemed harmless enough. An almost-grown boy was tending their donkeys and a few goats near a cart.

"Welcome," the man said. "Where are you going?"

Kheti pointed ahead. He wasn't going to say much until he was sure these people could be trusted. "Where are you from?"

"We've come from the capital," the man said.

Kheti had been hoping to hear news from the capital. "And what has been happening in the capital since the long darkness?"

"Do you truly not know?" The man frowned.

Kheti leaned on his staff. "Several men in our area died, but we have not heard about other areas."

"It was horrendous," the man said with a shudder. "Wailing in the middle of the night. Bodies laid out in rows in the street in the morning. Shop owners and slaves, priests and princes."

The plague had not discriminated by age or rank or wealth.

"It took me all day to bury four bodies," Kheti said. "How did they manage in the city?"

The man swallowed. "They had to burn the bodies, for there were not enough burial sites. The whole city was filled with the smoke."

"Did no one paint the blood on the doors?" Kheti asked.

"Very few. Many thought it would be both an abomination to sacrifice a sacred animal, and a sign of disloyalty both to Pharaoh and Egypt."

"My brother refused, and he died," Kheti said, with a frown. "Where are you headed?"

"We're going to join the Hebrews," the man said.

Kheti gave them a warm smile. So Kheti and his group weren't the only Egyptians doing this. Maybe there would be others. "To follow them to their promised land, you mean?"

The man nodded. "If they'll let us."

Kheti looked up sharply. "Do you expect it to be a problem?"

The older man rubbed his eyebrow. "Would you welcome your former masters just as you finally gained freedom?"

It was good to be reminded that just because Avraham and Sara had welcomed Kheti, others might not. Kheti would have to warn the others and impress on them that wandering around alone wasn't a good idea.

"And we've been avoiding towns and villages because other Egyptians might not be too happy at our decision. The Hebrews' god told them to ask their neighbors for jewels and gold and silver as they left." The man whistled. "Most people gave it to them."

Why had Avraham not asked them for anything? Papa would have been happy for gifts to be given for all their years of faithful service.

"Maybe our people were happy to see them leave," Kheti said.

The man grunted. "Probably, but it means much of the gold and treasure of Egypt is leaving with the Hebrews. Pharaoh won't be happy."

And an unhappy Pharaoh could be dangerous. Angry enough to chase the Hebrews and kill them, rather than force them to turn back? Kheti's stomach churned. Egyptians like himself might be treated as traitors, and their group was vulnerable with four women and two children. Kheti looked toward the carts where Tia and Nophret were folding up their sleeping mats and checking everything was secure. Had he made the right choice for them?

"Would you like to travel together?" the older man asked.

Kheti blew out a gusty breath as the tension eased out of him. He smiled at the man. "If we're going together, let me introduce myself." He told the man their names, and the man introduced himself as Rameses, surely one of the most common names in Egypt. The rest of Rameses' family held back.

"Shy," Rameses told him.

"Have you worked out what the tower of fire is?" Kheti asked.

Rameses shook his head. "We'll have to find out together."

Kheti would go and talk with the girls. They could always strike out on their own if the other family slowed them down, but for now, a bigger group seemed safer.

CHAPTER THIRTY-SIX

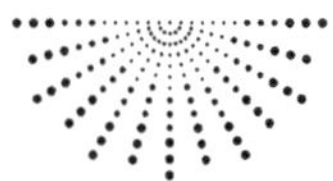

"I'm a little worried about going through there," Rameses said as he strode along beside Kheti. "If I was a bandit, that's where I'd wait."

Kheti looked at where Rameses indicated. There was a tumble of rocks on either side of the narrow path.

Kheti looked over to where Nophret and Tia were now skillfully driving their teams. "Maybe we should bunch up a bit and put the livestock in between the carts."

"I'll send my son and our cart through first," Rameses said. "Then your livestock and the two carts, and finally you and I at the rear."

Rameses sounded like he'd done this before. Kheti nodded and went to talk to Nophret and Tia.

Soon Kheti walked briskly behind the carts. He'd suggested that a slightly faster speed would make them a harder target and get them through the danger point more quickly.

"Keep your eyes down," Rameses said in a loud whisper. "There are people hidden up there. Have you got your staff?"

Kheti hadn't had any proper weapons, just his staff and a few farming tools. He'd given the tools to Iset and Nophret. Kheti wasn't sure that either of the girls would actually swing their weapons, but at least they had something to make them look more threatening.

There was a whistle from the rocks above. Out of the corner of his eye, Kheti caught a glimpse of one brown-robed figure, then another. How many were there? *Elohim, we are few. Keep us safe.*

"Stop," a loud voice commanded.

Kheti heard Tia gasp and his heart sped up to a gallop. Ahead of her, halfway up the rocks, a man with a bushy black beard stood, arrow at the ready, flanked by two other men. Kheti swiveled his head. There were others lining the two sides of the canyon. Ten or twenty at his count. They didn't have a chance.

"Keep driving, Tia," Kheti yelled.

"We won't have any of that," a voice said close by. Something whizzed through the air, and Kheti ducked and twirled out of the way. What? Why had Rameses taken a swing at him?

Kheti didn't wait to find out. He dashed toward the back of their two carts and leapt onto the platform so he could see more clearly.

"Quickly, son," Rameses called.

The first of the three carts turned left, blocking the path. Kheti had thought the son dopey, but he was dopey no longer. He was grinning at his father who now had his wife—if that was what she was—standing at his side.

"You may as well give up," Rameses said. "We've caught you."

Heart beating wildly, Kheti touched Tia's shoulder. "Stop. There's not much we can do. I can't risk you being hurt."

Tia called out "Whoa," and leaned back. Her face was pale. How must Nophret be feeling on her own at the front?

Elohim, is this how things are going to end?

Behind him, Kheti could hear the leader leaping from rock to rock. "Well done, Rameses. Your plan worked."

Rameses smirked. "Seeing a family man fools them every time."

It had certainly fooled Kheti. He should have taken one of the girls to talk with Rameses and his "wife" as the girls might have picked up clues he'd missed. Although maybe not, for this family—if they were even related—were obviously accomplished liars and actors. It didn't comfort Kheti that he was likely the newest fool in a long line of fools.

Elohim, you're the only one who can get us out of this.

"Put your weapon down," the leader growled.

Kheti dropped his staff on the floor of the cart and carefully turned around. Better to see what was coming than to be stabbed in the back.

The leader stared at him. "Not you again."

Kheti looked at the two men flanking their leader. Yep. The same men he and Yosef had encountered on the way back from the capital.

Tia tucked her hand in his. It was sweating, and he couldn't blame her. *Elohim, help.*

"Let them go," the leader said, his face pale as papyrus.

"What are you doing?" Rameses hissed. "They're ripe for the picking."

Tia gripped Kheti's hand harder. Beyond the leader, he could hear Nophret whispering. Was she praying? *Pray on.*

"This is the man who called down a plague on my head," the leader said.

Kheti wasn't going to point out that the gnats had had nothing to do with him.

Rameses muttered under his breath. Whoever he was, he wasn't the main leader. By the look that he was giving the leader, Rameses planned to do something about that in the near future.

"Come on, men," the leader said, bounding onto the first rock. "Let's get out of here."

Rameses swore, cuffed his son's ear, and grabbed the reins off his son before slapping them on their donkey's backside. The donkeys jumped into action. Within moments, the whole group of robbers was out of sight.

Tia threw herself into Kheti's arms. "I was so scared."

Kheti laughed shakily. "You didn't show it. Come on. We need to get out of this place before we're trapped again. Tia, can you go with Nophret? I'll take over here."

He sat down abruptly on the front of the cart as a trembling started in his legs.

Thank you, Elohim for saving us.

Elohim had listened to an Egyptian's prayer. Elohim cared. There was no need to doubt it any longer.

* * *

Kheti craned his neck back. The column of cloud or smoke or whatever it was soared above them. The tower of fire had been more obvious and more scary the closer they got. Their group had been passing Hebrew stragglers for a day already. No one had paid much attention to Kheti's group, each being intent on keeping up with the Hebrews in front of them.

Finally someone had smiled at Kheti, and he had taken Iset and Hepu to ask some questions. Kheti pointed at the pillar above them. "What's that?"

"Yahveh sent it," the man said. "It appeared shortly after we started our journey. During the day it's a cloud, and it's a fire at night. The fire allows us to travel in the dark."

Was Yahveh the name God had revealed to Mosheh? The name that Avraham had been reluctant to share?

The man's wife leaned around her husband. "When God wants us to move forward, the pillar moves, and when it stops we stop."

Iset raised her eyebrows.

"Are you coming with us too?" the man asked.

"We are," Kheti murmured. He wasn't willing to say it too loudly yet. His intentions and what was possible, might be two different things.

"There are many Egyptians already in the camp," the man said.

"Yes," muttered his wife. "Mosheh has welcomed them."

She didn't sound too pleased about it.

"Thank you for your help," Iset said, pulling Hepu close. She gently touched Kheti's arm, and they went back to their carts.

"What do you think?" Iset asked. "Is it safe to keep pushing on toward the main body of the camp?"

"We must," Kheti said. "That woman said Mosheh is welcoming Egyptians like us, and we need to find Avraham and Sara."

"Won't that be nearly impossible?" Iset continued. "There are probably hundreds of people with the same names."

"Perhaps thousands." Kheti's heart sank. None of them had anticipated how vast the numbers would be. This was already more people than he'd ever seen in one place, and they hadn't even reached the main group. How could they hope to recognize Avraham and Sara among crowds of people with similar coloring, all wearing similar clothes, and living in the same kinds of tents?

Kheti stroked his chin. Nophret would say that if Elohim intended them to find Avraham and his family, then he'd enable them to do it. He wished he had her faith. Already she was sprinting ahead of him in her knowledge and trust of Elohim.

CHAPTER THIRTY-SEVEN

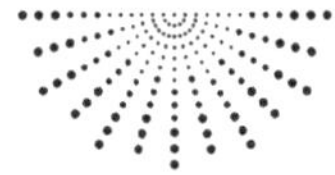

Kheti gasped.

"What can you see?" Tia called up to him from the cart which they'd parked at the base of the tree. From the cart, Kheti had been able to haul himself up into the lower branches of an ancient sycamore. It had been easy to clamber up into the higher branches and look over the Hebrews' camp.

"It's vast." He shaded his eyes and peered ahead. The plain was covered in a jumbled mass of carts and tents and people. People standing and chatting. People collecting water from the river. People preparing food.

Kheti turned his head to scan to the outer edges of the camp. That area was dominated by shepherds and herders seeking to find grass for their stock.

Far, far ahead rose the pillar of cloud. It hung in the air, motionless. Yet the Hebrews he'd met along the way said it could move at any time, then everyone packed up and followed. Awe tingled along his arms. What other people had ever had their God in their midst rather than distant and unknowable?

Between this tree and the pillar of cloud, there was a tent with a strip of red cloth fluttering above it. Surely that must be Mosheh's tent. They'd head halfway up the camp, but approach from the outside and set up on the outskirts. It would be easier to get feed for their animals, and also safer while they tested their welcome.

* * *

"Get away. We don't want your kind here," the woman spat at Tia.

Kheti touched Tia's arm. "Don't respond. We'll keep going. Nophret said Elohim has a place for us."

Tia set her face and directed the oxen in a wide circle around the woman's tent.

"Do you think we should do what Nophret suggested and find some other clothing, to make us blend in?" she asked.

"That's a good idea, but let's talk about it later," Kheti said. "First we need to find a place we can stop for the night." Then he intended to walk toward the main tent and find someone to talk to. He would feel better knowing firsthand that Mosheh welcomed Egyptians like themselves. He hoped their gift of papyrus would be accepted and gain favor in the eyes of the Hebrew leaders.

Nophret and Intef's cart drew up alongside.

"What about here?" Nophret asked.

Kheti looked around. There were a couple of tamarisk trees for shade, enough space for the animals, and he could hear the trickle of water nearby. "Yes, this will work."

Tia and Nophret had mastered the art of parking their carts next to each other and setting up. They'd be doing it many times in the months it would take to reach Canaan.

Once the camp was ready, Kheti strolled over to the girls. "Who wants to come for a walk with me?"

"Why don't you take Intef?" Nophret said. "Then we can do some washing and get the animals settled."

Kheti took his staff, just in case, and Intef bounded along beside him. Kheti looked back at their site and carefully noted landmarks. It would be easy to get lost.

A small boy ran out of a tent, crossing their path. Kheti stopped, and Intef bumped into Kheti's heel. Kheti wasn't sure if they should catch the child or not.

"Avram, Avram." A woman called as she dashed out of her tent. When she saw them, she flapped her hands and said something. He didn't understand the words, but the intent was clear. He bit the inside of his cheek. Was this how it was going to be here? Always viewed as a threat? As unwelcome?

Kheti put a protective arm around Intef's shoulders and nudged him forward. Intef looked up at him, eyes wide like a frightened calf, but he followed. Kheti looked forward to the day when Hepu was better able to play with Intef. Hepu brought joy to all of them, laughing and playing as long as Iset was close by.

They wound their way further into the camp. Kheti didn't know why he was making for the main tent. It wasn't as though Mosheh would have time to talk to someone as unimportant as himself.

They kept walking until they reached their goal. A long line of people waited outside the tent. Every so often, someone would come out of the tent, and everyone would move forward. Were the people waiting to consult Mosheh about something? The man must be exhausted.

The line didn't seem to shrink while they stood there. Intef tugged on his arm. Kheti looked down on him, smiled, and turned to go.

"Well, if it isn't the young man from Goshen," said a voice he'd recognize anywhere.

"Nanny!"

She was seated at the entrance of the tent next to where they were standing. Kheti walked over and grinned down at her. "So I've progressed to being a young man, have I?"

"You're here, aren't you?" she said. "It took courage to come. Making tough choices proves you're a man."

Her praise warmed his belly.

"Sit down, both of you." Nanny gestured to the ground next to her. "Who's your friend?"

"This is Intef, one of our neighbors. He's here with his mother and older sister."

"More courageous people." She patted Intef's cheek. "Doesn't say much, does he?"

Kheti dropped his voice. "He hasn't said anything since the last plague."

"Never mind. I always have plenty to say." She winked at Intef. "I'm glad we found each other. Everyone has been kind, but it's not easy to start again at my age, and I doubt I'll ever get my tongue around the language."

Kheti hadn't even considered that aspect. Hebrews had always spoken his language to him, but maybe they'd choose not to do that now. "Who are you staying with?"

"This is Mosheh's tent. He's treating me like I'm a family member." She sighed. "Not that Mosheh is here often, but he says that his wife and sons will join him soon."

And Nanny would appreciate having a family.

"What happened after you moved to Goshen?" Kheti asked.

"For starters, I didn't have to go through the last two plagues. It was eerie, looking out from the house and seeing the curtain of darkness descend. I did ask to be carried out into the darkness to experience it for myself but—" She shuddered. "We didn't linger."

Kheti shivered. He would have gladly escaped the darkness too if there had been a way. "And the final plague?"

"It was more of a celebration for us," Nanny said. "But oddly, a celebration prior to the event being celebrated."

"Obtaining freedom, you mean?" Kheti asked.

She nodded. "By that stage, I wanted the Hebrews to be free

almost as much as they did. Mosheh had proven to be a man over and over, but Pharaoh?" She tutted. "He was a disappointment at every turn. Stubborn, vacillating from yes to no, and just plain foolish, thinking he could challenge the Creator and sustainer of all."

"Were there any Hebrews who didn't offer the lamb?" Kheti asked.

Her face fell. "A few. A few who thought they knew best or that they could offer an inferior animal. One household used duck blood." She snorted. "As though Elohim could be tricked."

Kheti leaned forward. "And their sons died?"

"Of course." She brushed the corner of her eye. "But there were also Egyptians around us who were saved."

Because of people like Kheti's father and Nophret. People who'd taken Elohim at his word and acted in faith.

Beside him, Intef sniffed and wiped his eyes.

Kheti reached across and gripped his knee. "Are you alright?" he mouthed.

"Papa wouldn't listen," Intef said with a croak. "He wouldn't listen." Tears streamed down his cheeks.

Kheti leaned forward and wrapped his arms around Intef. "I'm so sorry." Intef's tears soaked into Kheti's tunic. Kheti had the same regrets as young Intef.

Nanny patted Intef on his shoulder. "You're a brave boy to come on this journey. A brave boy."

Intef gulped, wiped his nose with the back of his hand, and straightened.

"And he has the makings of a good shepherd," Kheti said.

"Really?" Intef asked, face bright with hope.

"Yes, and your sister is going to be excited to know you're talking again."

Nophret had been worried about her brother. Worried he'd deteriorate as her mother deteriorated every day, spending most of the day curled in a ball.

"Don't be a stranger," Nanny said. "Please visit. I'm so glad you had the courage to come. What happened to that other young man?"

"Yosef? He should be somewhere here, with his family." Kheti sighed. "I had no idea how many people there'd be."

"Impressive, isn't it?" Nanny asked. "We're waiting for men to join us from the mines near here, then we're turning south."

"Why south?" Kheti asked. "Northeast would be easier."

"Easier, maybe, but Elohim has told Mosheh that he doesn't want us to run into the Philistines. They're used to fighting and we're not." She shrugged. "There's barely a weapon among us."

"But south means we're going to be trapped by the Red Sea," Kheti said with a frown. "I have enough papyrus to make two small boats, but that won't transport my group, let alone this multitude!"

"I think Elohim might have thought of that." Nanny tweaked Intef's nose and he giggled.

It was all very well for Intef to laugh. The Red Sea was an uncrossable barrier, not some rivulet they could wade across.

CHAPTER THIRTY-EIGHT

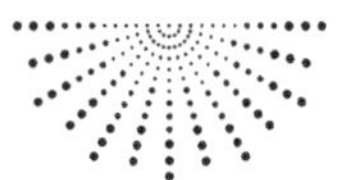

"What's everyone whispering about?" Nophret asked Kheti. "They've been moving from tent to tent, but they're avoiding us."

"I'll go and see if anyone will talk," Kheti said.

"Maybe it would be better if Tia and I went because—" she flushed. "We look less threatening."

"You're welcome to try," Kheti said.

Tia scooped up Hepu, and the two of them set off for the nearest tent. Kheti watched as they went from tent to tent. They never stayed long, and it hurt to see the looks on Nophret's and his sister's faces. Their smiles froze. Kheti saw them say something to each other before turning and walking back to him, heads down, and expressions glum.

"No one will tell us anything," Nophret said.

"I'm sorry you had to go through that," Kheti touched Tia's shoulder. "Little do they know what they're missing out on."

"And what's that?" Tia asked.

He grinned. "Having two intelligent women as their friends."

Tia flashed him a tired smile.

It made Kheti angry to see everyone ignoring them. Intef had come alive since their talk with Nanny and was now chattering constantly, as though to make up for lost time. Hepu followed Intef everywhere, and they especially loved the sheep and goats.

"I'll go and see Nanny," Kheti said.

"Can I come?" Tia asked. "I'd like to see more of the camp."

Turning to Nophret, Kheti asked, "Is that all right with you?"

"I need to stay with Mother. She's frightened about something."

It might be that she knew they were trapped between the hills and the sea. If Pharaoh changed his mind again, there was nowhere for the Hebrews to go except into the water.

* * *

Nanny was sitting at the entrance of the tent. She grinned her lopsided grin. "Who's this you've brought to see me? A special someone?"

"Of course." Kheti winked at Tia. "Nanny, this is my sister, Tia."

Nanny tilted her head. "I can see the resemblance."

Kheti sat on the ground. "We came because something is going on, but no one will tell us what."

Nanny put her head back and laughed. "And I thought you came for the pleasure of my company."

Kheti chuckled. "That too."

Nanny paused and then said, "Adonai has told Mosheh to turn back and encamp near Pi Hahiroth, between Migdol and the sea."

It relieved Kheti to know they weren't simply wandering around aimlessly. If Elohim had told them to move, then there was nothing to worry about. He didn't know how, but Elohim had never failed to keep his word.

"Pharaoh will think the Hebrews are wandering around in confusion, hemmed in by the desert and the sea," Nanny continued. "Elohim will harden Pharaoh's heart again, and he will pursue us."

Kheti gulped and Tia gripped his hand, her fingernails digging into his skin. Papa had always told Kheti not to poke a stick into a bee's nest, yet it sounded like that was exactly what Elohim was doing. What was he up to? Pharaoh would be madder than an entire colony of bees. He would come with the might of his entire army. Kheti glanced around. These people were farmers and miners, not soldiers. If Elohim didn't save them, they'd be trampled into the ground.

"Don't worry, Tia," Nanny said. "Adonai has said he will gain great glory through Pharaoh and his army, so all the Egyptians will know that he is Lord."

"How's he going to gain glory?" Tia asked, a tremble in her words. "Pharaoh has hundreds of horse-drawn chariots. What do we have?"

"Don't you remember the signs, we've just been through? Adonai is King of Creation," Nanny said, confidence in her tone. "He can make the wind, and the waters, and the creatures of the air do his bidding. I'm sure he is more than capable of beating Pharaoh's army."

Kheti wanted to say, "But Pharaoh's army is huge and terrifying," but it would be a waste of breath. If anyone knew the size of the army, it would be Nanny. She'd lived near the royal stables all her life. She probably knew more about the troops than any Hebrew, especially someone like him who'd never seen more than a few chariots together.

"Go back to your tent and be ready to move quickly. Pray. Don't worry." Nanny laughed. "Real men pray. They don't waste time worrying about things they can't do anything about."

Kheti straightened up. She'd been calling him to be a man, not a boy, since the first time they'd met. He'd go back to their carts and follow her advice.

* * *

Kheti was still praying when there was a scream, and then another.

"The Egyptians!" A man nearby pointed south. "The Egyptians are coming!"

Kheti jumped up on the cart, but all he could see were billows of dust.

"Come on, Intef," he called. "Let's climb the hill."

They scrambled up the rocky slope, dislodging stones that slithered behind them. Around them, others were doing the same.

At the top, Kheti and Intef turned, chests heaving, and looked toward the dust. Around them was a horror-filled silence as the sun glinted on metal within the dust cloud. Someone screamed and then said something in Hebrew.

Another called out in the common language. "Was it because there were no graves in Egypt that Mosheh brought us out into the desert to die?"

"Yes," another voice yelled. "What has Mosheh done, bringing us out of Egypt? Didn't we say while we were there, 'Leave us alone; let us serve the Egyptians'? It would have been better for us to serve the Egyptians than to die in the desert!"

Intef turned to Kheti, his eyes wide and frightened. "Are we going to die?"

"No." Kheti shook his head to convince himself. He had to stay calm for the boy. "Elohim will rescue us. Let's go and listen to what Mosheh has to say."

Kheti and Intef scrambled back down the hill, slipping and sliding in their haste. Kheti didn't know how Elohim would rescue them, but Nophret was sure to remind them all that Elohim was still in charge.

Reaching level ground, they went back to the carts. Kheti left Intef with the girls and promised he'd be back the moment he knew anything. Then he ran toward the center of the camp, fear gripping his heart. It seemed others had the same idea, and soon he was jostled from all sides.

When Kheti reached the main tent, the complaints he'd heard earlier were tossed into the air again.

Mosheh came out of the tent, and someone helped him up on a cart. Mosheh raised his hands for quiet, and there was immediate silence. To Kheti's surprise he spoke in Egyptian. Perhaps after 400 years, some of the Hebrews no longer spoke their own language, or perhaps there were more non-Hebrews than Kheti had yet seen. Whatever the reason a warmth filled his chest.

"Do not be afraid. Stand firm, and you will see the deliverance the Lord will bring you today," Mosheh said. "The Egyptians you see today, you will never see again. The Lord will fight for you. You need only to be still."

"Ooh," the people around Kheti said. Kheti swiveled his head. The pillar of cloud was lifting. It rose straight up and moved south. Kheti's heart galloped. Where was the cloud going? Were they supposed to follow?

"Look, it's moving between us and the Egyptians!" one man shouted, breathing the garlic from his last meal over Kheti.

"And it's turning to fire," another person said.

The fire rippled up from the bottom of the pillar, like a living, breathing thing. They were all used to the fire, but it must have been terrifying to the Egyptians who were not familiar with it. A warning for Pharaoh and his army to turn back before it was too late.

Mosheh jumped off the cart, pushed through the crowd, and strode off toward the shores of the Red Sea. The crowd surged to follow.

Mosheh climbed a high rock overlooking the sea. He raised his staff and stretched it out toward the sea. The fire and setting sun burnished the waves with glints of copper. A breeze blew in Kheti's face, quickly growing in strength.

Mosheh turned around. "Go and prepare to leave. We cross tonight."

"Cross?" said a man at Kheti's shoulder. "How do you cross without a boat?"

"Isn't that Elohim's job to figure out?" Kheti asked.

"What would you know, Egyptian?" the man snarled.

The mockery twisted in Kheti's gut, but he pushed past the man and headed back to their campsite. How dare this man say such things? He and the others had given up everything to follow Elohim. Elohim welcomed all who trusted in him. Papa had known that.

Reaching the carts, Kheti gathered his new family and repeated what Mosheh had said. By the end, he was almost yelling over the growing noise of the wind. A steady east wind. It reminded him of the winds associated with the locust plague. Elohim was master of the wind.

"So we're going now?" Nophret asked.

"Mosheh said to get ready so let's do it. Intef, come and help me water the sheep."

Kheti didn't need to give any instructions to the women. They had things in a smooth rhythm. First they'd make Nophret's mother comfortable on top of the cart, then they'd pack everything around her.

Kheti grabbed the waterskins. He'd fill those first from the little spring, before the sheep muddied the water. Across the sea, it was desert. They'd carry as much water as possible.

Kheti sent Intef to carry the water back while he allowed four sheep at a time to drink their fill. The fire pulsated above him. Was it brighter tonight than normal? Shadows flickered across the ground as the trees and bushes danced frenetically in the strong wind.

The first group of sheep finished drinking and the next group moved in. Kheti stretched his back and looked toward the camp. On all sides, people were dousing their fires. Black shadows went to and fro, carrying items of varying sizes. A donkey hee-hawed and others joined in.

A shofar blew. He wanted to yell at it to be quiet, that Pharaoh's army was close but there was no need, for no one in Pharaoh's camp would hear it. Not with the fire roaring above them, and the noise of the wind. If anyone doubted that Elohim was fighting for them, they only had to look at the pillar of fire forming a barrier between the two camps.

Would Pharaoh turn his army back? Unlikely. Pharaoh had never been anything but stubborn and reckless with his people's lives.

The next group of sheep jostled for their place. Already, other families were bringing their sheep. On the edge of the darkness, Kheti glimpsed pale shadows on the move. Where were they moving to? They'd be blocked by water on the far side.

"Hurry up, man," someone shouted. "They're leaving."

Intef jogged back to Kheti's side. "We're ready when you are."

Kheti pointed to one of the ewes. "If you lead her, the others will follow."

Intef scampered to follow his instructions. At the carts, Nophret and Tia were already seated and ready to go. Just in time too, for the first of the surrounding carts were moving.

The oxen lowed in protest at the night move, but they leaned forward and strained, muscles rippling. The carts rolled forward. Kheti and Intef followed with the sheep, and together they moved toward the shore.

They hadn't moved far when Tia called his name, her voice full of excitement. Kheti checked the sheep were all together and moved forward to see what she was looking at. Awe gripped him and goosebumps spread across his body.

In front of them, a column of carts and flocks and people were marching steadily forward, forward to a broad road that led as far as he could see. Ahead were tiny pinpricks of lights where torches had been lit. The light glinted on something that soared in walls on either side.

"Is it water?" Tia asked.

"It has to be. It wasn't there earlier." This time the wind had not brought locusts. It had divided the sea itself. Kheti shivered. After all that had happened, how could Pharaoh still defy this God?

CHAPTER THIRTY-NINE

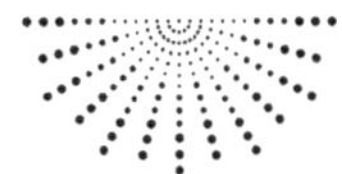

"Take it slowly and steadily, Tia," Kheti said. The sea bottom before them was mostly sand but there were occasional boulders to navigate around. "I'll check with Nophret then help Intef with the sheep."

Kheti had expected his feet to squelch. They didn't. He reached down and took a handful of sand and silt. It was dry as though it had been heated by the sun. Elohim thought of everything. Wind-dried rather than sun-dried.

Intef stuck as close as possible to Kheti. A large fire was burning where they'd entered the sea, and a group of men were handing out lighted torches. Kheti took one and moved to the front of the flock, near Nophret's cart. Her mother lay staring at the walls of water, eyes wide but no fear left on her face. A tiny smile graced the corner of her mouth. Was she beginning to trust herself into Elohim's hands?

The walls of water glinted in the light. Intef touched Kheti's arm and pointed. The dark shadow of some sea creature swam into view then disappeared back toward the north. Kheti shook his head at what he was seeing but kept his eyes open and his mind alert so he'd remember all the details. What a story he would have to tell his children one day. Children who would have the privilege of knowing Elohim from their earliest days.

Far ahead of them, torches were moving upwards. Kheti assumed the first people had completed the crossing and were now ascending the far bank. Kheti turned to looked back. Behind him he could still see the bonfire and the never-ending stream of people and animals. Could the crossing be completed in a single night? If he was Pharaoh, Kheti would have sent out scouts. What would they do when they discovered their prey were fleeing out of the trap?

Elohim, once again, show yourself greater than Pharaoh.

The crossing was slow, but eventually the ground beneath Kheti's feet began to rise.

Tia slowed the oxen down to negotiate around a particularly large group of boulders. Kheti checked that Intef was close by. Intef yawned. It must now be late in the middle watch of the night, but Intef was still alert enough to be trusted with the sheep.

Kheti went ahead and clambered up on Tia's cart. He held his breath as they mounted the last rise. Once they were back on level ground, he jumped off the cart and stooped to pick up a handful of desert sand, letting it trickle through his fingers. All around him were people doing the same, weeping and singing and kissing the ground. What must it mean to them to be free after four hundred years? He didn't know what he felt. Yes, there were glimmers of joy, but also the regrets of loss. Had he made the right choice for them all?

Kheti found a place to stop, and he and Tia unhitched and tethered the oxen to graze amongst the sparse grass.

Nophret settled her mother and Intef, and Iset also took the chance to curl up with Hepu. Nophret came over to him and Tia. "I couldn't possibly sleep. Let's go and see if Mosheh has had another message from God."

Linking arms to make sure they didn't lose each other, Kheti, Nophret, and Tia headed back toward where Mosheh was sitting on a rock and watching the endless procession. They sat on the beach and wrapped their arms around their knees.

After a long time in which Kheti might have fallen asleep, Nophret said, "Look. What's that black patch at the back?"

Kheti straightened up and rubbed his heavy eyes. "Where?"

She pointed and it took a few moments before he worked it out. "I think it's the end of the caravan. That last torch marks the last group crossing."

"And the pillar of fire is on the move," Tia said.

They craned their heads back as the pillar rose higher into the air. In the space below it, smaller lights pierced the further shore.

Tia clutched Kheti's arm. "Is that Pharaoh's army?"

Kheti swallowed. Pharaoh's army was immense. A tense hush fell over the crowd. The path was still open, and the army could still follow.

The light from the pillar of flame illuminated the scene below, where silhouettes of soldiers were frantically hitching up their horses. A trumpet blast bounced off the walls of water and the first of the chariots moved toward them, picking up speed.

The front group of chariots raced down the far slope toward the water-walled path and a guttural moan went up from the Hebrews all around them.

"Hurry," Tia said, striking her palm on her leg. "We must—"

"Wait." Nophret pointed to the end of the front line of chariots.

A horse's neigh of agony reverberated off the walls of water, followed by shouts and screams.

"What's happening?" Tia asked.

In the haze and darkness, Kheti wasn't sure. There were more screams and the crash of metal on metal. Several chariots emerged out of the gloom. Two chariots veered toward each other, crashed, and turned over. Another lost its wheel and scraped along the ground before hitting a rock and crashing onto its side.

Kheti stood up, pulling Tia and Nophret up as well. "Elohim is fighting for the Hebrews."

"Go back, our brothers. Turn around," Nophret murmured a prayer.

A cheer went up behind them, then another. Not everyone had Nophret's concern for the Egyptian army.

The final Hebrew carts and herds were now climbing the slope to the shore. More carts and people passed Kheti and the girls and the cheers intensified to welcome the final arrivals.

"Come on!" Kheti ran to follow the crowd. As he and the girls reached the place where the final carts were climbing the shore, everyone formed two lines and applauded them. Tia was laughing next to him, and he yelled with gusto. The last young man to step out of the cutting bowed from the waist as though he'd done something worthy of praise. Tia laughed, but Nophret tugged Kheti's tunic and used her chin to direct his attention toward the land they'd left.

The first glow from the rising sun was now illuminating the opposite shore, where soldiers were abandoning their chariots. Some stragglers fled back toward Egypt while others kept formation, marching toward them through Elohim's pathway.

The mood of elation around them shifted to fearful murmurs.

"Elohim! Be our strength. Be our salvation." A woman's voice cut clear and bright through the rising alarm, ringing through the dawn like a song.

The army had reached the halfway point, joined by a column of chariots that had survived the initial chaos of the descent. Egyptian military chariots were pulled by seasoned war horses and manned by skilled archers. The Hebrews were as helpless as a fallen nest of baby birds, unable to flee.

Mosheh stood on his rock. The rising sun cleared the horizon, bringing the swarming hordes of Pharaoh's army into full light. Mosheh stretched out his hand over the sea. Kheti's stomach cramped.

With a mighty roar, the water at the top of the high walls shot toward the sky then crashed down in a torrent.

The soldiers turned to run, but it was too late, much too late. The walls of water disappeared completely, flowing back into the gap, swishing Pharaoh's army out of the way as if they were mere ants, enveloping them into the deep, and settling flat and still in the morning sun.

Cheers filled the air, but a rock-sized lump filled Kheti's throat. Nophret's head was bowed, and tears ran down her cheeks. "Oh," she rocked back and forth. "Oh."

Emotions churned in Kheti's heart. Relief at being safe, but also bitter loss. The drowned army were his own people, and now the way back to everything they'd known was closed.

A small wave touched the shore, as if nothing but a gentle wind had bothered the Red Sea that morning.

Kheti took Nophret's arm and gently guided her back toward their carts, as Tia followed. But they didn't get far. Somewhere a tambourine rattled, and a woman was singing, the same voice as they'd heard before. Soon others joined, amplifying the words.

Kheti turned to the nearest Hebrew and asked for a translation. The words of the chorus were simple enough.

"I will sing to the Lord, for he is highly exalted. Both horse and driver he has hurled into the sea."

The words were repeated over and over. Soon, everyone around them was singing. A woman came into view. Her braided hair was silver, but she danced with the exuberance of a much younger woman. Kheti turned to the nearest Hebrew. "Who is she?"

"Miryam, sister of Mosheh and Aharon."

Kheti looked at her with interest. This was presumably the woman who had looked after baby Mosheh as he floated in the basket on the Nile.

"The Lord is my strength and my defender; he has become my salvation,"

The woman sang, and others repeated her lines.

"He is my God, and I will praise him, my father's God, and I will exalt him. The Lord is a warrior; the Lord is his name."

The tune was nothing like Egyptian music, but it twanged in Kheti's heart and soon he was able to hum the chorus. Tia hummed beside him, but Nophret continued to weep.

"By the blast of your nostrils, the waters piled up. The surging waters stood up like a wall; the deep waters congealed in the heart of the sea. The enemy boasted, 'I will pursue, I will overtake them.' But you blew with your breath, and the sea covered them. They sank like lead in the mighty waters."

With a sob, Nophret buried her face in his shoulder. He reached up and tentatively stroked her hair. It was soft to his touch. This leaving of theirs was not all joy.

"Who among the gods is like you, Lord? Who is like you—majestic in holiness, awesome in glory, working wonders?"

Miryam continued to dance and sing.

"The nations will hear and tremble. You will bring your people in and plant them on the mountain of your inheritance—the place, Lord, you made for your dwelling."

The dancers passed them, and the singing spread from one group to another.

Nophret lifted her head and brushed her hand across her eyes. "Can we go back to Mother? Please don't tell her what happened. My cousin was one of Pharaoh's soldiers." She choked back another sob. "He was so proud to be chosen. It would break Mother's heart to hear what happened."

It would break a lot of Egyptians' hearts to hear what happened at the Red Sea that night. Kheti looked at Tia, and together they trudged wearily back to whatever was next.

CHAPTER FORTY

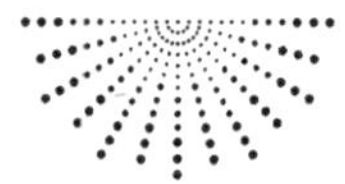

A few mornings later, Kheti was putting away his sleeping mat on the top of the cart when he heard Nophret say. "Mother dearest, let me comb your hair. You always liked that."

Nophret was hidden behind the flax mats that hung down around the carts to give a little protection and privacy. "I'd like to continue the story we started."

Kheti walked backwards slowly and then squatted against a rock and listened. What story would she tell?

"I already told you about the first two plagues, remember. Elohim is great and powerful, but he is also merciful. He didn't just wipe Pharaoh out. Let me tell you what happened next."

There was no sound from Nophret's mother. Every day she lay still, staring straight ahead. Nophret treated her mother with unfailing kindness.

"Elohim said to Aharon, 'Stretch out your staff and strike the ground.' Aharon did what he was commanded, and the dust of the earth became gnats. Do you remember those gnats, Mother? I've never itched so much in my life." Nophret laughed, a sound that somehow reminded Kheti of sunshine. "But my favorite bit of this story is that the magicians could not do this miracle. They came to Pharaoh and said, 'This is the finger of God.' And little did they know they were right." There was silence for a while, and Kheti assumed she was still combing her mother's hair. "Now, let me sing you a song I've learned. The tune goes like this."

She hummed the tune a few times, then sang in a lilting voice, "I will sing to the Lord, for he is highly exalted." He had thought she had said she wasn't going to tell her mother about the drowned army. She continued singing in their own tongue but she changed all the words in the middle.

Kheti grinned as Nophret concluded with the original words, "The Lord is God, and I will praise him. He has become my salvation."

Tears pricked his eyes. Nophret had lost her father, and her older brother, and probably her cousin, yet here she was, still praising Elohim. She was the sort of woman he'd have been delighted if his father chose as a wife for him, and he would have been honored to accept. He swallowed. Wife? Where had that come from?

"What are you doing here?" Nophret asked him.

Kheti's face warmed. He'd been thinking so hard that he hadn't noticed her exiting the space under the carts. "I was listening to your story."

"I wish I knew more stories of Elohim," she said, putting her comb away. "I'm sure there are more."

"Avraham and Yosef told me several."

"Do you remember them?" Her eyes were shining.

"A little, but Avraham would tell them better." Kheti sighed. "If we can find him."

They'd tried to make friends with those around them. It had become easier after they'd crossed the Red Sea, but it was still slow going.

"I've been praying about that," Nophret said.

He frowned. "Do you pray about everything?"

She nodded. "Sometimes I forget, but usually I'm reminded sometime during the day or before I fall asleep." She looked at him. "Would you be willing to tell us one of the stories you remember around the fire tonight?"

Kheti swallowed. "I'll do my best."

"That's all I'm asking. We could pray and sing too."

He grimaced. "Not sure you want to hear my croaking."

She grinned. "Then it's a good thing Elohim looks at the heart, isn't it?"

* * *

"I'm thirsty," Intef said, dragging his feet through the hot sand.

Two days before, the pillar of cloud had moved forward, and they'd left the sea behind them. They weren't going in the direction Kheti had expected. Although they'd filled every available container and waterskin, they had about half a day's supply left.

"See if you can go a little longer before you have a mouthful of water," Kheti said.

Intef kicked a stone. "Nophret gives most of the water to Mama."

Kheti ruffled Intef's sweaty hair. "Nophret is taking good care of your Mama."

"But Mama doesn't need as much water. She's not doing any work." Had Kheti ever whined like that? If so, perhaps he could now understand why Pentu got annoyed with him.

It was true enough. He'd asked Nophret the other night if she'd seen any improvement in her mother.

Nophret had said that her eyes seemed more focused whenever she listened to her daughter's stories and that her mother seemed to appreciate Nophret spending time with her.

262

Who wouldn't?

At midday, Kheti allowed them each two mouthfuls of water. Intef stared at everyone who drank, as though daring them to waste a drop. Afterwards, he sloshed the tiny amount of water left in the bottom and made sure Kheti put it away carefully in a shady spot.

"Elohim will provide," Nophret said.

"I hope he hurries up," Intef muttered as he returned to the sheep.

The sheep wouldn't manage much longer without water. They were already listless. Kheti wrapped a long strip of cloth around his head. It only gave the illusion of shade in this wilderness of Shur.

A shout went up from somewhere ahead. The word they'd been hoping for was shouted back.

"Water!" It was the first word he'd learned of this new language. Water, the most important thing in the desert. Just the thought of it made them pick up their pace.

Intef was jumping with impatience, but Kheti held him back. There was no point being trampled in the rush. When livestock were this thirsty, they could run down anything in their path to get to the water.

By the time Kheti and Intef reached the edge of the rise that led down to the water, people were trudging back up the slope, their faces gloomy.

"What's wrong?" Kheti asked.

"The water's bitter. That's what is wrong," a man snapped. "Undrinkable. Why did Mosheh bring us here?"

"Let me taste it," Intef said, and he was gone before Kheti could answer.

Intef ran for the edge of the pool and scooped up a handful of water. He put it in his mouth and immediately spat it out again.

"Why bring us here if the water is bitter?" the woman next to Kheti mumbled.

"You'd think Adonai would know better," said a man with a bushy beard.

"I'm sure he has a purpose," Nophret said.

Kheti turned to smile at her. He hadn't noticed Nophret's arrival.

"He's coming," the crowd muttered. "He's coming."

Mosheh was striding toward them. He went down to the water's edge and lifted his hands in prayer. Then he walked a short distance and stooped to pick up a piece of wood.

"What's he doing?" a woman asked.

"Shh," said another.

Mosheh tossed the piece of wood onto the surface of the water. "Now drink," he said.

Intef ran back down to the water.

He scooped up some water, slurped a mouthful, and smiled broadly. "It's sweet!" he yelled. "Sweet!"

Nophret held up the waterskins she'd been carrying. Of course she'd brought them. Kheti grinned at her and took two of them. Together they went and filled them. Her being prepared had spared them the crush. It would take most of the night to water this many people and animals.

As they left the water, Kheti heard Mosheh say, "This is what our God says, 'If you will give earnest heed to my voice, and do what is right in my sight, and give ear to my commandments, and keep all my statutes, I will put none of the diseases on you which I have put on the Egyptians; for I am your healer.'"

Kheti looked across at Nophret. Her eyes were glowing.

"Our God. Our healer," Kheti murmured.

"But we must remain faithful," she said in response.

Kheti nodded slowly as the determination to do so rose in his heart.

CHAPTER FORTY-ONE

"*How* beautiful," Nophret and Tia exclaimed together. After days in the desert, the springs and palm trees of Elim were a green oasis. The tension in Kheti's shoulders eased.

"Do you think we could swim?" Tia asked. "I never did get any more lessons."

There'd been no time. They'd just recover from one plague, clean up, and another would hit.

"We work first, sister, then we'll see."

It took far less time to water the animals than at the bitter springs, where there'd only been the single pool. Here there were twelve springs, each surrounded by palm trees. Kheti hoped they'd stay for a while, for they were all tired from the travel over hot sands and pebbles.

Kheti put salve on a sore where the yoke had rubbed one of the ox's shoulders. He'd expected far more injuries, but the pillar of cloud hadn't moved too far every day. The whole group moved at a pace which was not too fast for even the slowest among them.

"Can we swim now?" Tia begged.

Kheti couldn't resist her smile. "Ask Iset, if she and Hepu want to come."

"And Nophret?" Tia asked with a wink.

Kheti's face warmed. "I doubt she'll come. Maybe we'll be able to convince her later. I could carry her mother down to the water though."

It would do Nophret's mother good to get out, to see that there was a world outside the boundaries of her grief. If she could get interested in other things and other people, she might recover.

Although maybe Kheti was being unrealistic to expect her to change so soon. It was such a short time since the deaths of so many of their family members. Kheti's grief for Papa ached somewhere down deep inside. Would Papa be happy that they'd come? He only hoped Mama was content with her choice to remain behind.

Many people were paddling on the edges of the biggest pool. Kheti waded in. Oh, it felt so good to be wet instead of parched, cool instead of sticky hot. Tia followed him, confident he would look after her. He'd love to swim off on his own, but when Papa had given him the responsibility of the family, Kheti had known the responsibility would come with a cost. He was no longer free to do things on his own. At least, not until they reached the Promised Land. Once there, would they be able to find a place to settle? He doubted there'd be papyrus, but maybe they could find some land and grow crops.

When they were waist deep, Tia bobbed under the water. After letting her hair flow free, she rubbed it hard. Kheti did the same.

"Can you help me float?" Tia asked.

"I will, if you'll then let me swim a bit," he said.

She managed to float much more quickly this time, and Kheti left her practicing while he swam out into the deeper water. He hadn't been swimming long when a sharp whistle rang out. He looked up and saw someone bouncing up and down and waving from the shore.

Yosef!

Kheti swam for shore. Still dripping, he slapped Yosef on his back, grinning so wide the edges of his mouth must have reached his ears. "We've been looking for you."

"You came!" Yosef said, excitement in his voice. "We thought you'd stayed behind. Who came with you?"

Tia came out of the water and wrung out her hair.

"Tia—obviously—Iset and Hepu, and two neighbors and their mother."

"Hepu lives? Mother will be thrilled. She was praying for a miracle."

"Father rescued him." Kheti swallowed as his grief pushed for release.

"Come with me. My parents will be delighted to talk with you and your father."

Kheti drew in a sharp breath. "Papa—" Hot tears overflowed and he couldn't say anything more.

Yosef's face fell. "But he wasn't the oldest son."

Kheti shook his head and took a steadying breath. "Tia said Papa had been unwell for some time." He took another breath. "Rescuing Hepu was too much for him. He died before Elohim struck down Pentu."

Yosef touched his arm. "I am so sorry. Father will be, too. Your father was a man to be respected."

Kheti looked at the ground, chest tight.

"Come for the sunset meal, and bring the others," Yosef said.

"What, all of us?" Kheti asked.

"Mother will insist."

Tia squeezed Kheti's hand, her eyes brimming with tears. He squeezed back. Here, at last, was a welcome.

* * *

*J*ust before sunset, Kheti hoisted Nophret's mother into his arms. She weighed less than one of the sheep. Intef skipped at his side, while Iset and the others trailed behind him. They'd dug out some of their precious dried fruit and the last of the goat curds to take with them. Yosef had given them directions to the exact spring and the particular palm tree, but they couldn't have missed it for Yosef and Havvah were waiting for them.

"Tia! Tia!" Havvah called jumping up and down.

Hearing Havvah's greeting, Avraham and Sara came to the entrance of their tent.

"Welcome, friends," Avraham said, arms open wide.

A big lump rose in Kheti's throat as he carefully placed Nophret's mother on the carpet laid ready for them. Straightening up, he could only muster one shaky thank you and it seemed vastly inadequate. Avraham came close and enveloped Kheti in a hug. For a moment it felt like Papa was hugging him. Kheti pressed in to receive the warmth Avraham offered.

Avraham was slow to release him. "It is good to see you didn't come alone. Welcome Nophret and Intef. This must be your mother." He took the silent woman's hand in his and bowed. "Welcome to our home."

Kheti had forgotten Avraham had met Nophret and Intef when they'd fought the locusts together. It all seemed so long ago.

Sara had returned to the tent and emerged with some pillows which she used to prop up Nophret's mother. Nophret smiled her thanks.

The food did not take long to lay out. This far into their journey, there wasn't much variety left. What would they do when their meager supplies ran out? All around them were fires and families eating together, but the desert could not possibly hold enough food for them all. How would Elohim provide?

They ate the unleavened bread and curds and a few shriveled onion pieces steeped in olive oil.

"Thank you, Sara and Havvah. That was delicious." Avraham gave Sara a look of such tenderness that it brought another lump to Kheti's throat. Was this how things could be between a man and woman? Perhaps they could be for him too, if he chose the right woman. A woman who was kind and hardworking, a woman of faith and prayer. He knew someone like that.

Avraham asked for their stories. Between them they related their experience of the tenth plague and their journey, including the bandits.

"Praise Adonai for his protection of you all," Avraham said. "Now we've found each other, you must travel with us. Can you move your things over here?" He gestured to a clear space nearby.

Gratitude filled Kheti's heart.

Nophret covered her eyes, and he heard her sniff. To be welcomed after the many rejections was better than the refreshing embrace of the water in the springs.

CHAPTER FORTY-TWO

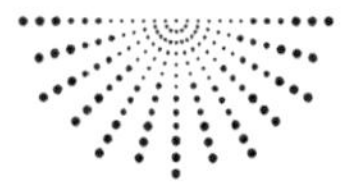

Wilderness of Sin

*L*ast night, Nophret had reminded Kheti it was one moon since the night that changed everything for them. One moon since the deaths of so many family members. She'd finished telling the stories she knew of Elohim, and Kheti had promised to ask Avraham to tell the many stories he knew.

"Kheti," Nophret said under her breath. "I've just ground the last of the barley to make today's bread."

"You mean we're going to starve?" Intef said.

"You weren't supposed to hear that." She tweaked Intef's nose. "I mean we have no more flour. I'm sure that Elohim has a plan."

Some of their neighbors didn't have Nophret's trust. He'd heard them whispering of the food they used to have in Egypt: cucumbers, melons, leeks, onions, and garlic.

"Let's pray for Elohim's provision," Nophret said as they ate their evening meal.

"You pray," Kheti said. He loved to hear her pray. Nophret

prayed as though Elohim was her father. Great and powerful, but near and compassionate as well.

Nophret paused and bowed her head, as though not willing to rush into Elohim's presence. "Oh, great and marvelous Creator. We praise you that you control the weather and the seas. That even the winds and waves obey you. We praise you that you can turn bitter water to sweet. We have no more barley or wheat. No means to make bread. We ask that you provide what we need. We know this is but a little thing to you, for we have seen you do far greater. Help us to trust you."

"May he answer your prayers," Kheti said. He took the bread, their precious last loaves, and tore them apart, handing a portion to everyone. Even Nophret's mother reached out her hand and took her piece.

* * *

Kheti poured a little olive oil on a sheep's leg. It must have caught it on a thorn the day before.

Avraham came over. "All of you come with me to Mosheh's tent," he said. "Many people are complaining and saying, 'We wish we'd died in Egypt. There we sat around pots of meat and ate all we wanted, but now you've brought us out into this desert to starve the whole lot of us.' How quickly they forget we were slaves, and many starved on meager rations and tasted the whip daily." He stopped short. "Not your father, Kheti. But come. We will hear what Yahveh has revealed to Mosheh."

Kheti put the stopper in the olive oil and stowed it safely away, then gathered the others. They followed Avraham to Mosheh's tent. There, a vast crowd had gathered. Kheti took his group to the outskirts of the crowd where they'd still be able to hear Mosheh speak but wouldn't draw unwelcome attention.

Mosheh was standing on a rock. "In the evening, you will know that it was Adonai who brought you out of Egypt, and in the morning you will see Adonai's glory because he has heard your grumbling against him." Mosheh and Aharon looked sternly around the crowd. "Who are we, that you should grumble against us?"

Mosheh waited while his words were relayed through the whole crowd. "You will know it was Adonai when he gives you meat to eat this evening and all the bread you want in the morning because he has heard your grumbling against him. You are not grumbling against us, but against Adonai himself."

Bread and meat for everyone? There were more tents than Kheti could ever count. How could food be provided for everyone, let alone distributed? Even thinking about what was needed made his head spin.

Mosheh turned and looked out over the desert to the pillar of cloud. In the blink of an eye, it turned into a pillar of pulsing gold. Kheti threw up his hands to protect his eyes. Awe filled him. Nophret had said Yahveh would provide, and now Yahveh had confirmed it.

"At twilight you will eat meat," Mosheh said, "and in the morning you will be filled with bread. Then you will know I am the Lord your God."

Then Mosheh and Aharon went back into their tent. Nophret looked at Kheti, eyes shining, "See, I told you Elohim will provide."

She had told him, but Kheti was at a loss how it was possible. Even if an army of bakers rose out of the sand, they could not provide enough bread for everyone to have even one mouthful. And meat. What kind of meat could be found for this vast throng in the desert?

* * *

"What's that sound?" Intef asked, hand cupped around his ear.

Kheti strained his ears to listen. There was a whirring, but not the scary whirring sound of locusts. This was a softer sound, a sound he'd never heard before.

"Look!" Intef pointed toward the setting sun. A low-lying dark cloud was approaching fast. Kheti stood and watched. The whirring sound was louder, and the dark cloud covered the camp.

"Birds," Intef yelled. "Nophret, come quick."

Nophret, Tia, and Iset came running just as the first of the reddish-brown birds landed awkwardly and ran across the ground.

"Catch them," Nophret yelled. "It's our meat." She grabbed at the first bird and caught it by a wing, where it struggled and flapped. Kheti came and put his hands round the whole bird until it calmed down.

"Here's a bag," Iset said. "Bring me the birds as you catch them."

Intef was darting this way and that, not catching anything. Hepu ran to help him, giggling as the birds ran away.

"Slow down," Kheti said. "Spread your arms wide and drive them toward Tia and myself." With a few false starts, and making sure Hepu only watched, they succeeded in catching enough birds for everyone.

"You kill and pluck them," Nophret said. "I'll cook them."

"Coming right up." Kheti's stomach grumbled. The birds were plump, and he couldn't wait to eat them roasted over the fire.

* * *

Someone was shaking Kheti's shoulder. He groaned and turned over.

"Kheti, isn't it time for Yahveh's bread to arrive?" Intef's voice was urgent.

273

Kheti kept his eyes shut and flapped his hand towards Intef. "You're welcome to look."

Intef left Kheti in peace, but he was back in a few blinks of the eye. "There's something I've never seen before all over the ground. Something white."

Kheti sighed. It was no use. Intef was not going to let him get a few more moments of sleep. Kheti stretched, got up, and rolled up his mat. "Show me what you mean."

Intef grabbed his arm and dragged him towards a clear area of ground. "When I got up there was dew on the ground, but in this patch and there—" He pointed. "Where the sun has dried the dew, it has left white flakes."

Kheti stooped and slid his fingernail under a flake. They'd formed a crust on the ground and lifted easily. He sniffed the flakes. They smelled faintly sweet. He stuck out his tongue. Whatever it was, it tasted a little like honey.

"Do you think it's the bread?" Intef asked.

"I don't know if it's bread, but I think it's edible. Let's see if anyone else knows, maybe Mosheh has said something."

With Intef skipping at his side, they wound their way through the camp. Everywhere the ground was now glittering like it had been covered in frost. More and more people were moving in the same direction they were. When Kheti and Intef arrived at the central tent, there was a hum of conversation, and everyone was asking the same thing. "What is it?"

Mosheh came out of the tent and raised his hand for quiet. They hushed immediately.

"What is this stuff?" one man called.

"It is manna, the bread Yahveh has given you. Yahveh has commanded that everyone gather as much as they need, one omer for every person in your tent."

An excited chatter of voices broke out, but Mosheh held up his hand again. "But no one is to keep any of it until morning. Only collect what you can eat in a single day."

Kheti and Intef walked back to their carts. "Could you be our manna collector?" Kheti asked.

Intef straightened up as though he'd been appointed as Mosheh's right-hand man.

"That would spare your sister the extra work and allow her to concentrate on cooking."

"I don't think it needs to be cooked," Intef said.

Kheti laughed. "But she will probably still try to cook it."

Intef was excited about the manna now, but he might not be so excited when he had to eat it every day until they arrived in the Promised Land.

As they went, the two of them collected all they needed for their group. By the time they reached their carts, the sun was well up the sky and the manna had melted away as if it truly was frost.

* * *

"What's that stench?" Nophret wrinkled her nose. "It's been getting worse all night."

Lately she and Tia had brought their sleeping mats out to the fire. The girls said the blaze of stars was awe-inspiring, and it was a waste to be inside when there was no need. It also gave more space to Hepu, who liked to clamber over everyone near him if he woke during the night.

Kheti joined the girls as they searched around their sleeping mats in case some creature had burrowed under them and died. They found nothing.

Intef sniffed and walked toward a container near his sleeping mat. He groaned and glanced around, looking shamefaced.

"What have you got there?" Nophret asked.

Intef held out the pot and she peered inside. "Ooh, disgusting. You'd better bury whatever that is."

"It's manna," Intef said, voice low.

Nophret looked at him, eyes sad. "We were told not to keep any."

"I thought it might not be there tomorrow, and I often get hungry at night."

"Well, bury it." She ruffled his hair. "We must remember to follow every part of Elohim's commands."

Intef nodded and then dug a hole with his hands, poured the slimy, maggot-ridden mess into the hole, before covering it.

He didn't do it again, and Elohim stayed true to his promise to provide fresh manna every morning. As Kheti had predicted, Nophret learned to boil and bake the manna. She made it into little cakes with the olive oil they'd brought with them and added an occasional pinch of herbs. It was surprisingly tasty and filling.

On the morning of the sixth day, Mosheh sent out a command for everyone to gather double their normal quota, for there would be no manna the next day, as it was to be a Sabbath, a day of rest, for everybody.

"But last time I saved some, it went bad," Intef said.

"One thing we should have learned by now is that if Elohim says something, we do it," Kheti said. "We don't need to understand how he works. We just do it."

"Like with the lamb's blood on the door?" Nophret asked.

Kheti nodded. He often found himself thinking about the ways Elohim had rescued his followers from the plagues.

Kheti reached over and put his hand on Intef's shoulder. "Avraham told me something about Elohim that I'd forgotten until today. When Elohim created the world, he worked for six days and rested on the seventh. That day was set apart as holy."

"What's holy?" Intef stumbled over the unfamiliar word.

"I think it means set apart for Elohim, but it emphasizes that our day of rest is special," Kheti said. "Tia, Iset, and Nophret do so much cleaning and cooking. Now they can have a day off."

"Maybe we can have extra time that day to enjoy the beauty around us and hear more stories of Elohim," Nophret said.

"And Nophret, I'd like you to teach me how to pray," Tia said.

"I'd love to," Nophret said. She turned to her brother. "You heard Kheti. We need double the amount of manna this morning. Then I'll bake the portion for our family ready for tomorrow rather than baking on the Sabbath."

Family! Nophret had called their motley group a family. Joy coursed through Kheti as he looked around their camp. They might not yet experience a general welcome among the Hebrews, but Avraham and Sara made up for that. Avraham's family members were constantly coming across to talk and share whatever they had, and they welcomed all of them into their tent, reminding Kheti of how Elohim had made them, as foreigners, welcome.

Intef laughed as he collected the day's manna. He was so different from the silent boy who'd set out on this journey.

Papa would have been so happy that Tia, Iset, and Hepu were with him, and Papa would have loved Nophret, a woman with a heart of faith like his own. A woman who was showing them all how to fix their eyes on Elohim and walk in step with him.

EPILOGUE

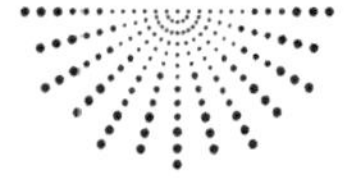

One year later

"Unka Cati," Hepu lisped as he toddled after Kheti. "Why kill little lambie?"

"It's Passover, and we've been invited to share it with Uncle Avraham and Aunty Sara."

Hepu clapped his hands. "Me like meat."

"Well, if we're going to have roast meat by sunset, you'll have to let me get on with it. I'm sure your mother would love your help."

Hepu's dimples showed and he headed back to the tent Iset, Tia, and Nophret had made from goat skins.

To Kheti's surprise, the sheep and goats liked the desert, and they'd had plenty of young. It was good to be able to share their abundance with the family that had made them feel so welcome.

"Good morning, brother," said a familiar cheery voice.

"Yosef, I need to make sure that I follow all of Elohim's commands as I prepare this lamb. Can you help me?"

Yosef came and looked over the two one-year-old male lambs lying there with their legs tied. "Those look perfect to me."

"I remember that we must not break the legs," Kheti said. "Was there anything else?"

"Brother, it is amazing to hear you speaking my language!" Yosef lowered his voice a little. "And to know you revered Elohim so much that you've been circumcised." He shuddered. "I'm glad I was too young to remember the pain."

Kheti grinned in response to Yosef's sympathy. Yes, it hadn't been much fun. There had been pain, but also purpose. He was now marked as belonging to Elohim. All the stories told of the ancestor Avraham were now his own history, and the promises Elohim made to his descendants were now part of his inheritance.

The lambs at their feet bleated.

"I wish more of our people were so committed. Many have not circumcised their children." Yosef shook his head and then looked up again at Kheti. "Abba loves teaching you our language, culture, and history."

Nophret and Tia had made rapid progress with the language, and Sara had taught them to weave and make curds and many other useful skills, including tent making. They no longer needed to camp out every night.

Nophret, Tia, and Havvah were virtually inseparable. Lately he'd noticed that Yosef and Tia were close as well. He would be delighted if that led somewhere. To see Tia so worthily matched, and to be able to call Yosef brother in another sense. It was Kheti's duty to see Tia settled before he married himself. He bent his head to hide his flushed face. Nophret said she was happy to wait, but he wasn't nearly so patient.

* * *

The sun was close to setting as Kheti and his family washed their hands and faces, smoothed down their hair, and carried the roast lambs across to Avraham's tent.

Avraham was at the tent entrance to welcome them. Behind them, the full moon was rising over Mount Sinai.

"Oh, that smells good." Avraham sniffed appreciatively. "Thank you for coming to join us."

Avraham didn't wish them a happy Passover, sensitive to the fact that tonight was also the anniversary of too many deaths. This first year had been hard, and Kheti's grief had ebbed and flowed. Little Hepu was beginning to remind him of Papa, something about his eyes and kindness towards all living things.

Sara had laid out their best carpet, and Nophret's mother was led to the place of honor. In the last few months, she'd relearned to walk and talk. While she didn't laugh, they sometimes saw her smile. It would have been hard not to smile at some of Intef and Hepu's antics.

Three moons after Papa had died, they'd reached Mount Sinai and there had seen fire and thunder and things beyond imaginings. Elohim himself had talked with Mosheh and explained how they could live in a way that pleased him, a way that would allow them to thrive as a community. Kheti got goosebumps recalling the words Elohim had spoken to them through Mosheh,

---

"You yourselves have seen what I did to Egypt, and how I carried you on eagles' wings and brought you to myself. Now, if you obey me fully and keep my covenant, then out of all nations you will be my treasured possession. Although the whole earth is mine, you will be for me a kingdom of priests and a holy nation."

A holy nation planted in the Promised Land. On difficult and dark days, Kheti imagined this new nation like a nation of lights.

Sara and Havvah brought out the unleavened bread and bitter

herbs. Once everyone had taken their places, Avraham raised his hands and prayed. "Thank you, our great and marvelous Creator, Lawgiver, and Savior. Thank you for providing manna for us every day and for meeting our every need. Thank you for the joy of family and friends and good food. Help us to never forget you."

A year ago, when Avraham had prayed in Hebrew, Kheti had only heard meaningless sounds. Now, it was as though Kheti had entered a new country. One day it might even be familiar. Kheti prayed he'd one day hear the praise of Elohim flow freely from his own children's lips.

Avraham finished his prayer and held up the bitter herbs. "These herbs remind us of the bitterness of our lives as slaves. Of course, due to the generosity and kind spirit of Kheti and Tia's father and Hepu's grandfather, our lives were much less bitter than many others, but still it is a hard thing to be a slave."

Kheti squeezed Tia's hand as she sat on one side of him. He missed Papa's kindness, but every day he aspired to be more like him.

Next, Avraham served the lamb. "Elohim saved us through mighty miracles, ten in all. He told us to kill a lamb to die in the place of the oldest sons." Avraham nodded toward Yosef. "Yosef, you and I and Hepu were redeemed by the lamb dying in our place. Let us eat and be thankful."

Avraham and Yosef both took a mouthful of lamb, then served the others.

Finally, Avraham took the unleavened bread. He handed it to each of them. "This is made without leaven to remind us that on that final night, our salvation came like a bolt of lightning, before the yeast could have worked its way through the dough."

He looked around the circle at them all.

"We must never forget the lamb or the meaning of the blood painted on the doorposts. The Lord's messenger saw our obedience and passed over. We were safe under the blood."

Kheti swallowed and tears prickled his eyelashes. Papa had said that. That he was happy to die under the blood. Had that been how Papa understood it? That he was ultimately safe, even if he died, because he lay beneath Elohim's sign of salvation.

As they ate, Kheti looked around the group, each so special to him. He silently thanked Elohim for Avraham and Sara and their open-hearted generosity to a family they could have held a grudge against. He was thankful for Yosef's friendship, made possible because Yosef too could forgive the past and see beyond Kheti's differences, as Yosef had done way back when they'd first met as children on the riverbank.

Kheti looked across at Iset. She'd had the courage to leave Egypt and trust him to provide for her. A widower had recently been coming to help her draw water and to take Hepu and Intef out to collect manna. *Elohim, provide for Iset and Hepu.*

Tia, full of fun and joy, willingly helped them all and already fit in with Yosef and his family.

And Nophret, her faith had been inspiring Kheti from the day he had first met her. Of all of them, she loved Elohim most and sought to honor him every day. When those around them grumbled and complained, she sang praises to Elohim. She led them all back again and again in worship to the one who had saved them.

There was still much that was strange and unknown in their lives, but Elohim remained their rock-solid foundation, the center around which all else revolved. Step by step, they were headed toward the Promised Land. Kheti couldn't say their journey had always felt like being carried on eagles' wings. But he'd seen with his own eyes, and now trusted in his heart, that Elohim was holding those he loved safe in his all-powerful hands and Elohim would continue to provide all they needed.

Every single step of the way.

ENJOYED PLAGUES AND PAPYRUS?

One of the best ways readers can thank authors is to write a review.

This book is independently published which means the only way it will be discovered is if readers tell others about it. Online reviews are a concrete way of doing this.

How to write a review – easy as 1-2-3

1. A few sentences about why you liked the book, or what kind of readers might enjoy this book. Even one word turns a mere star rating into a review.
2. Upload your review - the same review can be copied and pasted to each site. This blog post (https://www.story-tellerchristine.com/blog/reviews-the-how-and-where/) tells you where and how, for the priority sites.
3. If you loved the book please also share your review on social media. Anywhere you can spread the word is appreciated.

A book can never have too many reviews.

HISTORICAL NOTES

I have long pondered on what it must have been like for an Egyptian to go through the ten plagues and was excited to delve into the story.

Much is known about Egypt but it tends to be history of certain periods, or of the Pharaohs, rather than of the common people. What we know of Egyptian religion is also more on the level of the Pharaohs or concerned with death rites for the wealthy. I researched what I could and then extrapolated for Kheti's family.

Names of the characters

One of the difficulties about writing a story where many of the incidents are well known is figuring out how to make the story fresh. I decided to call the biblical characters by less familiar names to make us enter their world with new eyes. I consulted several places for how to better anglicize the Old Testament names.

Choosing Egyptian names wasn't easy as there were not a huge number of choices. The names we know are mostly gods, or royal names.

Names of God

You might have noticed that I used both capitals and non-capitals when referring to God. If it is written without a capital then the character is not a believer (yet).

I have tried to use the names that followers of God used in the days of the story. Hence names like Elohim, Adonai, and the Creator.

Pharaoh's capital

The capital moved around over the centuries. However, Rameses II made **Pi-Ramesses** his capital and it was in the eastern delta region. I have placed the capital in this story within a day's run from Kheti's home.

Plague timeline

I made the timeline about eight months. There are clues within the text related to harvest times. I asked myself about how long the news of each plague would take to travel? If the plagues were too close together it would defeat God's purpose (Exodus 9:13-16) of letting the whole world know God's name.

STORYTELLER FRIENDS

Becoming a **storyteller friend** (https://subscribe.storyteller-christine.com/) will ensure you don't miss out on new books, deals, and behind the scenes book news. Once you're signed up, check your junk mail or the promotions folder (gmail addresses) for the confirmation email. This two-stage process ensures only true friends can join.

Facebook: As well as a public author page, I also have a VIP group (https://www.facebook.com/groups/242910632748639) which you need to ask permission to join.

BookBub - (https://www.bookbub.com/authors/christine-dillon) allows you to see my top book recommendations and be alerted to any new releases and special deals. It is free to join.

DISCUSSION QUESTIONS

- Who were your favorite characters? Why?
- What were significant steps in their spiritual journeys?
- What were significant barriers?
- What were your favorite parts of the story? Why?
- Did you learn any new things about the biblical stories? Or ancient cultures?
- What were the original beliefs of Kheti and his family?
- Without written scriptures, it would have been easy to forget the Lord. How did believers remain in the Lord?
- Why ten plagues and not simply one big one?
- What were God's purposes for the Egyptians? (Exodus 9:13-16)
- Why might the Egyptians, who all experienced the same plagues, have different responses?
- Why was Pharaoh so stubborn?
- What attracted Kheti towards knowing the Hebrews' God?
- Choose a character and trace their faith journey.
- Which faith journey do you most relate to? Why?

- How did this story encourage or inspire you?
- What can we learn about sharing our faith from this story of God's reaching out to the nations?

Please feel free to write your own discussion questions. I would love to see them and am happy to include them for others if you give permission.

FICTION BY CHRISTINE DILLON

Prior to writing Biblical-era fiction, I wrote a 6-book contemporary Australian set of novels.

I prefer you to buy the ebooks/audio directly from my online store (https://payhip.com/ChristineDillon#). It uses PayPal or Stripe (Visa/Mastercard). This is the cheapest place to buy the books as there is an extra discount available from the code at the top of the webpage.

Book 1 is also available in Dutch, under the name *Verborgen Genade.*

Of course the books are available from a wide range of other stores.

The *Light of Nations* series will likely be at least nine books. The best way to hear about upcoming books is to subscribe and become a storyteller friend or follow me on BookBub.

ACKNOWLEDGMENTS

Although my first series of novels were contemporary Christian fiction, I am feeling very at home in the new genre. I've always loved history and research (one of my hobbies is genealogy) and I've been telling oral Bible stories since 2004.

Many years ago, I spent a year looking at the Old Testament and the many opportunities that non-Israelites had to get to know the God of the Bible. That study was probably the genesis of the idea for the *Light of Nations* series. Throughout the Old Testament people from other nations interacted with the Israelites and many showed superior faith to the Israelites. Think of Rahab, Naaman, Abimelech, and Ruth.

In Isaiah 55:11 God says that his word,

... will not return to me empty, but will accomplish what I desire and achieve the purpose for which I sent it.

I do not think this means that God's word will always lead to trust in him but it will achieve its purposes whether salvation or judgement. Who were some of the people impacted by the witness and words of God's people? I didn't want to write about the people we know about, as lots of books have been written about Rahab and Ruth. I wanted to write about some of the nameless others who represent people that we will meet in God's Kingdom where people will come from the east and west to form that multitude of nations around the throne of the Lamb. As Revelation 7 says,

---

There before me was a great multitude that no one could count, from every nation, tribe, people and language, standing before the throne and before the Lamb...they cried out in a loud voice: "Salvation belongs to our God, who sits on the throne, and to the Lamb."

I love the research part of writing, especially the Biblical research. In preparation for this story I studied the first half of Exodus and asked myself many questions. Questions that needed to be answered to write this novel.

I am thankful for my beta readers: Lizzie, Kate, and Dr Janson Condren, Old Testament lecturer at Sydney Missionary and Bible College. A special thank you to Laura Tharion who put in a tremendous amount of work. Her suggestions greatly improved this book.

My proofreaders continue to be highly efficient - Anne, Stephanie, Suzanne, Elizabeth, Lizzie, Roe, and Annie. Though excellent at their job, it is amazing that errors might still remain. Please contact me if you see one. One advantage of self-publishing is that I can easily sort these out.

Iola Goulton continues her editing magic and this time was more difficult as she was in the midst of publishing her own debut novel. Congratulations and may there be many more.

Thank you Joy Lankshear for another wonderful cover. I found it hard to choose this time as there were at least four options that I loved.

I was warned that switching genres would be like restarting. They were right. Thank you to readers who have trusted me enough to switch from contemporary to historical. I hope you find the same spiritual quality that you came to love in the *Grace* series.

*1-2-1 Discipleship: Helping One Another Grow Spiritually
(Christian Focus, Ross-shire, Scotland, 2009).*

*Telling the Gospel Through Story: Evangelism That Keeps Hearers
Wanting More (IVP, Downer's Grove, Illinois, 2012).*

Stories Aren't Just For Kids: Busting 10 Myths About Bible Storytelling (2017).

This book is free for subscribers. It's a taster book and includes many testimonies to get you excited about the potential of Bible storying. All these books have also been translated into Chinese.

Sword Fighting: Applying God's word to win the battle for our mind (July, 2020).

This book is also now available in German under the title: *Siegreich Sein: mit Gottes Wort.*

ABOUT THE AUTHOR

Christine writes both fiction and non-fiction. Her non-fiction concentrates in the areas of evangelism, discipleship, and spiritual growth/warfare.

Christine worked in Taiwan, with OMF International, from 1999 to 2021 and still works with OMF, but now based out of Australia.

It's best not to ask Christine, "Where are you from?" She's a missionary kid who isn't sure if she should say her passport country (Australia) or her Dad's country (New Zealand) or where she's spent most of her life (Asia - Taiwan, Malaysia and the Philippines).

Christine used to be a physiotherapist, but now writes story-teller on airport forms. She spends most of her time either telling Bible stories or training others to do so.

In her spare time, Christine loves all things active – hiking, cycling, swimming, snorkelling. But she also likes reading and genealogical research.

Connect with Christine
www.storytellerchristine.com/

facebook.com/storytellerchristine
pinterest.com/storytellerchristine
bookbub.com/authors/christine-dillon